# Mystic Charm

Sara Longmate

Published by Sara Longmate, 2023.

MYSTIC CHARM

**First edition. December 30, 2023.**



ISBN: 979-8223703631

Written by Sara Longmate.

# Table of Contents

To my incredible family and friends, thank you for being the wind beneath my writing wings and turning this dream into a reality. Your unwavering support and laughter-filled encouragement made the journey to publishing a breeze, and this book is as much a celebration of our shared moments as it is a product of my passion. Here's to the late-night chats, the coffee-fueled brainstorming sessions, and the countless times you believed in me when I doubted myself. This one's for you.

# Prologue

"**A**lex! Hey wait up."

Shane, the cutest boy at Jeffries Technical High School, called out cheerfully. I turned and saw him walking towards me. I didn't bother trying to open my mouth, because the words that may come out might instantly incriminate me. Labeling me a full-blown spaz, who was head over heels in love with him. He continued.

"Hey, so I was just coming over here to ask you something."

"Yeah?"

I said shyly, hoping it came out more coy than shy.

"There's a new movie playing at the Multiplex, something about vampires on a 100-year-old reveng e kick. You want to go? With me?"

"Vampires?"

I raised an eyebrow at him.

"Yeah, isn't that what all you girls are into now? I mean, I don't know but there's lots of blood and fighting."

I laughed into the jacket I cradled in my arms. I couldn't believe he was talking to me, and about vampires, of all things. I smiled, still a little shocked it was me he was talking to and not someone like Charlotte Davis.

"Yeah, maybe like twenty years ago. Go Team Edward."

I gave a little mock air punch with my last statement. Sarcasm remaining my defense, regardless of being shocked or not.

"So, you'll go with me to the movies?"

I wondered if he was the shy one now as he looked down at his sneakers. So I said the only logical thing.

"Yeah, I'll go with you, if you don't mind me swooning like all the other girls."

Raising my eyebrows and tucking my chin in a 'just like you said,' sort of way. He chuckled.

"Yeah, okay, bad assumption, all forgiven?"

His hands went up in the customary sign of defeat. I nodded my head and tried not to smile like some crazed freak show. I couldn't believe that Shane Dodson was asking me to the movies! I hope this wasn't some huge cosmic mistake that would later backfire in my face.

"Okay great, I'll meet you at the pavilion at seven?"

He said, looking at me with his beautiful blue eyes. I responded.

"Yeah okay, see you then."

He backed away wearing a confident smile. I couldn't help but to smile back.

Down the hall I could see Charlotte Davis, a bratty rich girl from hell, plant herself right in front of his locker (could she be any more obvious). Charlotte — it seems — goes out of her way to make my life miserable. She looks my way and evil oozes out of her over-lined eyes. Or at least that's what I think she's trying to convey with the look she's throwing me. Almost as if the wings of her eyeliner would lift off her face and come out and slap me. She was leaning on his locker, laughing, trying to be cute and flirty, but it sounded forced and skanky. Something I bet she'll be doing for the next 20 years of her life. I could feel myself seething, getting angrier as her laughter bubbled down the hall.

Shane Dodson. The cutest, cute boy of Cute-town just asked me out, and she had to get her nonexistent panties in a bunch and ruin it for me. Everyone knows she has the hots for Todd Roy, the senior QB, so why can't she leave Shane alone? I'm shamelessly watching their encounter by his locker, and she smirks at me. She was up to something. It was like I was watching a slow-motion recap of a sporting mishap where the athlete breaks his leg in three places. It's a horrible sight, but you can't look away. I was about to turn back to my locker to gather my next set of books when Charlotte takes one more look in my direction. She then leans in and kisses Shane. Before I could find out if he kissed her back, rage rushed inside me as if lava was forcing rock through the earth's core. I wanted her to get her slutty mouth the hell away from Shane!

Suddenly, without an ounce of warning, Charlotte flew backwards into the lockers, mimicking the movement of being pushed. A sick crack reverberated in my ears. I assumed that was her head on impact. She collapsed to the floor like her bones could no longer support her. Did I really witness Shane shove Charlotte into the lockers? That can't be possible. Shane would never do that. I looked over at him. He'd gone completely still. Arms splayed out he held onto the lockers behind him. His face lost its normal golden hue and went completely gray. There was a light sheen of sweat covering his forehead and cheeks. He was pressing himself into the lockers, trying to absorb into them. Something wasn't right. My heartbeat so hard I thought it would echo down the hallway. Taking a few steps backwards, uncertain of what had happened, yet all too familiar with the situation. I turned around and hurried out of the hall, hoping Shane hadn't noticed my hurried escape.

"All things must change to something new to something strange."
Henry Wadsworth Longfellow

# Chapter 1: City Mouse Has Officially Moved to the Country,

**Alex**

Karma is: *'The quality of somebody's current and future lives as determined by that person's behavior in this, and in previous lives.'* According to Webster Dictionary. If you're going by that definition, then my *"Past Lives"* must have really sucked. Little did I know how true that statement was going to be. My name is Alexandra Hart, and this is my story.

I could never fully process the idea of Karma or luck, fortunate or unfortunate events. I always thought those sorts of things were due to a person's will. What were they willing to fight for, to strive for, what were they willing to sacrifice to make what they wanted to happen? Were they willing or unwilling to do good? And it was that good — or lack thereof — that dictated their karma. So why then, when I try to do good or be good, or simply just your average juvenile citizen, does my karma suck so badly? With the logic of karma in play, I must repel luck. For I sure haven't had much of it these past 17 years because bad things always happen around me and to me.

---

I picked up my eyes from the notebook I've been mindlessly doodling in for the last, I don't know how many hours. I quickly realized how stiff my neck and shoulders were from holding the same position for so long. I feared my hand is now permanently claw shaped. I looked out the window and regrettably wished I hadn't. All I could see was miles and miles of the Rocky Mountains. Our car zigged and zagged between twin walls of rock and moss with occasional glimpses of the canyon below. I felt a fear of small places and a fear of heights simultaneously. I didn't even know that was possible. Keeping my eyes on the notebook in my lap was the only way I could hold off the crushing fear of death by car plummet or rockslide. I know I'm being a tad bit dramatic. But when you must drive miles away from the only home you know, because you've worn out your welcome from an entire state, you get a little dramatic.

I buried my face in my hands, unable to handle any more of the constant weaving of the car. Once we started leveling out, I braved the window to see we were descending into a valley. The valley opened to a green meadow basin like something out of a Thomas Kinkade painting. As we got closer, I saw a sign that read "Gold Creek Welcomes You" with an intricately carved horse and rider underneath. I'm convinced I was now in a Thomas Kinkade painting.

To take my mind off that this city mouse has officially moved to the country, I launched into the events that brought me here. My mother had abandoned me on the steps of a church as an infant with nothing more than a diaper and a blanket with my name stitched in one corner. The only witness was an elderly man who told authorities he thought he saw a car with Illinois plates across the lot leaving in a hurry, which could have been helpful considering we were in Minnesota. It was dark, and he wasn't wearing his glasses, so they threw his statement out. There weren't any other leads to be found, as the car was in a blind spot of the only security camera in the area. The case went cold, and they deemed me a ward of the state, which began my journey of mismatched and misplaced foster homes.

With a beginning like mine, and no roots to ground me, it doomed me to be labeled a "difficult case". Circumstances inevitably follow me regardless of where I live, which made me feel as unwanted as a canker sore. Making me a prime suspect for relocation when I was no longer a, "good fit".

Now I can't always explain why I was moved so many times. It could have something to do with the crazy things that constantly seemed to follow me. I believed the good people of Minnesota drew their own wacky conclusions to why those weird things happen when I was around. But regardless of the reason, one too many unexplained — and sometimes damaging — things had occurred. So, they kicked me out.

Believe me. I quickly packed my suitcase for my next stop, no question, no refunds. Now I've never read my Case Chart, but I know all the fluffy words they use to explain why I am being transferred — again. I have officially been through every Group Home and foster family in Minnesota. Which is why I find myself in a mountain town in Montana. "Silver Mountain Youth Manor" here I come. A.K.A., "This is Your Last Stop So Make It Work Manor". Hmm, Youth Manor like some kind of resort getaway. Somehow, I doubt it.

"Alexandra."

Clara Stonewell. My social worker snapped me out of my contemplation. Eunice, a short stumpy woman who wears way too much blush, has been my social worker ever since I could remember. She is the closest thing I have to any resemblance of a family. She's nice. But somehow, it always seemed like she couldn't get away from me fast enough. But that could be my trust issues talking. So here we are on this two-day trip riding in this tin can excuse of a car. My ass is so numb I can't tell where it stops, and the car seat starts.

"When are you going to stop using my full name and simply call me Alex? You know I hate when you do that."

I muttered in response.

"You were named Alexandra for a reason. I want to honor your name by using it in full. If you were meant to be called *Alex,* you would have been named as such. So, Alexandra it is."

Clara continued her tirade, but I tuned her out. It's the same script over and over. I told her to stop using it. She tells me how it's important; I get mad; she gets offended; round and round we go. If it was that damn important, maybe the scumbags who left me on the freaking church steps could have at least left a forwarded address. Or hell, maybe even a phone number! But like I've said, I've stopped listening. I'm too engaged in the view out my window. The town was so pleasant and perfect it resembled something you would see in a Hallmark movie. One where the single mom moves to a small town and falls in love with the wealthy widower. One who brings joy back into the town and into his heart. This can't be happening. This can't be where I'm going to be living. With all the bad luck that seems to constantly fall at my feet, it's going to be like letting Godzilla loose on Manhattan.

"Alexandra, are you even listening to me? We're here; help me get your stuff."

She sounded even more exasperated than usual.

"Oh yeah, sorry."

I tell her, sounding as unconcerned as possible. I know how much that ticks her off. I love to watch her get flustered and agitated in her power suites that are always one size too big. She lost a significant amount of weight recently and still hasn't quite figured out how to dress for her new body. She really is an amazing person, and I give her a hard time because she's the only constant figure in my life and showing emotions — positive ones — is hard for me.

I looked out the window to see where *here* was, and to my astonishment, it wasn't half bad. I mean, I don't know what I was expecting. I guess some old shack in the woods with doors hanging off the hinges and children coming out of every seam. Think Old Lady in the Shoe. But it wasn't anything like that. The town was charming; it was an old two-story red brick building with creeping ivy growing along the walls. It had flower boxes beneath every window that sagged under the heavy weight of the brightly colored posies and pansies. A pebble paved walkway, every shade of gray and blue, swayed under the sunbeams. I half expected Hansel and Gretel to come walking out with giant lollipops in their hands.

I climbed out of the car and of course when I say climb, I mean floundered and flopped like a fish out of water. Empty chips bags and water bottles cascading out behind me. My legs felt stiff from the hours of sitting. I was about to close the car door when I heard footsteps behind me. The hairs on the back of my neck trembled, every nerve in my body was alert. I could hear my heartbeat thud in my ears. I couldn't decipher why my body was reacting this way. It must be the newness of everything.

"You must be Alexandra Hart."

I turned to face the voice. I swear, I almost recognized it, but the memory was too hazy to fully recall where I could have heard it. I tried to shake the fog that settled in my mind because, of course, that was highly unlikely. I have never been out of Minnesota and the odds of running into someone I knew was, what, one in a million?

"Alex is fine"

I told the woman. When I turned to look at her, a flicker of remembrance came over me. But again, it was too thin I couldn't grasp the memory. It felt like water falling through cracks in your hands, you can hold it, but never long enough to fully fill your palm.

"Well, Ms. Hart, welcome to the Manor. May I help you with your belongings?" The lady said extremely politely. If she recognized me, like I thought I recognized her, she didn't make any movement to tell me otherwise. I took a harder look at her, unabashedly. There was something about her that made me uneasy. I couldn't tell if it was her grandmotherly warmth she was projecting, which my natural instincts wanted to deflect. Or because I felt drawn to her in a more familiar term, like something was — *calling me* — towards her. Like a message finally answered. As quickly as the thought came, it left, and it was just me and her standing outside her gingerbread house in an awkward staring contest.

"My name is Meriwether North. You can call me Ms. Mary."

She moved closer and extended her hand for me to shake. I shook it tentatively. Before I could say anything, she bent down to pick up my backpack. Ms. Mary was a hearty woman with skin the color of coffee with too much cream. She was a few inches taller than me, which wasn't hard for I stand a whopping 5'3". Her hair, what little she had of it, grew out in tight spirals that were ashy gray in color. But what I noticed the most were her eyes; they were the color of seaweed. A green, so green they were almost translucent. I could almost see the ocean stillness beyond her pupils. Looking into her eyes filled me with a sense of calm, like a wave had engulfed me, carrying me out to a sea of tranquility.

I forcibly shook my head to release myself from her gaze. The powerful wave dissipated, but it left behind the sensation of water licking at my toes. I felt a wave descending back into the ocean. Feeling connected to the sea gave me strength, calming my nerves over this big move. She smiled warmly at me and with my bag in hand, turned around to lead us up the pathway. I grabbed my only other luggage. It was an old trunk, Claraand I found at a secondhand store patched together with old stickers of bands I've never heard of and places I've never been. But I hefted it into my arms and followed Ms. Stonewell into the house.

"The others are at school right now. They shall be returning in a little while. It will allow you some time to unpack and settle in before making more introductions."

I heard Ms. Mary say over her shoulder.

I nodded at first, and then hurriedly said a quick "Thank you." Before she assumed I was ignoring her. We walked into the house where Ms. Mary led us to a small room right off the main entrance. I believed she called it a Mud Room. There was a long wooden bench and coat hooks all along the wall. It smelled like pine and lemon. I shrugged out of my heavy coat, feeling a load lighter, and hung it next to the others that were scattered around.

"Well now, how about a tour to familiarize yourself with your new surroundings?" she said cheerfully.

"There are now currently six residents in the Manor, you as well as two boys and three girls. My cousin and I are the Matrons of the Manor."

She continued, but I stopped listening sometime back as we walked in and out of rooms and up and down hallways. I found myself in awe of this place. I couldn't believe this is where I'd be staying. It was unreal. At one point, I was standing in the middle of a small hallway, revealing both a kitchen on the right and what I assumed to be the living room on the left. Only it wasn't like any living room I've ever seen. It was a large, open room with an enormous picture window cut out of the west-facing wall looking out onto the front yard. There was an equally large, wood burning iron claw-footed stove sitting in the opposite corner. The décor of the room cut this massive space into two very distinct areas. One half of the room where the windows were located had rectangle tables arranged in a stye that resembled an old study hall. Complete with small lamps built into the tables. The second half of the room was an entirely different story. The style of the furniture could have come from the early 1900s. Two large cocoa-colored tufted high-backed leather chairs flanked the massive iron wood stove. Each had its own little round mahogany table whose legs we intricately carved to look like tree trunks growing out of the wood floor. Little wine-colored velvet couches with delicate little legs scattered around. Complete with mismatched patchwork pillows. Some with tassels, or buttons, or rick-rack trim. And was that glitter sequence? No two pillows were the same, and they were everywhere! Little ones on the couches, large, overly stuffed square ones on the floor. There was even a pile of them stacked in a corner about ready to topple over, all varying in size and fluffiness. The two sides of the room were warring with each other, modern and vintage, both putting up a good fight, but in the end, no winners would be named.

I could picture previous owners sitting by a roaring fire reading or knitting by lamp light. This place was just too unreal. Ms. Mary must have noticed me admiring the furniture. She told me they were original pieces dating circa 1887 and have been in her family since they were manufactured. The entire house seemed to have an old-fashioned quality about it. I wonder if all the décor was an original piece passed down from generation to generation.

We came to the end of the hall and Ms. Mary nudged opened a door, gesturing for us to follow her inside. The door led to an office where, behind a large wooden desk sat a lady who stood up to great us.

"Hello, you must be Ms. Clara Stonewell and Miss Alexandra Hart. Please come in and have a seat. It is so lovely to meet you. I am Ms. Terra Westerly."

She said in an accent I couldn't make out.

She extended her hand in greeting, and I took it cautiously. She held my hand and instantly the smell of wet soil filled my senses. It was earthy and comforting. It filled the room like a living entity. I looked around to see where the scent was coming from. No potted plants or opened windows. It had to be something filtering in from a vent, but I couldn't see anything that would cause such an aroma. It had to be some sort of room freshener I couldn't see. I'm telling you; this place was giving me serious creepy vibes.

Ms. Terra took her hand away without breaking eye contact. I noticed her eyes were a rich brown, almost red in color, like clay or terracotta tiles (maybe that's where the name came from). With the break of contact, the scent suddenly vanished as well. Once again, recognition dinged in the back of my mind, but like with Ms. Mary, it was too faint to hold any barring. They must have that face, I guess. The face that makes you think you know someone.

I rubbed at my temples, feeling an all too familiar headache coming on. Since the dawn of time, debilitating headaches have plagued me. Which no doctor could tell me the cause other than, "get more sleep, drink more water, eat more protein." *Thanks, doc. That was not helpful.* To get my mind off the pounding between my eyes, I inspected Ms. Terra, who looked nothing like her cousin. Where Mary was all curves and warmth, Terra was all angles and rigidity. She was tall and slender with dark ebony skin and hair that fell in a wave of midnight blue braids down to the middle of her back. She had perfect posture and cheek bones that could cut glass. For a full minute we were locked in an unfaltering stare, her eyes were fastened on mine. It felt like they were digging into my soul. I felt trapped. My vision was blurring. The room became dark. Maybe it was the headache taking over my senses. I felt stuck in thick mud, constricting every muscle in my body. The feeling was viscous and dense. I was no longer in the office but in a pit of wet sand, the smell of earth cloying at my nostrils. I couldn't have moved if I wanted to. I blinked sluggishly, and the office came back into view. My eyes suddenly cleared, and I was in the house again, in the office, where I had always been. My muscles felt stiff and heavy. I took a step back and clumsily landed into a chair behind me.

*What the hell was that?!*

"Alexandra, why don't we head up to your room? You must be exhausted from the long trip."

Ms. Mary said. Clara agreed, patting my shoulder. The gesture was for comfort, but her eyes looked worried.

"Al-Alex"

I stuttered. Then I stood up and headed out of the room to follow Ms. Mary. I couldn't decide if I should feel amazed or violated. Something happened in that room. I didn't know what or how, but I knew something did. I wasn't in a position to question anything. Clara made it absolutely clear this was my last stop. I have exceeded all other options. I just needed to keep to myself until I was eighteen and then my life would finally be my life. I had to make this work no matter what.

We headed up a set of stairs at the back of the house to another long hallway with three doors along each wall. It reminded me of one of those dreams where no matter how fast you run, the corridor just never ends. My feet were silent scuffles on the intricately woven carpet down the hallway. The carpet was stiff from years of tread. The color had muted and melted into each other but still held some of its old glory, all gold and bronze. There was a heavy rose smell that seemed to come from everywhere. I wondered if they pumped it through the ventilation system, but of course, that was ridiculous. It must be some form of carpet powder used to clean this ancient runner.

We reached the third door on the right, and the contradictions from the bottom floor to this one was worlds apart. The room was so modern. Desk, nightstands, and rugs look to be straight out of an IKEA Catalogue. A set of bunk beds flanked one side of the room. Each bed held a plethora of items, from discarded clothing to books to stuff animals who looked like they've seen better days. On the other side was a single twin bed. It was empty of any personal items, aside from being dressed in a set of plain white sheets and a multicolored heavy patchwork quilt. My bed, I'm assuming. I dropped my trunk on the empty bed, letting out a deep breath from lugging it up the flight of stairs. I wondered if I'd be able to shop for my own set of bed covers. It would be nice to have something that was just mine. I had to leave behind my last comforter, which I bought with the pathetic "allowance" I had received from foster home #6, or was it #8, because it had caught fire. Totally not my fault, I swear.

Ms. Mary and Clara were talking about finalizing paperwork and before they excused themselves from the room, Ms. Mary turned to me and said in a gentle voice. "Well, dear, this is your new room. Please feel free to unpack and settle in. The set of drawers at the foot of this bed are empty and free for your use, as well as this desk right here." She placed my backpack on top of the desk she had mentioned, then turned to exit the room.

Clara grabbed me in a last embrace. There was a sense of urgency in her arms, and I wondered if this would be the last time, I saw Eunice. I hugged her back awkwardly. We were never the touchy feely type. Her perfume smelled of overly sweet fruit that always made my nose tickle. But it was a familiar scent, one I would come to miss. I felt a single tear slip down my cheek. I let her go. Before I could step back, she grabbed my shoulders with both her hands and looked at me firmly and said.

"You're going to be okay. You've got this. Keep your nose clean and your head down and you will get through this. You are an amazing person. I know it doesn't feel like it now, but you will find your way, you will find your place. And you will always have me. No matter what. Forever."

She gave me another quick hug and a deliberate nod, then turned to shut the door behind her before I could say anything back. I guess she wasn't good at saying goodbye either. I was left standing there alone in the room, my room, with a clearly undeniable awareness that my life would no longer be the life I once knew. Things were changing, and I knew there was no way I could stop it.

# Chapter 2: Roast Beast and Potatoes

### Alex

"Lay off it, won't ya? Besides, it looks better on me, anyway. I was gonna give it back, so you see no harm, no foul."

"Nora, I don't care. Don't touch my stuff."

I heard them before I saw them. Two girls were coming down the hall and either they were loud, or these walls were thin. But I was betting those voices belonged to the two beds on the other side of this room. The door opened in a rush and in came a blonde girl, who said.

"Fine, okay Paige, sheesh! Don't burn my head off or anything. It's my laundry day I'll just throw—Oh Hey!"

The blonde one must have realized there was another person standing in the room because her conversation came to an abrupt halt.

"You must be Alexandra! Ms. Mary said we'd be getting a new roommate. Howdy, I'm Nora. Top bunk."

She replied with a slight country drawl to her voice.

Nora is what I would describe as a living doll. Perfect blonde ringlets hung from her head and kissed her shoulders. I half expected two pink ribbons to adorn her crown like the ones you'd see on porcelain dolls in antique windows. Her eyes were a powder blue, like glass, like doll glass eyes. And from what I could hear, she had a problem with belongings. Noted.

"Hey, Alex, twin bed," was my response.

Her companion was an almond-eyed girl with severely cut bangs and stick straight chin length hair, dyed bubble gum pink. She headed straight for the pocket door on the other side of the room. Once opened, it revealed a bathroom with another identical door across from it. Something I knew to be called a Jack and Jill bathroom. There was one in Group Home #2, or was it #5? She walked into the room and rolled the door closed behind her, glaring at Nora the whole time.

"Nice to meet ya, Alex. That's Paige, bottom bunk. Don't mind her, she's a little bent out of shape, because..."

Nora raised her voice and turned towards the bathroom door.

"She's a little over dramatic over a silly shirt!"

Nora looked back and gave me a wink, and a sweet little smile spiked with guile. The bathroom door slid open, and Paige leaned out spitting her words towards Nora.

"Don't touch my things, especially without asking. Thanks Hun."

The last two words came out with an emphasized twang accent.

Wow, what did I step into? Nora took Paige's place in the bathroom, and Paige now stood in front of me. Very pixie like in her build, she resembled a little Japanese Anima character complete with navy blue knee length jumper. To see her, I had to tilt my head down. She stared at me for a second, assessing, then asked.

"What'd you do to land here?" She paused and continued. "There's always something."

She raised an eyebrow in my direction. I didn't plan on telling her anything. Why should I play show and tell with a stranger? I don't know her. I guess you could call me distrustfully cautious, but hey, can you blame me? Besides, this wasn't Swap Your Sad Story Hour. I had almost forgotten she was in front of me as I lost myself in the thought of why I was here. Surely, I had till dinner before they interrogated me. I haven't even unpacked my socks yet.

No matter how many times I've replayed the story, it always sucks to tell it. The reaction was always the same; the story of an abandoned baby being left on the doorstep of an old church warrants the same response; pity and sorrow. Well, I'm not sad, and I need no one's pity. It's always been just me. Well, me and Eunice, but she doesn't count, and I like it better that way. No one to disappoint, no one who judges. Here it's going to be different. No one knows about the incidents that follow me. There are no eyes scrutinizing my every move. No one will look at me with suspicion and doubt. This would be a fresh start. Once and for all.

"Earth to Alex, you in there? You don't have to answer, especially if it's going to make you all catatonic. It was just a question."

Paige's words interrupted me from my reverie, and I lowered my eyes in embarrassment. I've got to stop doing that. I need to pay more attention to people or they will start thinking I really am a freak. She walked away from me. I heard her muttering something to herself. Good job Alex. Great first impression.

Nora joined us from the bathroom and spoke in her drawled voice.

"You'll tell us. Eventually. Everyone's secrets always have a way of coming out. Nothing stays hidden for long."

Nora paused for a moment, then slowly turned and headed up to her bed. I scrunched my nose and wondered if her comment meant to advise or to threaten.

"Sorry, it's just been a long couple of days on the road, you know."

I hoped they would take my unanswered question as fatigue instead of avoidance. The last thing I needed was for my new roommates to become my new adversaries and start questioning my sanity.

"Mm-hm" I heard Nora say.

Yeah, on the road to making fast friends. I let out a breath and turned toward my bags and started unpacking.

A voice boomed into the room startling me. It was a matron on the P.A. system. The girls didn't react to the intrusion. They gathered their book bags, taking things out and adding things. I had zero idea what was happening, so I stood there and listened to the message playing overhead.

"Good afternoon residents of Silver Manor. I hope your day has gone well. It is now time for Study Hall. Please gather your books and we will see you downstairs. Alexandra, I expect you in the office. Thank you."

"Ooooh, the office. See ya later, Alex." Said Nora.

She climbs back down her little ladder. Nora and Paige giggled their way out of the room, backpacks in hand. Yup, we'll be BFFs by the end of the week. Well, not a problem. It wouldn't be the first time I was deemed a social outcast. I was fine by myself. Sometimes I preferred it.

The office. What could call me to the office so soon after my stay? I looked around the room, wondering if I should bring anything. Since I had nothing to bring, I headed downstairs. I stood at the office door it felt like I was here not 20 minutes ago. Oh wait, that's right, I was. Has it really been less than an hour since I arrived at this weird new place? It seems like days have passed already. I bet the seat would still be warm from when I last left it.

I had an uncanny sensation I was walking away from one life, one filled with suspicion and rumors, and into a new life. One with the pulse of hope and unknowing beginnings. If I could only learn to not be such a freak, maybe I could make this place stick. It was one of the nicer places I have been. If I could get used to the altitude, I'd say this little bumpkin town would be a pleasant change of pace. Some place where a girl like me could hide away. The door in front of me brought me back to the present. I raised my hand to give a knock, but before my knuckles could hit the wood, I heard a voice coming from within.

"Come in Alexandra."

I turned the knob to let myself in and there, behind the imposing desk, sat Ms. Terra.

"Come, child, have a seat."

"I prefer Alex."

"Of course."

Ms. Terra was gentle and inviting, not at all like the first impression I had earlier. Gone was the tense feeling of wading through mud and in its place was warmth. Fire from a hearth, radiating down to my bones. I pulled a chair out and sat down. Ms. Terra looked at me for a moment. Pulled out a file from her drawer and instead of a voice full of warmth as I was expecting, her voice was the personification of professionalism.

"I can see from your file you are vulnerable to migraines. How are you handling that?"

She narrowed her eyes to take me in, waiting for my answer.

"They're... manageable."

I said, wondering where she was going with this.

"Mhm."

She said cryptically, writing something down on what seemed to be a dictionary size file in front of her. I looked down at my lap and restlessly pulled on a snagged fingernail, shamelessly avoiding her questioning stare. She glanced back down at the file and continued.

"You also seem to have a problem with behavior issues. In your last resident, there was an incident of pushing a young girl into a locker bay, resulting in a concussion—"

I abruptly interrupted her.

"I didn't touch her, she must of —"

Ms. Terra raised a hand to stop my rebuttal. She looked at me above her wire rimmed reading glasses. I sat back against the chair in defeat, knowing no matter what I said, it wouldn't make a difference. She lowered her hand and inhaled slowly, a smile returning to her face.

"We won't have any scenes like that here, will we?"

"No, Ma'am."

I responded the only way I knew how, although I felt it was just an empty promise. I had no control over those other incidents, so how could I have control over things that have yet to happen? She put the file back in a drawer and explained the expectations of the Youth Manor.

"You will start school tomorrow. The guidance counselor will have your schedule and your teachers will have your books. We use the local school bus; the stop is just down the lane. Breakfast is promptly served at 7:00am. If you're late, you'll miss out, but there are always granola bars or fruit you can grab on the way out to catch the bus..."

She explained the day-to-day routine. I zoned out somewhere between breakfast and curfew. What happened to my resolve to try to pay more attention to people? She looked down at her watch and told me.

"Shall we go outside to meet the others?"

I stood up from my chair and mumbled to myself,

"Off to the firing squad."

I thought about having to replay the same stories to a new crop of kids. It becomes very monotonous. I should hang a sign from my neck that says.

> Hi, I'm Alex the Orphan Child who seems to be a magnet
> for odd occurrences, watch out.

I refused to be the weirdo at the table. I decided to meet my doom head on. I lifted my chin, straightened my shoulders, and put one foot in front of the other. I followed Ms. Terra out of the room toward the waiting kids who would be my companions for the next however long I would live here.

We entered the Study, and immediately four of the five heads shot up in my direction. Restlessly, my hand worried at the hem of my shirt. I tucked them inside my jeans' pockets instead. I would not let them see how nervous I was. I could see Ms. Mary occupying one of the high-backed chairs next to the wood stove. Ms. Terra cleared her throat and addressed the room.

"Everyone, this is Alex Hart. She will be joining us here at the Manor. She comes to us all the way from Minneapolis, Minnesota. As we all have roots in distant locations, I know everyone will go above and beyond to make her feel at home."

She had a very pleasant way of speaking. You couldn't help but feel at ease listening to the cadence of her voice. I released the breath I didn't know I was holding and bit down on my lower lip, determined to not let my nerves get the best of me. Sensing my discomfort, she rubbed my shoulder ever so gently and continued with her speech.

"In honor of our new resident, we have made a special dinner for her welcome, and therefore Study Hall will be dismissed early. When I call your name, please raise your hand to help Alex associate your name to your face."

She started listing off names, and hands went up accordingly. I will never remember all these names. I felt bad for not paying closer attention. But the slow encroaching headache amped up a few degrees and my brain could not allow for anymore new information. I tried the best I could to keep the pain off my face and look as normal as possible.

I did, however, recognize the two girls from earlier. Nora gave me a friendly wave, and Paige nodded in my direction. I scanned the other faces around the tables, pleasantly surprised at how normal they all seem to look. One boy sat facing me. All broad shouldered and sharp-chinned with shaggy black hair that hung around his ears and forehead, desperately in need of a comb or a haircut. The boy across from him turned in his chair to look at me. He was tow-headed with a hairstyle that you knew took forever, but the goal was to look relaxed and unkept. He had a very lean body structure not lacking in strength. His eyes locked with mine, and instantly they looked familiar. They were the same powder blue I had seen earlier in my room. The same blue as Nora's. Siblings? Related, at least.

Everyone was focused on me, wondering who I was. Trying to unlock the mysteries that brought me here. I know that's what I'd be doing if I was in their position. It dawned on me, if something brought me here, something had to bring them here as well. I took a harder look at these teenagers in front of me. I tried to decipher what their history was, drugs, vandalism, Neo-Nazi take-overs? It could have been anything; okay, I was hoping it wasn't the latter but given my set of circumstances, who knows?

I blinked hard, trying to stop my mind from rolling with the What-If's on these kids' rap sheet. Through the quiet murmur of the students' unanswered questions, I noticed a mousey brown hair girl sitting off by herself. She had a history book and a pad of paper attempting to look busy. Ms. Terra must have called her name because she shifted nervously in her chair. With a quick movement, her left hand shot up for a moment.

The girl, Chrissy, looked at me from underneath a mountain of curls which came out in every direction, fighting for open space. Her eyes knit together. And as quickly as she looked up, she looked back down at her pad of paper, murmuring to herself. Her lips moved in silent cadence as she had a conversation with no one in particular. Hey, we all have our issues.

Ms. Terra finished her introductions. Thank goodness! She then herded us into the kitchen. The warm scent of rosemary and garlic flooded my senses. Until that moment I didn't realize how hungry I was. We all sat down to a pleasantly perfect first meal of Roast Beef and potatoes.

# Chapter 3: Seen Any Good Implodes?

**Alex**

On this chilly late winter morning, the school doors stood in front of me like the wall of Oz, foreboding and dominating. I was expecting a little window to open and a tiny person scowling at me and saying, "No one sees the Wizard". Okay, maybe I'm being a little theatrical. It's just high school, right? However, the building was enormous and made of stone standing three stories high. A monolith of masonry standing guard over an ancient fortress.

"Ya'll coming? Or are ya gonna stand there with your mouth open, wishing the building would implode?" Nora said.

"Yeah, I do that every morning. Trust me, it doesn't work. You might as well go in." Said Paige.

Nora and Paige came up behind me. I didn't realize I was gawking until they had pointed it out. Man, I needed to get my shit together and not look so out of it all the time. That was a sure way to get me on the fast track to Freak Town.

"You've got to give a girl some credit for trying. I was sure hoping for some imploding. It's been a long time since I saw a good implode."

My sarcastic wit coming out in full force. I was eager to ease the awkwardness of the moment.

"Come on, I'll walk you to the G.C. so you can get your schedule."

Paige walked off; I had no other choice but to follow. I waved at Nora as she walked into the building and in the opposite direction. Nora and Paige, I found out after dinner last night, weren't all that bad. As far as I could tell, they were just typical teenage girls, albeit a little "drama-centric". I was feeling better about rooming with them; maybe I would make some real friends after all.

I fell into step next to Paige. She was a fast walker and didn't bother to turn around to see if I was following. Somehow, I doubted if she would have noticed if I wasn't. I got in step with her and nervously asked, "what's the G.C.?" She stopped and looked up at me, one eyebrow raised, and replied.

"The Guidance Counselor, you know, to get your schedule? How are you to know what classes you're in without one?"

Okay, maybe the word friend was a little early. "Oh" is all I could say to her exasperated tone. She shook her head at how clueless I was and continued to walk toward the office. I reached an arm over my shoulder to adjust my backpack, it felt like a weight pulling me down. Which was unexpected considering there was nothing in my backpack, but one folder and a small pencil bag filled with various office supplies. It was a gift from Ms. Mary. I chalked it up to nerves. No matter how many times I started a new school, it was never easy. The crowd of kids around us was growing thicker, and we were finding ourselves having to bob and weave our way down the hall.

I was a little distracted in my head and didn't see the person walking directly into my path until something suddenly bumped me in the shoulder. Hard. I stumbled back a few steps and immediately turned my head to see who it was that rocked me. I could barely make him out among all the other students, but the blonde bed-head hair looked strikingly familiar. The guy I was searching for turned to look at me as well. There, staring back at me, were those same powder blue eyes that were staring at me over dinner last night. And his look wasn't a friendly one.

At the end of the corridor was a set of double doors. The kind you would expect to see in old black and white sleuth movies. Stenciled into frosted glass was block lettering informing us this was the Guidance Counselor, and front office. The only thing missing was a cloud of smoke as the door opened.

"Here" Paige pointed to the door.

"I gotta go to humanities but his office is in there. You'll be okay, right? You won't need me to take you to your first class or anything, you can read a map, right?"

Her tone was casual. I don't think she meant it as a dig but was curious if I could get around on my own. I bet she hoped I didn't need her to babysit me all day. With a rushed tone she added.

"I mean, I have a group project to present right now, and I just don't want to be late, or anything. Uh, yeah. So, I'm going to go."

"No, it's okay, I'll manage. It's just high school, right?"

I said, so she knew her statement did not offend me. I sighed and pushed open the door. There was a desk in the entrance with two ladies behind it, one answering the phones and the other stapling packets together. One lady looked up in my direction.

"Can I help you?"

Said Lady Number One. I walked over to her.

"Yes, I'm Alexandra Hart. Today is my first day."

"Oh yes, right dear. Let me pull up your file. Have a seat. It will only take a minute."

Lady Number One clicked a few keys at lightning speed. Lady Number Two took pages in her packet and continued to assemble them while giving me a sideways glance. I headed to where there were a few chairs lined up against the wall. The office was pleasant. Full of banners from winning teams and plaques of achievements, the office was abuzz with phones ringing and students coming and going. Unexpectedly, I noticed an open interior door with two figures on the other side.

# Chapter 4: Maybe It's The Lights

### Alex

"Don't forget what I said."

"Yeah, yeah, duty. Got it."

I looked and saw an older man and a male student having a conversation. The older man was wearing a collared shirt and tie, his neck looked like it was struggling to break free. He was a larger man, maybe 6'3", 200 lbs. He looked rather uncomfortable in his white-collar get-up. Immensely out of place liked he'd prefer to be wearing anything else than the tie and blazer. The door read, *M. Patrick; Guidance Counselor,* the illusive "G.C." I presumed.

The boy was about to turn when Mr. M. Patrick stopped mid-sentence and glared at me. He looked over the boy grabbing my attention, narrowing his hazel eyes at me. In that moment, I could almost swear his eyes reflected light from the office halogens. It reminded me of cat's eyes frozen in place by headlights on a highway. Whatever he was about to say stopped short on his lips. He leaned in and whispered something in the boy's ear. The boy's shoulders stiffened; I saw his fist clench at his sides. Whatever the man whispered to him, it wasn't good news.

The boy was tall but a few inches shorter than M. Patrick. His hair was dark brown, with strands of copper and gold weaved into it. He combed it back in enormous waves as if he was running at great speeds and the force of the wind blew it back in chocolate golden tuffs. His shoulders were broad. He was wearing a dark canvas jacket tailored to his build, it fit him like a glove. His jeans were dark and cuffed at the bottom over his Chuck Taylor Converse Shoes. I blushed, noticing I'd just been staring at this guy, to no avail.

"Miss Hart, here is your schedule."

Lady Number One broke the trance I was under. I took the outstretched papers which were my schedule and a map of the school grounds. She pointed me towards my first class. Standing next to me was the boy from the door. He handed the secretary a slip of paper.

"Mr. Alder, you have first period with Mrs. Huan. Why don't you show Alexandra where to go? Alexandra, this is Jason Alder. He's a junior like you and will show you to your first class. Isn't that right, Jason?"

The Lady looked at me but asked him. Oh god, is this happening? I was mortified, yet hopeful that he'd say yes. He turned to look at me pausing before he answered. If I thought the back of him was hard to look at, then the front was beyond comprehension.

This boy, this guy, in front of me had literally taken the breath out of my lungs. My lips hint of blue from lack of oxygen. His face was angelic, strong cheekbones and lips making cupid jealous. His skin sun kissed. The sun warmed him from the inside out. He was beautiful. But beyond his beautiful and perfectly placed face I noticed his eyes. They were an alarming green, a forest canopy filtering out all sunlight. I have never seen eyes that color before. When I looked again, I saw a similar flash, like I had seen on the Guidance counselors. Maybe it was the lights, although I had my doubts.

He ran a hand through his luscious hair which cascaded over his forehead and hooded his eyes from me. I could still feel his gaze. His lips twitched in a grin for a fraction of a second. It felt like hours before he answered.

"Yeah" was the only thing he said.

His tone was nonchalant, yet cautious. He gave me a halfhearted smile revealing the hint of a dimple. I blushed, my face and neck instantly flushed a muted pink. Physically, I could feel myself getting redder by the second. I must have looked drenched in red food coloring.

# Chapter 5: Townies

### Jason

Jason hated it when his uncle called him into the office to talk. It wasn't bad enough, his dad insisted he have a family member employed at the school, for Jason to attend. But did it have to be as the Guidance Counselor? And did it have to be Patrick? Mikael Patrick wasn't Jason's blood relative, but his involvement in the family has been a constant role since before Jason was born. He was his father's right-hand man. Which meant anytime, and every time Jason screwed up, stepped out of line or couldn't...control himself, his dad was going to hear about it via Patrick. Patrick was one of the few members with a bachelor's degree. His happened to be in Human Resources, allowing him to be employed by the Missoula County School District. Jason lived outside of town, deep in the mountain forest surrounding the valley. For over 100 years the town sat on land his father's family owned. Yet he has never attended any of the public schools in the area until this year.

Most of the townspeople weren't aware who Jason Alder or his family were. Especially the new residents who were migrating en masse from the surrounding big cities wanting to try their hand at country living. It was the elder generation who had deep roots and knew the stories that followed the Alders. The stories have gone quiet. The legends are too far away. The Alders establishing the town no longer held any importance to the new majority.

Jason's family and his people live on the back end of their land. They coexist away from the locals. They keep to themselves whenever necessary mingling when it's unavoidable. They had their own school and General Store. Which sold your quick fix last minute supplies such as milk, cereal, and small bags of diapers. It would hold you over till you could make it to the public Safeway. If they couldn't grow it, raise it, or make it themselves, they purchased it in town.

Rumor has it the Alders were the first inhabitants of the land. Through every war, every Western take over, every gold hungry pioneer, the Alders held on to the land. It's sacred land, and one day it will be Jason's land. The only residents who knew the Alders owned the land were a few city officials and retirees. The Alders like it that way. So, when Jason expressed his desire to go to the local public school, the idea didn't thrill his father. Too many variables, too many unknowns, and too many secrets hidden just below the surface.

For Jason to attend, his father needed to ensure there would be safeguards. Which meant Mikael, — the no nonsense strict as arrows graduate from Eastern Washington University — Patrick, who was now going to be Jason's supreme babysitter, for all things school related. It wouldn't have been Jason's first choice of chaperones, but he needed to get off the familiar land. He did not need to be, Alder-Junior-boy-Prince, for a few hours of the day. So, he'll take what he can get. It was hard to get away when his *uncle* kept insisting on calling him into his office for talks. But it was the price he'd pay for some resemblance of freedom.

The new girl in the office put Mikael on edge. Mikael leaned in and gave Jason a quick warning about said girl. Saying she didn't seem right. What did he know about teenage girls? He hated townies. Hate might have been too strong a word, but he distrusted the local people who weren't part of the inner circle. He felt thoroughly displaced having to play Guidance Counselor to all the self-absorbed sheltered town kids, but an order was an order. Luckily,

Jason was a senior, so he would only have to play Guard Dog for a few more months.

After the warning to stay away from the unassuming wide-eyed girl, Jason instantly felt a slight pull in her direction. Imagine an invisible finger tugging on the hem of your shirt, strong enough to feel it but not strong enough to take seriously. Jason, knowing what he knows about the unexplained, could fight the sensation; a weaker man would have ended up in the lap of whoever was calling him. But he kept his feet planted.

Mikael dismissed him gesturing toward Mrs. Morals' desk before retreating to his office in a huff of annoyance. Jason leaned on the high counter handing Mrs. Morals the small piece of paper, excusing him from his morning class. He had an important appointment that morning. The girl who he needed to stay away from, openly gawked in his direction. Jason was used to the stares he received from the local female and sometimes male variety around town. He knew his physical appearance and relaxed manner attracted all types of attention. He tried not to lean into it too much. He would never return any of the attraction he gained from the locals. He knew what was in his future, and getting together with a townie wasn't it. But that didn't stop him from having fun with them now and then. He was a teenage boy, after all.

Before Jason dismissed the girls' stare as just another admirer, he paused for a moment. He took a beat and looked at her, really looked at her, and immediately felt something different. This girl was different. He could sense her heart rate was quickening, her body heat rising. It surprised him she hadn't passed out because of the unnatural rhythm of her heart. What was even stranger was how his heartbeat in rhythm to her own. Two people falling into step with each other, he needed to get out of this space. Maybe something really was off with her after all.

Who was this girl? Once he got himself back under control, he assessed her thoroughly. There was nothing that struck him as odd or out of place. She seemed like your typical average teenage girl. She was short, not childlike, but pocket size. He bet if he were to hug her, the span of his arms would engulf her. He immediately shook the thought from his head. Why was he even contemplating hugging her? She had soft light brown hair waving down her back like ripples in a lake. It gathered over one shoulder, a hand nervously twirling the ends. Her soft delicate fingers were painted an electric blue. The paint was chipping off, the edges looked jagged. Signs she bites them. Her face was soft and round, with a set of full lips, and a nose that turned up in a point. But her eyes were the most fascinating feature on her face. They were as round as quarters and completely gray. Not a dull gloomy gray but a metallic almost silver blue, a gray so deep you could get lost in them. He let out a breath and inwardly smiled because not only was she having improper thoughts about him, but he was allowing himself to have them about her. Something completely out of his character.

Mrs. Mendez asked Jason if he would take Alexandra to her first period class, their first period class. He had to go to his appointment, but he could at least walk her to the door. Jason had a unique set of abilities, one of which was being able to hear the interworking of what others were thinking. Call it a gift, or a curse, but it was one of those family secrets his father was worried would be exposed with his attendance at the school. He was, however, extremely good at hiding and turning out the constant barrage of chatter that engulfed him to no end. Especially the thoughts of the wishful thinkers hoping Jason would reciprocate their attention, because he never did. Not only was it not allowed for him to get close to outsiders, but he hasn't wanted to get close to anyone, not since his mother died. Which is why he was completely surprised when he kept finding his thoughts coming back to the girl standing in front of him.

Returning to the present, he cleared his head of all thoughts of the girl. A difficult feat especially when her cheeks flushed, coloring her cheekbones a soft hue of pink making her even more attractive. How was she doing this to him? How was she able to get under his skin so easily? Alexandra. Her name was Alexandra and Mrs. Mendez asked if he'd take her to her first class. He'd take her anywhere. Jason mumbled out a single syllable in reply, not wanting to say anything more. He needed a moment or two to pull himself together. He heard the warning from Patrick, but he also couldn't deny something about this girl was too strong to ignore. Jason needed to find out why he was so drawn to her.

# Chapter 6: Oddities

**Alex**

I gathered my papers as Jason led the way. He held the door open watching me exit the office. We were quiet, methodical; I felt his eyes following me. I instantly felt self-conscious, wished I wore my green blouse instead of this old AC/DC shirt. After a few beats he spoke.

"Hey. Alexandra, is it?"

He said with a quiet confidence that made him even more attractive.

"Alex. It's my first day."

I stuttered. My tongue utterly tied in knots; it surprised me I could speak at all.

"Yeah. Mrs. Mendez mentioned it back in the office."

He said it affectionately, not sarcastically. I probably would do the latter, stating the obvious and all.

"Oh, right."

I cursed myself for being so lost in my words. He went on.

"Where are you from?"

I hated that question. He must have sensed my unwillingness to answer. Before I could think of a witty lie to deter him from pressing further, he said.

"It's just I know you must not be from around here. The town is small, so if you're an outsider, everyone knows."

*Great!*

"You don't have to answer if you don't want to. I just thought a little idle chatter would ease your nerves." He told me.

Now not only does he think I'm nervous, but he must also think I'm a weirdo. Good going Alex, good going. He smiled to himself and gave his head a little shake. My thoughts must have been written all over my face, but before any more time could go by and all points confirmed what a weirdo I truly was, I decided to continue with the conversation.

"I think I'm from Minnesota. Minneapolis Minnesota. I mean..."

Shit, I didn't want to say that. He gave me a sideways glance, and I could sense his mind was turning over my last statement. Oddly enough, he let it go. My eyebrows knitted together. How could he not want me to explain? It's not every day someone claims to not know where they're from. I didn't know what came over me to tell him that. I started feeling a headache coming on, and all I could think of was, not now, I don't need this now. I willed the headache to go away, knowing it wouldn't help, but hoping anyway.

My headache turned into a full-blown migraine; I doubled over in pain. I felt a hand at my elbow keeping me on my feet. I was mortified. I was having a wicked migraine from hell in front of this super-hot boy. The migraine was like none of the others I've had before. It was consuming. Every sense was on overload, to the point where I felt nothing at all. Like being in a depravation chamber, all dark and encompassing. I squeezed my eyes shut and covered my ears. I was afraid I was going to hurl whatever was in my empty stomach. I missed breakfast forgetting about the grab and go muffins that were discussed yesterday. I've got to start paying more attention. My lack of follow through was neither here nor there. I needed to get this headache under control before Jason called the nurse and solidified my mortification of the day. But underneath all the pain, I quietly heard a voice calling to me.

*Alex. Alex, are you okay?*

The voice was in my head. I felt the voice with my body more than heard it with my ears, and then the headache was gone. Just as fast as it came, it went away.

I straightened up. Moving away from Jason's hold of my elbow, making sure to move slowly. I did not want to agitate my head, which felt like it went through a vise. I looked around to see what kind of spectacle I had made of myself. Fortunately, there was no one around, no one but Jason. His green eyes full of worry. I gave him a weary smile, hoping it showed everything was okay. Somehow, I don't think he bought it.

"I should take you to the nurse." He said.

He ran a hand through his hair. Something I was gathering as a nervous habit.

"No. I'm fine, really. It's just a little headache; I get them all the time."

Whether he bought the excuse I couldn't tell, but there was an even bigger issue than a meltdown in the middle of the school hallway.

"I heard you. But I didn't hear you. I mean, I didn't hear it with my ears. I mean, it sounded like it was in my head. But that's impossible. I mean, that's crazy. Oh God, listen to me. I'm babbling. I'm not a crazy person, I swear. It just sounded so strange. Oh my God, I'm going to shut up now."

Any hope of me not turning tomato fucking red went out the window. I was so red it surprised me I didn't light up the whole damn school. I looked at Jason now, ready for him to bolt as far away from me as possible. To my surprise, he didn't. He was standing there, staring at me. Smiling at me.

"You talk a lot." He said through a smile.

"Yeah, that happens when I get nervous. I can't seem to turn off the sound. It's very annoying, especially when I start to say things to fill the silence. It's like I can't stand awkward silence, so I feel the need to fill it to not make others as uncomfortable as I feel and... I'm doing it again, aren't I?"

"Well, for what it's worth, I didn't say anything." Jason chuckled.

I wondered about his statement. I knew what I heard, but I filed it away to deal with later. He stared at me a moment longer. Wondering if I was going to pass out from an aneurism or something. When he felt confident, I was telling the truth, we continued down the hallway. We made it to class as the late bell rang. Saved by the bell, you could say. I found an empty seat in the back of the class and Jason found the seat right next to me.

"Don't you have an appointment." I said.

Masking my embarrassment with false confidence. I thought I'd have the class period to ponder the oddity of what happened. Now it seems I will have an audience.

"Not anymore." He replied.

# Chapter 7: Secrets

**Jason**

He watched Alex walk into the hallway, moving deeper into the belly of the school. He kept pace with her but gave her ample room so she wouldn't feel crowded. Her thoughts were a jumbled mess of nerves and first day jitters. He thought about trying to ease some of her anxiety and fill the air with idle chitchat.

"Hey. Alexandra, is it?"

The reply he received from a simple question of, "where are you from" threw him for a loop. Was she unsure about where she was living? Or was she trying to be funny? There was something strange about this tiny girl next to him. But before he could dive deeper into her history, everything suddenly went quiet. Like a light switch clicking off, all of Alex's eternal noise swiftly and abruptly shut off. In its place was a deep sense of pain, and not the emotional kind but the agony kind. Alex was in pain, and tons of it. He reached for her elbow to prevent her from falling over as the pain was physically making her unable to stand. What was wrong with this girl? What was happening to her?

Jason tried to talk to her, but his words were hitting deaf ears. He wanted to help, but there didn't seem to be anything he could do outside of carrying her back to the nurse's office. Which is what he wanted to do. Jason could feel her pain, but more than that he could sense it. The pain seems to take on \a physical form, phantom like. It was alive, trying to fight its way through Alex's body. Jason wanted to help her. He could feel the impressive amount pain she was under. Somehow Jason knew there was something he could do. Something that might stave off the agony that possessed her. He knew, however, if he was going to help Alex; it had to be now. If she was as different as his uncle hinted at, maybe it could work.

He concentrated on the space where her thoughts should have been. Where now existed, an angry black cloud swirling around like a hive of disturbed bees. He imagined blowing it away like smoke from a fire, a cloud of ash and soot; he pushed through the cloud and spoke to Alex. He wanted her to hear him. In his pack those who have gone on their Spirit Journey were granted the gift of Spirit Talking, where you can push your thoughts onto to others. It came as natural as breathing. It was another one of those secrets they couldn't get out. It took more concentration to keep out the thoughts than it did to send them. But Jason never Spirit Talked with anyone who wasn't in his pack. He didn't know if she could reciprocate in the same way his pack could. He silenced his mind and attempted to reach her.

*Alex, Alex are you okay? Do you need help?*

The swirling cloud in her head froze in place, like a dog being snapped out of its destructive behavior. It slithered away; mad it could no longer cause any more damage. Alex was once again just as she was. Her thoughts returning, white noise in the background. Slowly she stood, she seemed to be fine. She tried to convince Jason she was okay, but he didn't buy it. Something happened, and it wasn't a simple headache. She interrupted his inner dialogue.

"I heard you. But I didn't hear you. I mean, I didn't hear it with my ears. I mean, it sounded like it was in my head. But that's impossible. I mean, that's crazy. Oh God, listen to me. I'm babbling. I'm not a crazy person, I swear. It sounded so strange. Oh my God, I'm going to shut up now."

It worked. She heard him, Jason thought. He didn't think it would work, but it did. Normal humans shouldn't be able to hear him. Sure, you run into the occasional clairvoyant, or another tribe member gifted with Spirit Talking. But mundane's or, non-paranormal's shouldn't be able to hear him. Maybe she's of the clairvoyant variety. He knew she wasn't a tribe member. There were other tribes like Jason's, but his tribe was the biggest of its kind. There aren't many around nowadays. If he assumed she wasn't clairvoyant, what does that make her? He wasn't ready to hear what that answer might reveal, so he brushed it off. He has secrets of his own, and if he wasn't ready to reveal his, then she was owed the same patience until she wanted to reveal hers. In time they\\\\\ would all come out. Secrets always have a way of coming out.

# Chapter 8: In a state of shock

**Alex**

I thought my embarrassment was at max capacity because of the incident in the hall. That was nothing compared to the feeling that came over me when Jason followed me into our shared class and took the seat next to mine. I wanted to hurry and sit down, gather my wits before anything else could happen. Knowing he'd be gone because of his previously scheduled appointment would have given me a brief respite from his questioning eyes. But now, out the window, that plan went. There was nothing more I could do but pretend to be engrossed in our — hopefully soon to be—upcoming lecture. I had no textbook to look at, so I busied myself with a blank notebook and pen from my backpack. I could feel Jason's eyes watching me and, in my peripheral, I dared to glance back at him, only to have him quickly look away. What was he thinking? What did he think of me? I continued to ponder what was running through his mind about what happened out in the hallway. But before I could come to any conclusion, Mr. O'Dell interrupted my train of thought.

"Good morning students, before we begin today, we have a new student joining us."

Mr. O'Dell, our Civic teacher, was a slender young man who had a voice that was nasally and registered at a higher pitch than I would have imagined a man's voice to be. Maybe the bow tie around his neck was too tight. The blush that had just dissipated not a moment ago returned faster than lightning. I hated being called out in front of the class. No matter how many times I was the new student, it was always rough. Why did teachers think that was an acceptable way of introducing a new student? It just makes our anxiety run rampant.

"Everyone, this is Alexandra Hart."

He motioned for me to stand up. *Oh god, and I have to stand up.* Just paint a sign over my head. *ATTENTION: Here stands the New Kid!* I heard a soft chuckle coming from Jason's desk, humiliation now fully complete. Great. I turned to glare at him. I hope he was enjoying my death by mortification.

"She's new, not only to our school but to our town. Make her feel as welcomed as I'm sure you all will."

Whispers blew through the classroom, a subtle wave of voices murmuring in unison. Mr. O'Dell turned back towards his desk and began riffling through it, papers spewing out every which way. He let out a loud "AHA" when he came to what he was searching for. He held up a textbook in one hand like it was a relic to be admired; and from the tattered binding and faded cover, it might have been. Mr. O'Dell walked the book down the aisle and laid it gingerly on my desk.

I took my seat, eyeing the book as if it would sprout legs and walk away. When a red-headed girl in a cheerleading skirt and oversized letterman's jacket laughed in my direction. Her red tipped fingernails covered her mouth, but not before she started whispering something about my appearance. Two other girls giggled not so quietly at whatever she had just said. Letterman wearing cheerleader never once breaking eye contact. Right on cue, the typical high school mean girl must make the new kid the token outcast. No big deal, nothing I haven't dealt with before. If she thought a few whispered remarks were going to make me cower before her, she had another thing coming.

"Alexandra, isn't that an old lady's name? What rock did she crawl out from under?" Retorted Letterman Jacket a lot louder than necessary and the class erupted in muffled chortles.

I rolled my eyes at her, wanting nothing more than for her to shut up. I mouthed the words to myself, putting all the animosity I could muster behind it. I hated that she was making snide comments at my expense. Without warning, Letterman Jacket stood up, her chair clanging loudly behind her as the force of her sudden movement knocked it off kilter. Her hands were grasping at her throat, her mouth moving wordlessly. The gaggle of girls around her all stood up to attend to her unknown needs. Letterman Jacket's eyes went wide with gathering tears that were about to spill over. I couldn't take my gaze off her as she looked around at her posse. Her unsaid cries for help garnered only confused and worried expressions. Jason kicked my chair, a slight nudge that broke the unconscious hold the situation held over me. I shook my head, regaining my composure. Blinking away the fog. Letterman Jacket stumbled towards the teacher. Mr. O'Dell, in a state a shock asked the mute girl.

"Moira, what's wrong? Do you need the nurse?"

Moira grabbed her throat. Her eyes full of tears. But before Mr. O'Dell could say anything, words fell out of her mouth like water being released from a dam.

"My throat. My voice. I couldn't. My voice."

Moira continued to babble aimlessly, not making any coherent sentences. Mr. O'Dell instructed one of the other girls to take Moira to the nurse's office. The two of them walked out of the room, Moira still muttering quietly to no one in particular, her friend rubbing her back as the door closed behind them.

The class was in utter disarray, a million-conversation happening at once. Mr. O'Dell was trying and failing to get the class under control. Everyone was talking about Moira. Everyone but Jason. He was looking at me. I couldn't meet his stare. I didn't know what happened any more than anyone else did. I rubbed at my temples, the remnants of my earlier headache simmering under the surface. Jason's phone trilled in his pocket, breaking the hold we were under. He read the message that appeared on the screen. Cursing under his breath he shoved his phone roughly into his pocket. Apparently, he didn't like whatever the message said. Jason looked at me once more and moved his mouth as if to say something but thought better of it. He grabbed his backpack, whispered something to Mr. O'Dell and left the class.

My eyes followed Jason. A deep sense of relief from my head to my toes washed over me. There's something about that boy that makes me both uncomfortable and intrigued, two very dangerous things. But I needed a minute to process everything that happened since I missed breakfast that morning. And I knew I couldn't do that with him staring at me all first period. So, I was happy with whatever it was, that called him away.

I surveyed the room. Mr. O'Dell had given up completely on today's lesson. He told everyone to read chapter 5 and proceeded to dabble on his computer, while no one attempted to open their book. Everyone carried on their conversation like we were patrons at a coffee shop and not students trying to learn about the judicial system. To my right sat a friendly looking blonde girl who offered me a kindhearted look. She leaned over and whispered her name.

"Hi. I'm Melissa, but you can call me Lissa."

"Hi. Alex."

We started a simple conversation about nothing. It was nice. I found out she was in my next class. Which was amazing because they filled the school with an overabundance of hallways. Getting lost in our conversation was an easy thing to do for the remainder of the class. Lissa and I fell into step with each other. Our conversations came easy. She was inquisitive without being probing, sympathetic without giving pity. Maybe I finally found a friend. I was thankful, not only for her empathy, but mostly for her kind smiles. It seemed too long since someone smiled at me. A true genuine smile rather than one's full of fake concern from foster parents who share no actual concern. Maybe I really could get through this.

The day continued better than it had started, the incident in Civics completely forgotten. Even my headache was tolerable. Nothing a little Advil couldn't fix. Maybe I would go to the nurse after all, if for nothing else but to get a little medicinal help. Lissa and I walked to our next class side by side. The walk across campus to our English class was where I learned Lissa was born and raised in this little town. She and Moira were once best friends, growing up competing in rodeos together, particularly barrel racing. Their families all grew up together, which isn't hard in a town as big as this one. But as the story goes, one girl grew up faster and decided boys were more important than friendships, and Moira wasted no time in kicking Lissa to the curb. If Lissa had any doubt their friendship was indeed over, Moira spread a nasty rumor about her family. Something about losing the family farm because of the illegal sale of horse meat. I guess it was bad, because all of Lissa's friendships were suddenly severed. No one wanted to be seen with the girl who sold and ate horse meat. The truth Lissa later told me was that her family came upon hard times and the bank had a hold on their farm, which they almost lost. But with major downsizing and hard work, they could maintain the payments and keep the farm in her family's name. Her family raises horses for the local ranchers and rodeo folks in the area. They even sold a horse to a local jockey who was a minor celebrity in town. But those types of sales haven't happened in a long while.

Moira has had her eye on Lissa's prized Arabian ever since she won her first barrel race at 13. It quickly became apparent that Lissa was the superior one in the arena and Moira wouldn't stand for it. Even tried to buy the horse out from under her, but Lissa's dad refused the sale. Soon after that, the rumor took off like a wildfire through town. Lissa realized it was because of Moira, the coincidence was too great. She knew, no one ever refuses Moira Devereaux

Ever since Lissa's fall out, she tries to simply get through the day. Something I can relate to on a molecular level. Lissa has continued to compete in the barrel racing circuit, hoping it will be her ticket out. She wanted nothing more than to get as far away from this little town as she could. I couldn't blame her.

# Chapter 9: Text Message

**Jason**

Once Jason decided to skip out on "his appointment" he knew he would have to answer his dad when he returned home later that afternoon. Part of his agreeing to let Jason enroll in school is that it wouldn't distract him from his responsibilities, and today was his day to lead patrols. He quickly shot a text to Mato.

**Jason: Something came up. Cover for me.**

**Mato: Again! Your dad's gonna tan my hide.**

**Mato: This better be about a girl. You need to get laid.**

**Jason: STFU I'll tell you later. Just do it.**

**Mato: Sure sure.**

Jason put his phone away and decided since he was breaking all the rules now, he might as well do it in full. Jason followed Alex to the back of the room to the only two empty seats in the class. Good thing they came in late, or they might not have been able to sit together. He wanted more time to figure this girl out. Something was strange about her, and he needed to find out what it was. If not for his own curiosity, but also for his pack. He needed to make sure his family was safe from anyone or anything that could jeopardize their way of life.

Mr. O'Dell was a new teacher this term, a transplant from the big city. Try as he might to be everyone's friend in class, it often became awkward and forced. So, it didn't surprise Jason when Mr.

O'Dell thought it would be a great exercise if he introduced Alex to the entire class. Hoping this would help facilitate some friendships among the students. Little did he know how much Alex despised being the center of attention. Jason couldn't help but smirk and watch the car crash of awkwardness take place as Mr. O'Dell began his introductions.

"Everyone, this is Alexandra Hart."

Exactly as predicted, it completely mortified Alex. As much as Jason hated listening to her inner thoughts — he tried to stay out of people's head — her thoughts were too entertaining to ignore. He could visualize the giant neon sign above her head flashing annoyingly, introducing her status as the new kid. A laugh escaped his lips, and he immediately regretted it. Alex turned to look at him, eyes full of irritation. He laughed again. Jason's attention quickly shifted from Alex's plight because a new conversation was stirring on the other side of the room. Moira, "Queen Bitch," was up to her usual self. She was already planting her dominance over the new girl and made some totally bitchy and expected comment at Alex's expense. The class giggled along with her because they would rather go along with the teasing than go up against Moira, weaklings, all of them.

Jason was about to step in and say something to Moira, but before he had a chance, a deep sense of foreboding washed over him. Like a sound wave pulsating through the class. He scanned the room quickly to see where the feeling was coming from, but everything seemed in its place. Then he turned to Alex who was glaring daggers at Moira. She obviously heard what Moira was saying and didn't appreciate it, either. The black fog that filled her mind earlier was back, and he could no longer hear her internal thoughts. The Fog swirled with a furry all around her like an invisible aura only he could see. Right then a clash of metal on linoleum reverberated through the class coming from Moira's side of the room. Moira, who never stopped talking, went instantly quiet and from her desperate grasping of her throat, looked like it was an involuntary decision. Her thoughts, however, were not quiet. She was screaming expletives in her head, completely freaking out, wondering why she suddenly lost all control over her voice. She was struggling. Something had happened to her, but Jason couldn't figure out what it was. He turned back to Alex, whose thoughts were still guarded from him. He could feel the dark fog weaving around her, creeping closer in Moira's direction. Her eyes were distant and glassy, almost like the fog was so thick in her head it was coating her eyeballs. He kicked out with his foot, jolting Alex out of whatever trance she seemed to be under. Alex's eyes cleared, and she shook her head, blinking away any remaining haze. Her thoughts came back. Jason could hear her inner monologue going over what happened. She was confused; she was concerned for Moira, wondering if she was okay. Weird, this was all too weird. Now, more than ever, did he need to figure out who or what Alex was.

Jason's phone buzzed once. Shit. He knew instantly who it would be. His friends didn't normally call or text him during school hours, and he didn't have any other outside connections. So, if his phone was going off in the middle of the day, there was only one person it could be.

**Dad: Home. Now.**

# Chapter 10: Fictional Spanish test

### Jason

Jason was racing down the highway towards home. He didn't need to hurry, he just liked driving fast. With Jason's unique set of abilities, he always knew where the cops were, which made getting a speeding ticket nearly impossible. At the entrance to his family's ranch, he saw his dad's pickup parked by the wooden fence. His dad stood leaning on the cab, a stern looks on his face, arms crossed over his chest. Shit. His dad was pissed. Jason parked his motorcycle next to the truck, not caring that he blocked the entrance. No one would be coming by. He removed his helmet and tried to form some sort of excuse for why he ditched patrol.

"Can it. Don't even start. I know exactly why you didn't show up for patrol this morning."

His dad cut him off before he could even take in the breath to speak. Spirit Talking was both a blessing and a curse. This was the curse part. He couldn't hide a thing from his dad. Because he could always just read his thoughts and find the truth for himself. It sucked. Imagine never getting away with anything as a kid, because your thoughts were never truly your own. There were ways to hide or block people out, but it required lots of concentration and training, and it was usually only the elders who could master it. Jason was better at it than most, but it took a lot of concentration. Hopefully, one day, it will be an easy feat. His dad lectured him on all the usual points, family duty, place in the pack, yadda yadda. It was always the same thing. There was so much pressure put on Jason's shoulders, which was exactly why he wanted, needed, to get off the land now and then. Attending the public school was the best way to do it. If his dad wanted him to one day be Chief, then his dad needed to know the decision would be his and his alone. Jason needed to discover what else was out there before he could just blindly take up the role. His dad hated this train of thought. He came from a generation of accepting the role you were born into and doing what needed to be done. His dad blamed Jason's need for answers on the "youth of today and the computers they hold in their pocket" he hated modern technology and swore it would be the downfall of all mankind.

"Patrick told me a new student enrolled today. He also told me he informed you to keep a wary eye out. And then not even ten minutes later, Mato is telling me you got stuck at school because you missed a Spanish Test. You're not even in Spanish. What's going on Jay? You know our agreement. Pack matters come first. You need to set the example for the others. What message does it send when the future Alpha is ditching patrols because he's taking a fictional Spanish quiz? You lead patrol once a month. We've already made sure they would accommodate it into your school day. You can't now suddenly blow off your responsibilities. It sets a poor example. Are you paying attention to me?"

"Yes sir. Sorry, it won't happen again."

"Damn right it won't happen again, because if it does, I'll pull you from that school so fast you'll wish you really had a Spanish test. Now tell me, what's the real reason you blew off patrol this morning?"

His dad softening, he relaxed his arms and shifted his stance. He never could stay angry at the boy. He was a good kid, and he didn't want to push too hard. Jason tried extremely hard to not think of the girl and what happened that morning during Civics. He was not ready to discuss that mess. So instead, he focused on what happened before class, the headache. But was careful to avoid thinking about the black fog that came with it and answered his dad.

"The girl that Patrick was talking about, she got sick or something and I wanted to make sure she was okay. So, I walked her to class, and wanted to stay. Sorry, I know it was dumb. But everything's fine, I won't do it again. I need to get back because I really have a test, but in English, not Spanish and I did actually study. I want to make sure I didn't spend my time in vain. Can I go now? Or is the interrogation still happening?"

"Stay away from her. This isn't a suggestion. Am I understood? The ramifications of what this situation could bring to our tribe, go way beyond you and me. I know you'll do the right thing. You have a big heart. You get that from your mother, but sometimes it's necessary to follow your head and not your heart."

Jason could sense his dad was over with the lecture and knew he was in the clear. His dad was a softy, and Jason knew it. The last thought Jason had before got back on his bike was, if I hurry, I just might get there in time for lunch.

# Chapter 11: Do you have a reservation?

### Alex

Finally, it was time for lunch. Lissa was a member of the Drama Club. They were in the thick of set design and fabrication for their upcoming performance. During her lunch hour a few times a week, she went to the theater hall to help work on the set. She invited me to tag along, but I wasn't ready to be the odd man out just yet. I was also predictably famished, realizing I hadn't eaten all day. I left Lissa and followed the drove of students winding their way onto the commons. Once outside, I could see the cafeteria building directly in front of us, topped in large blue metal letters that read Mountaineer Café. Café made it sound like it was some sort of upscale restaurant but as I got closer, I could see it was just a typical high school cafeteria inside of their gymnasium. The "Café" part was a food window where the kitchen ladies dished out today's meal of the day. There were a few refrigeration cases where the students could grab salads or drinks. The overcrowded café-gymnasium was too much for me. I needed space and air, especially after everything that happened today. Now that Lissa was gone, there was nothing that kept my thoughts from drifting back to Moira's episode in Civics. I grabbed a soda and a triangle packaged sandwich. It said it was turkey and cheese, but I couldn't have told you if that was indeed true. The turkey was grayer than it should have been, and the "cheese" looked like it was a piece of plastic food I used to play with when I was a kid. But it was food, or at least I hoped it was, and I was starving.

Rather than sitting inside the crowded building, I tried my luck outside. The weather was holding up. Clara had told me it would most likely snow toward the end of the month. It being in the mountains of Montana and all, and coming from Minnesota, I was no stranger to snow. But it was nice being able to eat outside in the crisp winter air. I was in no hurry to sit like pickles in a pickle jar once the snow came.

I saw Nora and Paige sitting on a bench surrounded by a group of boys, a few I recognized from my morning classes. I didn't feel in the mood to socialize, so I walked on, praying they wouldn't notice me. They didn't, too lost in their own conversations to be aware of anything else. I have never had any close girlfriends before. Back home, everyone stayed away from me. I did, want to be friends with my new roommates. I wasn't sure however, how to go about it. But with them and now Lissa, maybe I would make some actual connections this time.

I found a large, raised grass planter that decorated the inside of the outdoor seating area and sat down with my soda and sandwich. In between bites of my lunch, I opened my backpack to take out my notebook. I journal. Constantly. It's one of the things in my crazy life that has been a constant, that and run. But right now, I need to write. It's freeing. There is something so powerful about it, putting words on paper where before had never existed. It strips you away to the bare essence of your being, leaving you naked with only your thoughts and ideas.

"This seat taken?"

A voice startled me, making me jump in my seat. I was lost between the white lines of my notebook. When I looked up, there stood Jason in the glare of the sun. I could only see his silhouette because the sun behind him was shadowing everything but his outline. Even that was too much to look at. The boy was beautiful, a statue made of earth and clay. I raised my hand to my forehead, gathered my wits, and replied.

"I don't know. Planters are in high demand. Do you have a reservation?"

He crouched down next to me and gave me a halfhearted smile and chuckled through his nose. He rested his forearms on his knees.

"Are you always this witty or is sarcasm your only defense?"

"I'm always this witty. But if sarcasm was an Olympic sport, I would hold the gold medal."

He chuckled again. God, he was so cute. The throaty sound coming out of his mouth was like a wind chime drifting in the breeze. I wanted to sit and listen to it all afternoon. He adjusted his position, so he was sitting across from me, leaning against a tiny tree. I thought for sure the fledging sapling would buckle under the weight. He stared at me for a long time. I stared back, not wanting to be the first to break eye contact. It felt like we were playing a game of chicken, and I didn't want to be the one that broke first.

What could he possibly find that would be worth staring at? I was beyond average and did not stand out in the least. Yet he refused to look away. The one thing that might gain attention could be my eyes. They were a very peculiar color of blue, practically gray. Who wants gray eyes. Claraused to say I had eyes like a summer storm, both dangerous and beautiful at the same time. When you hear your eyes look like a storm, it sounds like something to be afraid of. A girl who resembled destruction and mayhem. A little on the nose, considering how bad luck seems to follow in my wake.

"You have beautiful eyes." Jason whispered.

It was so quiet I thought I might have imagined it.

"What? I mean, thank you. I find them odd." I said self-consciously.

I was not one who accepted compliments easily. Probably because I'm not usually the one who receives any. However, it was odd how he complemented me on the one thing I was just thinking about. That was a strange coincidence. He sat there for a moment, trying to read my expression, and suddenly I felt nervous. Afraid of what he might find if he looked too closely. He started speaking again and broke the spell I was under, bringing me back to the conversation.

"No, I think they're very interesting. You can tell a lot about someone through their eyes."

I blushed beat red. He smiled at me, a slow, purposeful smile. My heart was beating in my throat. I couldn't help but hope and pray he wouldn't bring up anything that happened in Civics today. That was the last thing I wanted to talk about.

"How's the rest of your day been?" He idly picked at some grass.

Good. It seemed we might bypass everything that happened this morning. With a sigh of relief, I played along.

"As good as can be expected, you know the same old high school, just a different campus. It's been an optimal day." Sarcastic remarks are never too far from my lips.

"Ah, Ladies and Gentlemen we have an optimist."

He said as he made a grand gesture, waving an arm above his head. I rolled my eyes to show him he wasn't getting to me, but really, I did it to hide the embarrassment I was holding back.

"Are you always this loud, or are you just a Smart Ass?" I retorted.

"Ouch."

He said as he settled back on the grass. He looked at his watch.

"Well, we have about 30 minutes left of lunch. Tell me all you can about your life in under 29."

My eyes bulged out.

"Wow, you don't waste any time. You just jump right in."

My comment did not faze him at all, and he continued.

"This morning, I asked you where you were from, and it seemed like you didn't quite know. Now forgive me for prying, but it's not every day you come across a pretty girl who doesn't know where they're from. Are you in the Witness Protection Program and you goofed by letting on that you were somewhere else when you should have said something else? It's okay, you can tell me I'm a cop."

Holy hell, what just happened? That was the longest speech I've heard him say all day. I didn't know what to process first. The fact that a cute boy who I was gawking at this morning tried to drag me to the nurse's office because of a wicked headache from hell now thought I was in the Witness Protection Program. Or the fact he called me pretty. I bit my lip, and felt my heart quicken. I was completely surprised. No way was I going to read too much into the, pretty, comment. But was I going to tell him my sob story? I diverted the conversation by avoiding his questions all together.

"You are not a cop, and we only have 27 minutes, and my story would need the full 30, so why don't we start with you? Other than your name and your love of the nurse's office, I know nothing about you. You could be a serial killer and I would never know until it was too late."

I laughed uneasily. I was trying too hard to sound casual when the truth was, I was never more stressed out.

"That was a quick change of subject." Said Jason.

He brought a closed fist to his mouth and started talking into it.

"Note to self: don't ask personal questions."

He ran a hand through his hair, and it was a movement so perfectly perfected it made me shutter. I needed to get myself under control. A look flashed across his face for a hot second. Was he blushing? As quick as it came the look disappeared. Ever so nonchalantly, I heard him say.

"You know I'm simply a run-of-the-mill prodigy son destined to take over the family business, whether I like it or not. You know, boring." Jason winked.

"Oh, is that all?"

If he wasn't going to tell me who he really was, I wasn't going to push. I had my own truths pressed close to my heart. He stood up and brushed the grass off his jeans, gave a little shake of his head and shrugged his shoulders,

"I'll see you in 6th."

And just like that, he walked away. Even though I wasn't going to pry I did wonder about his awkward exit. What was that all about? The bell rang to signal lunch was over, and the last thought I had before collected my belongings was, what did I have for 6th period, and how did he know I had it?

# Chapter 12: The Jewel

### Jason

Jason decided to not attend his next class and instead he headed for his bike in the parking lot. He wanted to call Mato and chew him out for the horrible lie he gave his dad, thus getting him in trouble. Next time, he'd have to come up with a better excuse and make sure Mato and the boys knew it backwards and forwards. Next time? Jason couldn't believe he was thinking about the next time he would defy his dad because of this girl. This was so out of character for Jason. He was the ideal son. Jason never rebelled or got into trouble, or even gave his dad a curt reply. He knew his place; he knew his lineage. Jason was the next Alpha, and he acted accordingly. But lately, something has changed. He had doubts, questions. Was this really the path for him? Was this what he wanted? Or was this just the expected path he was to take because of who his dad was? Now more than ever did he wished he could talk to his mom.

Jason's mom was the Jewel of the Tribe. She was kindness personified. Mother Earth herself would be proud to call her daughter of the land. She died two years ago; she had cancer. All the medicine men in the world couldn't heal her or any of the western medicine his dad insisted she go through. Jason hated watching her go through chemo. He watched her lose weight, lose hair, lose her fighting spirit. He didn't know what was worse, the cancer that was invading her body or the chemicals pumping through her claiming a cure. It was horrible. And he couldn't help but to think, somehow it was his fault.

He huffed out a loud breath. Jason hated thinking about his mother like that, so he stopped thinking about her at all. He knew it made him more closed off and hardened, but he didn't care. It made him feel better keeping people at arm's length, to keep them from getting too close. He used to take his mother to her Chemo treatments, where they would spend all afternoon talking about life and other things. She made him promise he wouldn't close his heart off, that he would let the wind and the land guide him through life and love and walk the path that was true to him. His mother always wanted him to find a partner. One that would be strong enough to take his stubbornness, but soft enough to teach him what it means to love. Jason always shrugged it off. He wasn't interested in any of the girls in his tribe. Jason knew he would have to choose a mate eventually, but it always seemed so far away. He had plenty of time to find someone. Then she died, and finding a mate was the last thing on his mind. With the passing of his mother, he thought his heart had closed forever, and he was fine with that. He didn't need love to lead the pack. Look at his dad. He was a widower and leading the Tribe just fine. His dad didn't need a partner, and neither did Jason.

With all this thinking about his mom and finding a partner, he couldn't help but have his thoughts come back to Alex. Alex, the strange girl who blew into his life and uprooted everything he knew. He, more than most, understood the meaning of extraordinary things. But she was beyond anything he knew. Was it her that caused Moira to suddenly go mute? Is that even possible? He couldn't prove that she had any involvement but the look in her eyes when Moira had her—episode—was undeniable.

When he kicked her foot, everything went back to normal. It had to have something to do with her, he just didn't know how. But despite the oddness of her behavior and the black cloud that seemed to physically follow her, she was rather beautiful. She didn't think much about her appearance, however, Jason sure did. In a strange way, she reminded him of his mother.

Not in appearance, but in spirit. She was unaware of the presence she held. And like his mother, when she entered a room, you knew. Her presence commanded attention. There was something dreamlike about her and it drew Jason to her. He could try to fight it. He knew he should fight it. But he couldn't help thinking his mom would want him to find out more. She was always telling him to follow his gut, and his gut was telling him something put her in his path for a reason. Jason decided right then that he was going to find out all he could about Alexandra Hart.

# Chapter 13: Edgar Allan Poe

### Alex

After lunch, I headed to my humanities class. I looked around to find an empty seat and on all the desk was a copy of the class syllabus. Which was strange because the semester started three months ago. Why was the teacher just now handing out the outline of the class? I busied myself reading over the class assignments outlined on the paper in front of me. The fortunate thing for me was that I've read most of these books already. Hopefully, this would be an easy class. Someone tapped my shoulder and when I looked up to see who it was, I was pleasantly surprised to find Lissa grinning from ear to ear.

"Hey, we're in three classes together isn't that great! And good thing because this class is a major snore. The teacher is like 100 years old and always forgets what he's talking about and that's only if he decides to teach anything at all. My mom is on the school board and is trying to get him transferred; they can't fire him because of some union issues. But I swear it's the easiest class you'll ever take."

I loved how Lissa could start such a simple conversation about anything at all, and she also didn't need help from me to keep it going. The teacher, who looked like he was trying to win an Edgar Allan Poe contest, messy hair and all, really could have been 100 years old. Or maybe we disturbed his noontime nap. He was pushing into the class a huge boxy looking television connected to a VCR player, yes you heard me correctly, a VCR! This really was going to be an easy class. Mr. Lang, the name printed on his belated syllables, turned off the lights and pressed play on the ancient VCR and To Kill a Mockingbird played on the screen. Lissa continued to have a conversation at me, I say at me, because really, let's face it, I wasn't doing much to keep it going. Bet she could have a conversation with a coat rack and illicit the same response I was giving her. I made a note to myself to add more, uh huh's, and yup's, and head nods to seem like I was following along. I wanted to have a friend. I never realized how alone I was in Minneapolis until I came here. Being alone was just what I was. Being one of many troubled foster kids in houses where, regardless of your struggle, you were already unwanted. Went a long way in solidifying a girl's understanding of how alone you really were in this cruel situation. But this place, this mountain town cut off from the hustle and bustle, it felt different. I didn't want to be alone anymore. I wanted to have someone I could trust and call a friend. Lissa was nice. I was glad she was in three of my classes. I believed I really could get through this. Maybe this really would be my last stop.

"Well, at least we got the syllabus."

I picked up the paper in front of me. It was double spaced and one sided.

"Yeah, every teacher is required to hand out a syllabus outlining the class curriculum. It isn't, however, specified when it must be handed out, just that it needs to be. What a joke, right?"

We continued like that for a few more quips and anecdotes. My mind kept drifting away from our banter and falling back on Jason. What was his fascination with me? Was he just trying to figure out how big of a freak I was and once he found out, would plaster some reputation, ending humiliation all over the school? Or did that only happen in bad teen movies? As if reading my mind, Lissa asked me about the one thing I didn't want to talk about.

"I saw you talking to Jason at lunch today, how'd you snag that lunch date. He's hardly spoken a word to any of the girls here since he transferred last fall. And that's not from lack of trying. He's ignored so many girls that there have been rumors going around that he is betrothed to some native princess. Either that, or he's gay and doesn't want to come out of the closet yet. I don't blame him if he was. The guys at this school can be real jerks sometimes and the girls too, for that matter. I mean, you've met Moira. So, what's your secret? How'd you do that?"

She looked at me and gave me a cheesy grin, while wiggling her eyebrows at me.

"I don't know what to tell you. He simply sat down next to me. I didn't *do* anything. And as for as the betrothal goes, he didn't seem to be betrothed to anyone, girl or guy."

I told her, trying to hide my guilty smile.

"Alex, you are bad! You know that? But now that you caught Jason's attention, there's going to be some feathers ruffled from the top cats around here. I'd watch your back if I were you. But tell me, is his voice as utterly lushes as his lips? And I bet he smells great. Does he smell great? Like danger and sex? You know he rides a motorcycle, don't you? The red and black one in the parking lot. I've seen more than a few boys' eye go green with envy whenever they see it."

Her infectious giggle as she spoke was hard to ignore. I smiled at her, a genuine, pure smile that I felt deep in my core. This was good. She was good. I gave her elbow a friendly slap,

"Now, who's the bad one? I bet you wish it was you on the grass instead of me."

"No doubt! Can you blame me!! He's gorgeous."

We both laughed in our notebooks, giggling and gossiping like schoolgirls. It was a welcome event. It was nice to feel at ease with normal teenage issues, not the fractured past I knew. However, the easy banter of our girl talk came to an abrupt holt. Moira walked in the door, dressed head to toe in school spirit. A sweater so tight it surprised me she could even breathe. And a skirt so short I prayed she was wearing panties. Two other girls followed her in, in their cheer attire, both just as beautiful, but no one filled out their uniform quite like Moira. The whole vibe of the room changed. It felt like they sucked the sound out. I guess word of her earlier mishap was making its way through the halls and everyone waited to see what Moira would do next. If the phrase Looks Could Kill had any bearing, this girl perfected it. Her pristine white sneakers made a soft thud on the carpeted classroom floor as she made her way to where Lissa and I sat frozen in our seats. Her skirt swished and the leather in her jacket squeaked. It was like everything about her announced her presence. She placed both of her perfectly manicured hands on my desk and leaned over to whisper words full of fire.

"I have no idea what the hell happened in civics today, but I know you had something to do with it and I will find out. I never break a promise and just so you're aware, Jason is off limits. Don't delude yourself because he spent 30 minutes with you at lunch today. There is no way I guy like him is going to be anything but bored by a girl like you. He needs someone of higher caliber, someone who will only add to his perfection, not someone who is going to drag him down. I run this school, my mother is the principal, and my father is on the Council. I suggest you get back on your broomstick and fly to wherever the hell you blew in from. I can make your life a living hell. Welcome to Gold Creek."

She stood up slowly and looked across from me to see who it was I was talking to, as if she'd only just now realized she was standing in a class full of people.

"Oh, hey Lissa, how was your horse-I mean lunch? Or is it the same thing these days?"

She and her harem of girls wickedly laughed as they walked away, but not before she mumbled "Witch" under her breath. She said it just loud enough were the immediate people around us could have easily heard her. I hoped they heard bitch, instead, because I'd rather they think of the latter than the former. Class continued with no further incidents, aside from a few wayward glances in my direction from Queen Bitch. Although poor Lissa looked as if her spirits were crushed, the joyful attitude we started the class with was nowhere to be seen. Class ended in silence from the both of us. We walked each other to the end of the hall where we parted ways; her going off to A.P. Trig; me going to Spanish. There was a comforting vibe in knowing I'd see her again tomorrow. Hopefully, we could put Moira out of our minds and be able to have a bitch-free day.

I suddenly remembered that according to Jason we had 6th period together, and after Spanish would be my 6th period. My heart was fluttering at the thought of it. Was it because I was hoping to see him again, or because I was afraid Moira wouldn't be too pleased?

# Chapter 14: I Heard Him

**Alex**

There was no avoiding it, it was time to head to my last class of the day; Gym and I had a serious case of elephant butterflies dive-bombing into the debts of my belly. The nerves weren't because of my hatred of P.E., but come on, who likes showcasing their lack of sport skills in front of 50 of their not so closest friends? It was because I knew Jason would be there. Jason. Just thinking about him made the butterflies spread their wings like an overachiever on Adderall. I was dizzy with nerves. It was weird how he knew my schedule. He must have read it on the paper this morning in the office. Before I could contemplate anymore of the ins and outs of Jason Alder's speed-reading abilities, I ran right smack into something hard and warm. We both said.

"Ow!"

"Ow? You ran into me."

I took a step back to see who the voice belonged to before we could debate who ran into whom. I recognized him; he was the boy from the Manor, the same boy that ran into my shoulder this morning. It suddenly flooded me with the realization we were the last few people out in the hall, and my gut was telling me I did not want to be caught alone with this dude.

"It's Alex, right?" He said.

His voice was smooth and had a county lilt to it, like Norah's, his twin sister it turns out. Only his sounded a little more forced, a little too cowboy perfect if you catch my meaning. If I didn't know that his sister had a similar yet not as pronounced accent, I would have thought he was putting on an act.

"Going to gym? Looks like we're in the same class. Ain't that my luck? I'm Neal."

"Uh, yeah." Was all I dared to say.

Neal, the tow-headed boy from last night's dinner, stood there in front of me, tall and lean. His stance was confident, almost aggressive. The sinking feeling that I shouldn't be alone with him was growing extremely fast. I remembered the ache in my shoulder from earlier. There was no way it was an accidental brush. He bent his chin down to inspect me and his powder blue eyes were so alluring and seductive it was hypnotizing. I took a slight step back; we were still too close for my personal bubble. He seemed dangerous, and I didn't want to be alone with him any longer than I needed to be. I side-stepped him and slipped my hand around the knob of the locker room door. It was a heavy door, and it caught me off guard. It groaned as it opened, blocking out whatever Neal might have said to my back. But it sounded something like, "See ya 'round."

The P.E. assistant helped me locate my locker and a new pair of gym clothes from the ASB Spirit closet. She said they were already purchased along with an ASB card. She told me the card gets me into dances and sporting events at half the price and she said it with such zeal like she fully believed it was the highlight of my day. I don't think going to school dances was really my thing. Or at least I've never been to one before, so what did I know. Once I dressed in all my flattering red and gold gym gear, I made my way into the gymnasium and towards the only middle-aged person in the room. I had to laugh a little to myself. This man was a stereotypical gym teacher. Exactly like the ones you'd see on a Wednesday night sitcom, tight red shorts and a potbelly trying to escape the bottom of his *Gold Creek High* windbreaker. The man spotted me and waved for me to come closer.

"You must be my new recruit."

He told me as I got closer.

"I'm Coach Jenson. We're halfway through our Basketball Bracket and right now we're scrimmaging. Take one of those blue vests and join the game on the left-hand side of the court. You'll find the captains of the teams have a White C on their vests. They'll tell you where to go."

He didn't say anymore, just blew the whistle that hung from his neck and jogged over to a game in session, yelling something about foul play and aggressive hands. I stood there for a little, thinking about the direction my "Coach" had given me. I broke it down word by word. Okay vest, blue. I grabbed one out of an ancient cardboard box being held together by tape and prayers and put it on. I didn't dare think about when the was the last time these things had a good wash. He said something about the left-hand side. Did that mean my left or his? I knew what Stage-Left was, I highly doubt there was such a thing as Basketball-Left. Good God, can't I stand here until the bell rang?

"Hey!"

Someone ran up to me. I turned toward the voice and my breath caught. It was Jason. He was smiling, a full toothy smile. It was amazing; I had half expected his teeth to sparkle and a sign for Colgate to drop from the rafters. He had on a blue vest like mine, only he had a big C stitched on it. Captain, of course. His gold cotton t-shirt hugged his body with just enough tension. You could trace your eyes along every muscle of his core. He was a tree, standing strong and majestic. It was wonderful.

"Hey Alex, you're on my team."

Blush. I need to stop doing that.

"Just so you know my basketball skills are seriously lacking, if you want to bench me, I'll take no offense."

He chuckled and his hair fell in his eyes as his head shook in denial of my claim of athleticism.

"Come on. I'm sure you're not that bad."

He said, giving my shoulder a friendly nudge. How I wanted to touch my shoulder, still warm from his hand. I looked at him uneasily and thought Newton, meet brick wall but followed anyway. I was managing on the sidelines well. Coach was too busy referring to the other games to notice the new girl avoiding any actual participation. However, I couldn't escape the entire period. Unfortunately, Coach approached me with a tilt of his head and a raised eyebrow.

"Is there a reason you have yet to enter the game?"

Before I could come up with an acceptable excuse, he blew his whistle, calling Jason over to us on the sideline. Jason approached us with an apologetic look, for who, I didn't know, but he gently took hold of my elbow and lead me to where his team was playing. He quickly told me where I needed to stand and what I should expect to do if and when a ball came into my path, I immediately stopped listening because I knew right away this wasn't going to end well if they really expected me to contribute.

There I was in the thick of the game, trying incredibly hard not to get elbowed in the eye while the other players bounced and dodged around me. I was more of a hindrance than anything else. I blocked a few people, or at the very least I stood there, annoyingly waving my arms up and down. In all my fake blocking attempts, I didn't notice Neal was one of the opposing players. He must have noticed me at the same time I noticed him, because right then he gave me the sleaziest grin I have ever seen on a boy. I instantly felt exposed and wished my too short shorts would magically turn into floor length pants.

At some point, I found myself under the net, which I knew now was the "rebound zone," when two large guys leaped into the air to fight for the ball as it came down from its arc. Before the players' feet came back to earth, the ground began to tremble. The parquet flooring was rolling, quick and fluid like water. I could no longer hold my footing and me hitting the deck was inevitable, as it was for the boys above me. I was going to be the cushion that broke their fall. Before the domino effect of, student bodies - hitting student bodies - hitting floor, could play out, something caught my attention. Neal was standing still among all the chaos, glaring at me.

As quick as it came, everything was as it was, still and unmoving. What was that! Is all that went through my mind. I never knew Montana could even have earthquakes. I thought they reserved those for the coast locked states. Before anymore contemplation of movement between plate tectonics could happen, I was suddenly aware of a sharp pain shooting up my ankle. I cursed internally as a searing hot pain throbbed up and down my leg. I saw the two boys who had been fighting over the ball earlier were now on top of my legs. We were all knotted together in a collage of students. Feet were rushing toward us and voices were murmuring around our heads. Hands grabbed my shoulders to prevent me from getting up. Other hands intertwined around the boys' limbs to help them untie legs from each other. The once smooth and shiny floor was now littered with cracks and jagged pieces.

Now that we were finally all free from the mess, my ankle hurt more than ever. The hands that were on my shoulders were now under my arms, about to help me to my feet. I turned my head around to see who the good Samaritan was, and, of course, to my utter embarrassment, it was Jason. He looked at me, concern written all over his face, and then I heard him ask me.

*Alex, are you all, right?*

Only his lips didn't move. I slowly shook my head from side to side and waited for the headache to come like it always did. But it didn't, and I don't think I was imagining it this time. I heard him. He narrowed his eyes. This time his lips moved.

"Alex, are you alright, can you stand?"

Jason pulled me up to a standing position and I tried putting my weight down on both my feet, BAM. A shock of pain coursed through my left leg, and I was heading toward the floor again. If it wasn't for Jason, I would have been on the floor. Lucky enough for me, he moved his grip and kept me upright. By this point, there were about a dozen adult staff members pouring into the gym to assess the situation and help the wounded. I could hear the faint sounds of sirens in the distance. Did we just experience an earthquake? In the middle of Montana? I had a sinking feeling that my bad luck had found me. It took all I had to not lose my lunch all over Jason's shoes.

Neal was nowhere to be seen amongst the chaos of students. First responders were now on the scene and other students were slowly coming out of their classrooms. The school had to be evacuated to access the damage. I don't believe anybody was seriously hurt. Nothing had come crashing down, nothing except me.

# Chapter 15: Like a Fuzzy Dream

### Alex

Jason maneuvered my arm, so it hooked around his waist that way I could put my weight on him as he helped me walk to the nurse's office. He looked shy, which seemed out of character for him, but it was endearing all the same.

"Shall we go then?" He said.

I took one hobbled step forward and a string of curses screamed in my brain. Jason winced, then bent his knees and wrapped his free arm around my legs to pick me up. My cheeks burned, and it was not because I had landed on the gym floor. We started walking again, no one said anything in the awkward silence. I couldn't take it anymore. I had to say something.

"I heard you."

He glanced over at me.

"Earlier, in my head. I heard you ask if I was okay, but I didn't see you move your lips. I know it sounds crazy, but I know what I heard. Maybe I'm in shock, but something strange happened. You can't tell me it didn't."

My gut put pieces together, but my mind was not letting the pieces stick. It was all too strange. Too unexplained, I was however, a magnet for the unexplained. So why then was it so hard for me to believe this could be another one of those strange occurrences that always seem to follow me. Maybe my desire for a permanent "mishap-free" place to live was stronger than I thought.

His jaw clenched and his grip around me tightened a bit. He didn't look at me, just continued down the hall towards the nurse's office as if I said nothing at all.

"I know what I heard. Are you going to talk to me?"

I deserved to hear some answers. He stopped walking and looked at me. I think he was weighing the words in his head. Going over what exactly it was he was about to say.

"You're right."

He said, so low I barely caught it.

"I am?"

*I was?*

"You deserve to hear some answers." He intoned.

My eyes widened. Had I said that last part out loud? I didn't think so, but then how did he answer me?

"You don't have to."

My mouth opened. To say something, to not say something, I didn't know.

"Put me down."

I told him, completely on edge now. He hesitated for a second.

"Put me down."

I said with a little more confidence. A sad look cut his face, but he collected himself again and did as I asked. When he put me down, I braced myself against the lockers next to me, trying to hide the pain in my ankle.

What was going on? How was he answering questions I hadn't asked? Who is this guy, what is this guy. I had to get away from him. I had to clear my head. Maybe I hit my head harder than I thought. Maybe this was all some crazy dream because of the concussion. This was an illusion. Any second now, I was going to wake up with drool on my face in the middle of the gym floor.

I couldn't really be thinking about this. It's not possible for people to what, — read minds — that's crazy. My head was spinning. This wasn't happening. It couldn't be. I took a strained step in the direction we were headed in just a moment ago. I moved one inch, but the pain was too much. It made a blinding light blaze behind my eyelids. There was no way I was going to make it on my own to the nurses' station, not when I couldn't place both feet on the ground. Hell, I didn't even know where I was even going.

Why didn't I wait for the paramedics in the gym? Why did I allow this boy I knew nothing about to separate me from the rest of the crowd. Oh god! I was going to wind up on some docu-series for kidnapped girls. This isn't good, I need to get back, I need to find people. Why were the halls so empty. Didn't we just have some freak earthquakes happen? My mind was spinning with unanswered questions, each one getting more and more dark as I spun out of control. I tried again, but this time I almost collapsed over myself. A searing pain vibrated through my heel and ankle. I tried breathing through it in a feeble attempt to seem strong.

His hand caught me before I could stumble too far. I jerked away from his touch.

"Please, let me help you. I'm not going to kidnap you. The gym felt... wrong. I can't explain it. And I knew there would be first aid equipment in the office. I can bandage your ankle if the nurse isn't there. I just knew I needed to get you away from the gym. You're in too much pain to go yourself. I won't hurt you. I'll answer any question that I can justify answering. Just please let me take you."

He seemed so concerned, so honestly helpful. But I couldn't shake the unnatural feel of his voice invading my head.

*Please.*

There it was again, the voice in my head. It wasn't the same as hearing sounds with my ears. I felt the words he was saying, like a fuzzy dream I was trying to remember. I could see the words he was saying.

"Stop it! Whatever you're doing, you're in my head. Stop it."

I tried to control my breathing. I was getting frantic. Between the pain in my ankle and the unexplained weirdness of what was going on here, I wasn't able to handle it. I swallowed hard to get myself under control. I stood there just looking at him. He looked so hurt and wounded, so small and frail, yet still as beautiful as a wild animal. I bit my lower lip, weighing my options. None of them were good. I leaned toward him and without saying anything, he cradled me gently and began walking toward the nurses' station.

We took a few steps more, no one wanted to break the silence first. I tried, without success, to be as far away from him as possible. But since he had to carry me, it was a futile attempt.

"You don't have to be afraid of me." He whispered.

"I didn't say I was."

Okay, that came out a little bitchier than I had intended, but the situation called for a little attitude. A smirk showed up on his face. I frowned at him.

"You're cute when you're trying to be mad at me."

He said, the calm confidence slowly returning.

"Okay, Stop! You really need to answer some of my questions, or I will find my way to the nurses' office without you."

I blurted, my face heating up out of anger and embarrassment. He took a deep breath, looked me right in the eye, and said.

"Okay fine. What do you want to know?"

He stopped walking and waited for me to answer.

"How can I hear you in my head? Can you read my thoughts? Can you do it all the time? Is there a way to get you to stop? Can you read everyone's thoughts or just mine?"

The words were falling out of my mouth like water through a sieve; there was no rhyme or reason they just kept coming.

"You talk a lot." He laughed. I didn't think any of this was funny.

"Sorry, you're right. It's not funny, you're...very amusing to me. Honestly, I didn't know that you could hear me when I tried to push my thoughts out to you. It was a long shot for sure. At first, I thought it was because you were...something familiar to me, but I can say that's a no. And yes, I can read all your thoughts all the time, and there is a way to block your mind from me, but it takes practice. And yes, I can hear everyone's thought not just yours."

He was saying all this as if it was the most common conversation to be having with someone. We could have been talking about any mundane issue; do you prefer hotdogs or corn dogs? But this wasn't mundane, this was insane. This was some plot line out of a sci-fi novel, not something that happens in your everyday life, but I guess my life has — at times — not been so "everyday". So why then was it so hard for me to believe that this was another one of those not so everyday things?

I looked — no, glared — at him to explain further. No way was I going to be some open book to have my every thought at the mercy of one cute boy.

"Okay Okay! You have to imagine your thoughts locked into a safe, or behind some concrete fortress. You know, unattainable, in such a way they're not sitting out there for anybody like me to read easily. It takes too much concentration, so I live with being an open book; unless you're my dad, then it's block, block, block." He said that last part with a smile on his lips.

"Of course, for me and others like me, we have learned restraints against reading each other's thoughts, you know, invasion of privacy and what not. And besides, when you have friends like mine, you really don't want to know what they're thinking all the time. It will change you." This time, a full chuckle came out. "But then again, I've had all my life to deal with this, so really it's nothing new to me." He continued back toward the nurse.

"You know you're an expert at answering my questions without answering any of my questions, and in the process, making me think of new questions all together. It's rather annoying. Are you trying to be annoying or stalling until we get to the nurse, so you don't have to answer?" I was getting frustrated. He shook his head again and this time his expression changed, almost remorseful.

"I'm not trying to stall. I have secrets, and they aren't mine to expose, if you know what I mean."

He sounded nervous. I felt bad for pressuring him to spill the beans. Almost. My head was spinning with the many questions I wanted to ask, but the ever-present nurses' station was coming into view. I knew our moment of privacy was coming to an end. Damn.

"Maybe I can meet you sometime and we can talk." He asked before I could say anything more.

"Yeah, talk...sure."

I didn't know what to say. From what I could gather, the Matrons ran a tight ship. I couldn't picture them letting me out for an evening when it was only my second day at the Manor. But I also couldn't live without knowing what was going on. I couldn't decide what to do. I looked at him. He was standing there holding me, looking so forlorn and lovely. How could I say no to someone who was so amazing to look at? Besides, it's not like breaking the rules was a new concept to me. I'd find a way to see him. I had to, and if I was being honest with myself, I wanted to.

Jason's smirk came back. Of course, he already knew the answer I was going to give him. Great, this was going to take some time to get used to. What was I getting myself into? I was about to open my mouth in reply, but before I could, Jason interrupted me.

"There's a little café around the corner. By the way, tomorrow *is* Friday. I'm sure you'll be able to get away for some coffee. I'll pick you up, and yes, before you ask. I do know where you live. Everyone knows about the ladies who live in the cottage in the woods." I shut my mouth and my teeth clicked, okay that was going to take some getting use too. Having a conversation without the conversation part was odd for sure.

Jason, who was still carrying me, kicked open the door next to the Guidance Counselor. Apparently, this was also where the nurse's office was. Jason walked into the room slowly, placing me on the tall table that sat in the middle of the room. He then went around to the main office doors to see if he could track down the actual nurse. Who was probably busy with the other students in the gym. I did not want to be put in an ambulance on my first day at a new school. Especially over a sprained ankle. I was hoping we'd find a nurse quickly and get the situation resolved with as little fuss as possible.

# Chapter 16: No Going Back

### Jason

As Jason watched with utter amusement of Alex's attempt to block the players in the key, he couldn't help but laugh to himself. He guessed she wasn't joking when she said she had zero clue what she was doing. Before he could move towards her to help block the two players, who were almost double her size, he sensed a disturbance under his feet. He hit the deck of the court, landing on all fours, keeping his balance as he witnessed the entire gym floor shook underneath him. An earthquake? Montana hasn't had an earthquake in over 40 years, Jason thought. Jason had to work hard to filter out all the inner voices of the surrounding students, all of which were in high panic mode. He had to find Alex. Where was she? He heard her before he found her. She was in pain, and from the look of it buried underneath 200 pounds of boy.

The earthquake lasted less than a minute. The chaos it left in its wake was everywhere. Floorboards cracked and splintered. Students walked around confused and shocked; staff members tried to get the situation under control. Jason was by Alex's side untangling the guys who fell on top of her. He looked her over, she seemed relatively fine. Her heartbeat was elevated, her pupils were dilated, she was going into shock. Jason thought right away he needed to get her to the nurse's office. He knew the paramedics would be here soon, but he didn't want to wait for them, besides he knew the nurse. She was a family friend, so to speak. Without thinking about it, he reached out to Alex through Spirit Talking and quickly regretted it. He needed to stop getting too close to this girl. He wasn't ready to reveal secrets that weren't his to reveal. But he also couldn't deny the attraction and pull she had over him. Nothing like this has ever happened to him before. He needed to get ahold of himself, but he also couldn't walk away until he knew more about her. Or at least that's what he told himself rather than believing that he's developing genuine feelings for this strange, strange girl. Once Alex was on her feet, he knew right away there was no way she'd be able to walk to the nurse. He would also bet that Alex was the type who liked to be in control of her own decisions. He decided he would help her in any way she would allow him to.

Alex agreed to allow Jason to escort her to the nurse, but she insisted she do it on her own feet, which Jason knew right away would be a battle she would lose. He could feel the elevated heat coming from her ankle. Which most likely meant it was broken, if not broken, then severely sprained. Alex gave in and allowed Jason to carry her the rest of the way to the nurse. Which meant there was no escaping Alex's interrogative questioning. There was nowhere for him to go but to face her questioning stare. Alex didn't waste any time voicing the thoughts running through her head.

"I heard you."

*Damn,* Jason thought. He was hoping his spirit message hadn't gone through. There was no denying it now. She had the gift. Or at least a way to receive it. Jason didn't know how much of his story he should disclose. He knew he would get shit from his dad, regardless of what he said. There was no turning back now.

"You're right."

It shocked Alex that he finally answered and admitted something was going on. Jason figured the cat was out of the bag and he might as well stop fighting it. Without thinking about it, he answered her unvoiced questions. He instantly wished he hadn't. His response made Alex's sense of intrusion jump tenfold. She demanded Jason put her down. His initial reaction was to deny this request. He knew her ankle wouldn't support her, and being in his arms would be the safest place for her right now. If Jason was honest with himself, he didn't want to put her down. He likes the feeling of her in his arms. She was soft and fragile, and warm. Reluctantly, he placed her gingerly back on her feet, and she immediately stumbled into the lockers behind her. Jason's arms involuntarily twitched in her direction, ready to catch her if she fell.

Her inner monologue was a whirlwind of confused questions he wasn't quite ready to answer, not here. His first concern was getting her off the ankle in questions and get her seen by the nurse. Whether she liked it or not, he refused to let her walk herself to the nurse. His pleas weren't getting through. He was about to give up when suddenly she leaned towards him, and he took it as her white flag. He gathered her up in his arms and continued to the nurses' station, trying to answer what questions he could. Throughout his conversation, Jason weighed what he should and shouldn't say. He knew he probably shouldn't say any of it, but there was something about Alex — *Alexandra* — that made him want to tell her. Jason knew he couldn't fight the feelings bubbling up from the deepest part of his core. He needed to a way to talk to her, in private, where he could try to explain the things, he knew he shouldn't.

He persuaded her to agree to meet him for coffee. It's settled then. He'd see her tomorrow night, and he knew after this day there was no going back.

# Chapter 17: Very Normal Things

**Alex**

The Nurse delayed my release from school, making sure nothing was broken. She wrapped up my ankle from my toes to mid-calf. When she had rolled my pant leg up to expose the ankle, what was revealed was a leg every shade of blue imaginable. I was definitely going to be feeling that in the morning.

Obviously, I had missed the bus, but instead of calling the Matrons to pick me up, the nurse informed me she had already contacted them and told them she'd take me home. Apparently, the manor was on her way home. I guess everyone really did know the Matrons. That's small town living for you.

I told the nurse to drop me off at the lane, rather than driving up to the house. I didn't want it to look like I needed an escort home. She was a little hesitant at first. I told her the two little Advil's she'd given me were kicking in and I hardly felt a thing. I felt bad for lying, but not bad enough to let her drive me to the house.

Walking down the lane, I will admit, was more of a hassle than I thought it was going to be. My ankle hurt like hell, and I was probably doing more damage by walking the short 200 yards to the door than was utterly necessary. I didn't mind all that much. It was a nice crisp winter day. It gave me time to take in my surroundings, to take in a moment where it was just me. To breathe. The wind picked up, bringing with it the scent of rain on the horizon. Trees were turning all colors of fall, bright red, muted orange, sharp yellow. It really was beautiful. For that minute, I was alone and normal. Just a girl walking home, crunching on the fallen leaves, thinking about the English paper that was due on a book she has yet to read.

Of course, that's not what I was. I was a girl who sprains her ankle after being used as a human crash pad because of some crazy earthquake that she was half convinced wasn't caused by natural consequences. Who was also making friends with a boy who could apparently read minds. *What a fantastic first day.*

The lane ended, and the only thing in front of me now was the large Manor. Standing guard was not one, but two Matrons with arms crossed against their chest standing on the stoop waiting to hear whatever story I was about to concoct. Before I could open my mouth, the two Matrons looked at each other with the same knowing expression. They pointed their eyes toward the front door, and all was left for me to do was walk through it, because really, what choice did I have?

I was dreading the confrontation we were about to have. Here I was, first day at a new school, second day in a new program and I was already breaking rank and showing up late and damaged. I mean, I had a good reason. Two giant boys used my legs as landing gear. I will be the first to admit I am not always one to follow the rules, but I think it's a record to break them in the first 24 hours of relocation. So, I was kind of proud of myself but very mortified at the same time.

Ms. Terra pulled out a chair for me as she made her way around the desk to take her place. I sat down, put my schoolbag on the floor, and prepared for the lecture. But instead of letting me have it, we sat there for a minute, staring at each other. Okay, when does the tongue-lashing take place? Mrs. Terra leaned over her desk and clasped her hands together before she spoke.

"Alexandra, how was your first day?"

I said nothing, waiting for the follow up question which I knew was coming she asked again.

"How was your first day?"

"Oh, other than the nurse's visit, I guess it was okay."

I felt strange having a seemingly normal conversation. She continued. "About the nurses' visit, what happened? I heard the earthquake occurred during 6th period. We felt it here as well, but it sounds like it was a lot stronger at the high school. Was everyone okay?"

She said it like it was the most normal thing to happen. You know the ever-present threat of earthquakes in the hills of Montana. The ones that remarkably disturb your education in the physical art of basketball, yet no one gets hurt. Oh wait, except me! Then there's the even more normal event of boys who can invade your thoughts without batting an eye. All very normal things.

Then it happened again, the headaches that have been coming far too often as of late. It seems I can't shake them. My senses ran on overload. Everything seemed so loud, yet I couldn't hear a thing. I had to shut my eyes suddenly because of how overwhelmingly bright the room suddenly became. Squeezing the side of my head, hoping to help shut out the lights, the sounds, the feelings that something was trying to push its way out of my brain. I wanted it to stop, but it got worse, way worse.

# Chapter 18: What's with all the whooshing?

**Alex**

I thought I could hear Ms. Terra saying my name, but the words were too far away and too fuzzy to comprehend. The only thing I could concentrate on was the last thing that we were discussing before the headache from hell rendered me useless, the earthquake in the gym.

My headache became stronger, but my vision was clearing, not the — open your eyes and survey your surroundings kind of vision — but a vision, vision. Images were slowly coming into focus behind my shut eyelids, all fuzzy and jerky, watching a movie through a projection reel. The more I focused on the images, the less of a problem my headache was.

Once I submitted fully to the vision, I became part of it. It suddenly whooshed me back to 6th period, straight out of the twilight zone, sort of whooshing. I was a little dizzy from all the whooshing, but I got my bearings and took in my surroundings. I was standing in the gym watching myself attempt to play basketball. This was the strangest thing I have ever encountered in my life — me watching me — definitely an out-of-body experience. I realized quickly I was merely a spectator. No one seemed to notice an exact double of myself standing mere feet from them. It was a very weird and disturbing thing to see yourself from outside yourself, talk about identity crisis.

Note to self, get a haircut, my ends are looking a little scary. Anyway, I looked around, trying to figure out what was going on and why I was being shown this scene. I've seen enough sci-fi movies to know that when the main character relives a part of their past. It's usually because there's some sort of message they need to uncover. So, I guess I need to find some sort of clue, but I was clueless. What was I looking for? I surveyed the scene in front of me to see if I could notice anything unusual or out of place, but the only thing I saw beyond the game at play was Neal. Everything was moving in slow motion, except him, he was not moving at all. Except on closer look, I saw something, his lips, he was mouthing something and looked to be in deep concentration. A bead of sweat was dripping down his forehead, his hands clutched tightly at his sides. I turned my head to see what he was looking at so intently, but the only thing in his line of sight was me.

Suddenly the whooshing tunnel came back, and I was unexpectedly — and might I add — not so gracefully thrown into a new vision. A vision I did not recognize. This was not a memory recollection like the basketball game. This was something else entirely.

I found myself standing on the outskirts of a crowd of people. People, who were gathered around one individual, like they were having an impromptu town meeting. The crowd was dressed in old fashion clothing; think Little Women or anything out of a Bronte novel. The women wore long plain dresses with bonnets and the men wore trim suits with hats. I wanted to get closer. Maybe I would get a better look at the woman in the middle of it all, she wore a red velvet cape, with gold stitching intricately sewn along every hem. The crowd was bathed in soft gas lamps, which made the stitching on the cape shimmer. It glowed from the inside out. The people who had gathered around her hung on to every word she spoke. They were in awe of her. A few of them dressed in similar capes, however, none were as remarkable as hers.

I made my way to the crowd of people ensuring I stayed in the shadows of the nearby structures. The woman leading the crowd came into focus. Instantly, I felt hit in the chest. I couldn't breathe, I couldn't move, I just stood there gaping mouth on the floor. The woman I was staring at... was me. Or at least I thought it was me. The woman was older, maybe in her late 40s, but her facial structure was unmistakable. High cheekbones, oval face, dark eyebrows, and her gray colored eyes, the color of an impending storm on the horizon were unmistakably my eyes. What told me irrevocably that the lady in front of me was me, was the overwhelming gut feeling. It was me, an older me, but me. What the hell.

I had to find out what was going on. Was I really seeing this? Did the fall in the gym today make me lose my mind? Was this what happened when you got a concussion? You see historical events resembling yourself. I wasn't ready to accept the fact that I was crazy. There needed to be another reason why, I was seeing what I was seeing.

A sharp breeze blew through, hushing the crowd. A man walked across the open space between the gathering horde. He wore a cape of his own, black and nothing like the beautiful red one. Hers was glorious and powerful. His was dark and dangerous. So black it was void of any color, any light that would have bounced off it was instead swallowed up, it had red symbols etched into the bottom, symbols that looked frightening and intrusive.

He pulled his hood low over his face. He vocalized with a voice I didn't so much as hear but feel. It rumbled through my bones. Lingering fingers of ice trailed down my neck and around my ribs. It was consuming. I wanted to run away from the voice, it was so hypnotic I couldn't move a single hair if I wanted to. I felt the effect his words had on the Lady. It was almost as if a thin veil connected the two of us and in that moment; we were experiencing everything together. All I could sense, however, was immense sadness and hurt. I can't explain it, but I knew what she was feeling and why she was feeling it. He betrayed her. He was plotting against her. Against what, I couldn't say, but I knew I was right.

He spoke. I couldn't make out what he was saying, but the Lady felt threatened. She knew she had to protect the gathering people around her. The man's voice was escalating, his words coming out faster, stronger and angrier. The Lady was becoming enraged. She raised her hands towards the sky, a billowing wind burst through almost as if it was bending to her will. Blustery puffs circled around her in a cyclone of power, leaves and debris. It was growing stronger with every passing second.

Out of nowhere, an inky black smoke cloud exploded through the crowd full of noise and electric sparks. I shielded my eyes and reflexively crouched from the noise. When I stood up, the wind had died down, and the dust had settled, and the man was gone. Before I could glance back at the woman, my vision was gone too. I was back in the office at the Manor. A confused look on my face and minus one headache, no after effect, no lingering pain, nothing. The only thing left was the connection I had with the Lady, who may or may not be me. And she was in some real danger. That man, the one she had once trusted turned against her, leaving her fearing for her life. I felt a similar feeling of fear that afternoon, when I had... when I had bumped into Neal. Was the Neal in my vision making the earthquake happen?

What was going on? I couldn't take it anymore. Now I was really getting a headache, but the normal stress one that normal people get. When I opened my eyes, I remembered I was in the office with Ms. Terra. Oh god, what does she think of me? I slowly opened my eyes to accept whatever weird allegation she was about to give me. She said nothing. She just sat there, slowly nodding at me, a faint smile slinking up her face. After a moment, she looked at me and said, "How are those headaches, any better? Are you noticing anything different?"

What is she talking about? Does she know? Should I tell her?

"It's okay Alex, you can talk to me I'm a pretty good listener if you give me a chance." Ms. Terra said warmly.

"I don't know what it is you want me to say? They're just headaches, you know, nothing special." My nerves were creeping up fast.

"Alex, you can tell me. I can answer some of your questions." She said.

There it was. The one thing I was hoping beyond hope I would not hear. The thing I hoped would discredit everything I was thinking about, everything I thought I was connecting. I was almost hoping to be crazy rather than have things explained rationally. I didn't think my mind could handle the idea that maybe there might be an explainable reason for the years of weirdness that surrounded me. My eyes just widened, and my jaw dropped. I didn't have the slightest idea what I was supposed to say back.

Ms. Terra continued, dodging the deer in the headlights expression I was giving her. "I am sure you have noticed that things do not always seem as they should. Odd events maybe, unusual occurrences perhaps, and every time a headache was right behind. Have you any idea why this is happening?"

What?! What was going on? For as long as I could remember, I have had to suppress my ideas of things seeming off. Maybe there was a rational explanation why weird, unexplained things seemed to happen when I was around. Of course, when they happened, I had no good explanation, and of course I never confessed to having anything to do with the weird occurrences. But then, like clockwork, I was on the next boat to my next posting. Making my rounds through every group home and foster care in the greater area of

Minneapolis, like a person carrying the last strain of a deadly virus threatening to affect the surrounding people. Fun, I know right?

Now here we were, me and my superior, talking about 'odd occurring's? Not happening. What should I do, tell the truth, get kicked out before I have even a chance to get settled, move on to yet another group home and continue to do that till I'm 18? Or should I just lie, and wait till things get worse, wait until someone gets hurt? Again.

"Alex, it's alright, you can tell me, you're in a safe place. You were brought here for a reason, and so I ask again. How are your headaches? Please tell us before someone gets hurt."

I let my head roll down to my chest in utter defeat. There is no reason to hide anymore. I took a deep breath and on the exhalation; I looked right at her and started talking.

# Chapter 19: No Denying it Now

**Alex**

What seemed like hours later but was only 45 minutes, I told Ms. Terra everything. Well, almost everything. I told her about what happened in Gym, and with Moriah, and about my accusations of Neal. She did not like that very much. Her eyes widened and her lips pursed together. Either out of anger or frustration, I didn't know. I told her about the other schools I had attended and some of the strange activities that happened there. Like the dog that kept barking under my window in St. Paul. How I wished a cat burglar would snatch him up, then how the next day he was gone, leaving the owners distraught with his disappearance. I divulged everything from my past, and it was empowering, almost renewing. Like with every secret I was holding onto a 5-pound brick, and I was taking a chisel and removing them one by one. My head was almost dizzy with how light I felt, and the best part was there was no sign of a headache coming. For once, there was no blinding pain bringing me to my knees, leaving me wanting to pull my hair out. And that, above all else, was the weirdest thing of all.

What I didn't tell her was about Jason. I don't know why. Something just told me to keep that last secret to myself.

"Alex, before you leave, there's one more thing."

Ms. Terra stood up and walked to her floor to ceiling bookshelf and began to read through the many spines of books that lined her shelves. She "ah-ha'd" and then pulled out a brown leather-bound book from one of the lower shelves. It was small, about the size of a diary, like the kind little girls have with a small lock to keep people out, but you know a simple bobby-pin would crack it in no time. She brought the little book over to the desk and set it in front of me.

"Alex, do you know what this is?"

"No, should I?"

I reached for the book to get a closer look. There was nothing remarkably special about it. It was plain, with no title on the cover or spine. If you didn't know it, you would think it was just a blank book. But once opened it filled with — poetry? In a language I couldn't read. Great! Super helpful. Why did I need a book of old poems, anyway?

"Keep the book with you, Alex. You may come to find out that it will bring you answers."

After the odd exchange between Ms. Terra over some old book, she granted me leave to go to my room. She also excused me from study hall, which I was incredibly grateful for because the last thing I wanted to do was sit in a room full of people I barely knew. Especially one who I thought might have possibly caused an earthquake in the middle of gym class. As I lay there on my bed in my empty room, I thought about what Ms. Terra had said, about how all the kids were here for a reason, a reason like mine. Did they hear voices, did weird things happen to them as well? It was confirmed that Neal indeed had something to do with the earthquake because once Ms. Terra let me go to my room; I saw her make a beeline for Neal's room and she practically dragged him out by his ear. I laughed a little to myself, remembering the memory. It was hilarious. My mind couldn't stop reeling from the many possibilities of my housemates.

Before I could ponder any more on the ins and outs of what the other residents in this house could or could not do. I turned my attention to the book I was holding in my hand. Ms. Terra informed me the book was not a book of poetry as originally thought, but a book of spells. Spells? Way more questions than answers, but I took the book and filed the questions for another day. Ms. Terra seemed to believe the book belonged to me. She couldn't tell me how she knew that, just that it did, and if I read through it, it would help me to understand some of my lineage. As well as being a book of spells that could one day come in handy. What did I know about spells? Furthermore, how will spells help me, help me do what exactly? And in a language, I couldn't read.

I changed my thought process and switched it to my headaches. She told me my headaches served a purpose — other than driving me to get a lobotomy. She told me that my headaches were a sign. Instead of fighting them, I needed to embrace them. They were blocking something trying to get out. And once I embraced, rather than prevent, things would start becoming clear.

I dug my head deeper into my pillow. Ugh! What was she talking about? Thinking, blocking? What was I some kind of Jedi? She couldn't have been more cryptic if she was Yoda incarnate. How did one go about embracing a headache? The whole definition of a headache is that your head... aches. You want nothing to do with it. Ugh again! I was more confused now than ever, and even more confused because now I wanted my headache to come just so I could try to process it. Now this crazy place was making me want my headache. What was going on? Headaches, spells. I needed to find answers, but all the information that was swirling around my brain was too much for one girl to take. I needed to lie down.

I ended up falling asleep and slept through dinner. I only woke up because I suddenly felt someone poking me.

"Is she dead?"

"She's kind of pale."

"She arrived looking pale."

I swatted at whatever device they were using to poke my cheek and opened one eye at them.

"Can I help you?" I said, my voice rough with un-use. Giggles. My bed flopped to one side as the two girls positioned themselves on my twin bed, moving my legs out of the way. I guess no invitation was needed. I sat up on my arms and drifted up the bed, waiting for whatever it was they came to tell me.

These girls, after getting to know them a little, didn't seem so terrible. They were a bit moody, but what teenage girls weren't, it was all part of the package, I guess. But regardless, their snide remarks and occasional evil looks weren't half bad if that meant I could make some real friends.

"So, why were you in the office?"

Nora said in her twang that I couldn't determine whether it was endearing or annoying.

"Nothing gets past you, does it?" I shot back.

She looked at me, totally unaffected by my snide remark.

"It's a small house. News travels fast and secrets don't survive. So, you might as well just tell us now, because eventually we'll find out." She had a point. And that brought something to my attention. I wrapped my arms around my knees and stared at the geometrical pattern of the quilt I was sitting on before saying anything more.

"Since you're asking me personal questions, you won't mind me asking one of my own, right?" I didn't give them a chance to respond. "What brought you two here? What about the others? Why is this place so different? Yesterday after I showed up, you asked me what I'd done to get myself here. What have you done? Answer me that, and I'll tell you why I was in the office."

They stared at each other for a moment. No one saying anything, I could almost see the secret conversation between them. Can they read minds too? Paige was the first to speak. Her shoulders swayed as she took a deep breath.

"One of the unspoken rules is that we keep our mouth shut until the new recruit figures it out on their own. It lessens the blow, so to speak. We're only allowed to unravel secrets that are ours to unravel. You know it's the polite thing to do." She cocked her head ever so slightly and gave me a pointed look. I'm sure she vows by the 'it's polite' rule.

"So... are you going to tell me?"

"Okay, fine, sheesh! You sure don't like a buildup for suspense, okay I'll tell it straight." Paige was still stalling, but I would wait if that meant I would get some answers. "We are, special. Well, I am regardless, but let's stay on target. We all have special... abilities."

"Abilities, like what, tell the future?" I said skeptically.

"Well, if you let me finish without interrupting, I'll tell you."

I sighed and leaned into the wall. I glanced at Nora, who couldn't look more bored as she picked at her manicure keeping one ear on Paige.

"We are what some would call witches, however, that would be incorrect because in fact we are, Mystics. The two are closely related with just a few minor details here and there, which I won't get into now. Witches are known more for their spell casting, you know; love potions, future telling, curse giving that sort of stuff. We're more like conduits. We act more like a medium between the visible world and the invisible spirit world and have the ability to manipulate the elements—you know like—earth, fire, water, air, that sort of stuff. So, we're more elemental magic than spell casting magic. But that's not to say that we don't spell cast, that's for the more advanced and knowledgeable Mystics, and that's it in a nutshell."

Nora piped in cutting Paige off to add her own take on what they were.

"Some of the elders, especially members of the White Coven have mastered the art of Spell casting. Some of the spells are serious bad ass magic type shit. Or so I've read, when I ease drop on the

Matrons when they have their Circle gathers. Or from the books I swipe when I'm bored and want some late-night reading. Pretty scary shit. And of course, there are your typical boring love spells and healing tinctures. But that's lame."

If I thought my head was spinning before, now it was in orbit. This was all crap. I can't believe any of this. They were totally messing with me.

"We aren't fucking with you, if that's what you're thinking?" Nora finally joined the conversation and eloquently, might I say. I sat there, gaping at the both of them.

"Wait, let me get this straight, so you are honestly sitting there telling me you–er- we, are some kind of witch or whatever? That we have control or unnatural pull over elements? That's what you're telling me? No joke?"

I buried my forehead in my knees and hoped the darkness of it all would erase whatever circus fun house I had entered. That, along with the crazy vision and the earthquake, was just too much information. A groan escaped my lips as the poking started up again.

"I mean really Alex, what did the Matron tell you, anyway? You had to of had some kinda clue or idea, I mean you're not that big an idiot, right? Didn't you ever feel like something was off about you?" She looked at me up and down. "And I totally mean other than your horrendous fashion choices." She added with a sneer and a smile, if that was even possible. I peered over my arms that were still holding tight to my knees and saw that Paige had taken to poking me with the pencil she was holding.

"She didn't tell me anything. She sat there as I told her things from my past, and then I had this strange vision about... nothing, it was all too weird." I decided to tell them, even if I didn't believe it all myself. The girls both looked at each other, neither one of them wanting to get deeper into what I had just divulged.

Curiouser and curiouser.

I bit my lower lip and furrowed my brows before I asked my next question.

"So... if this is all true, and I am in no way saying it is, then what does that mean about you two? What do you do?"

My words came out hesitantly and my eyes moved from one girl to the next, not knowing who was going to talk first, if either of them would speak at all. But true to form, they did. I have a feeling they will always speak. Nora was the first one to say something. That infamous look came back on her face. I look between cunning and alluring. It was hard to not get sucked in.

"I am an East Bound Mystic. I have ties to the earth, which means I could move mountains if I wanted. It's pretty awesome. Okay, maybe not mountains, but it's still pretty awesome."

She batted her eyes and looked at Paige. I guess summoning her to continue where she had left off. Paige rearranged her sitting position and told her side.

"I'm a South Bound Mystic. I control fire. There are four types of Bound Mystics: North, South, East and West. Each of them has ties over a different element. Earth, Fire, Water, and Air. Now you know what we are, what are –Ouch!" Paige said, as Nora's elbow jabbed into her side.

"Whatcha do that for?" Paige rubbed her bruised side.

"You forgot to tell her about the 5$^{th}$ element!" Nora said while leaning in toward Paige as if holding back some great secret.

"You don't honestly believe that do you, Nora? For like ever, no one has had ties to the 5$^{th}$ element. You really think AC/DC here could be Sonya incarnate? No offense." Paige said, giving me a half-hearted expression.

But I was a little offended. I didn't know if I believed all this fairy dust they were smoking. Nora was now sitting up on her ankles, looking like a child who discovered where her parents kept the Christmas presents and couldn't wait to tell everyone.

"There's a story about, the Divine Coven, it was the last time the Mystics had a true coven and a true High Priestess." Paige rolled her eyes, but Nora continued.

"The High Priestess. Her name was Sonya, she was the most powerful Mystic of them all. Her element was Spirit. Like mind control and telekinetic and—nesis—, all that shit. Well, some bad shit went down, and it destroyed her coven. But before it could destroy her as well, she cast this powerful spell, binding her soul and encasing her spirit in some unsuspecting Commoner fool. Rumor has it one day her spirit would 'awaken' in a child. And that baby would like rule the world or something. Ever since the *downfall of the Divine Coven'* there hasn't been a real coven in the traditional sense. We fool around with our elements like some stupid parlor tricks. That is if you don't get caught by the Matrons."

"Real scientific, Nora, good going. Do you ever listen in class when we take Elemental Magic from the Matrons, sheesh! Besides, they let us practice, but they don't want us to abuse it, there's a limit. If you overdo it, it changes you. Remember that one kid, Bobby? They had to bind his powers because he couldn't control his need to use it, kept blowing shit up and stuff. If you're not careful, they'll do that to you. You know with great power comes great responsibility."

"Did you just quote Spiderman?" I said, astonished.

"What's wrong with the web-slinger?"

"Nothing. He's my favorite Marvel character."

"Nerd alert!" Nora said, breaking the mood and bringing the attention back to her.

"Well, besides the whole historically inaccurate history lesson, yes there is a $5^{th}$ element, but like Nora said, no one has controlled it since Sonya vanished some odd years ago. So yeah, your possibilities of being a Spirit Wielder are slim. So back to the question at hand: what can you do?" Said Paige, who tried unsuccessfully to pull her hair back behind her ear, but it was too short. It sprung back out again.

I didn't say anything. I mean, what could I say? I didn't have any pull with any elements. I didn't have any control over whatever it was I did.

"What, you don't believe us?" Paige said. I heard a twinge of irritation in her tone.

"It's not that I don't believe you, it's just this is a lot to take in, you know? I don't have control over anything, I swear. I can't control wind or water or make the floor move like I saw Neal do."

"Like you saw who do?" Nora cut me off and glared at me.

"Today in Gym. During the earthquake when those two boys landed on my leg, thus the wrap. I think it was Neal." Nora's facial expression was a mixture of shock and irritation. I could tell she was fuming.

Under her breath she said. "That's why he went to the office. I swear if he gets us kicked out of here, I am going to bury him under six feet of soil." Still in her frustrated state she turned towards Paige.

"Paige, demonstrate it, would ya? Maybe that will speed the process along and she'll tell us what she can do."

Paige simply shrugged, licked her middle finger and snapped. Now there was no denying it, on her finger was a tiny flame hovering right above her thumb and index finger. A flame! On her finger!

Oh god, it's true. It's all true.

# Chapter 20: What do I tell the Master?

### Neal

Neal stood in a cold cement room with one small table and two small metal chairs. The room was once a basement for the shop above. Now, both the shop and this basement were abandoned except for its new occupants, who weren't in the market to open up any kind of retail shop. Neal stood, trying to hide the uneasy twitch in his leg. In front of him sat a thin man in a trim suit. He was very pale and very tense. The man pinched the brim of his nose under his wire-rimmed glasses and gestured for Neal to take a seat.

"Were you successful?"

"I don't know what you were expecting, but I did as I was told."

Neal tried to hide his emotions. The man sat up straighter in his chair and slammed his clenched fist down on the table.

"Did you not tell me you could identify the girl's true ability? Is she the one the Master's looking for? What do you have to say for yourself?"

Neal sat there in the chair and swallowed hard before speaking again.

"I did — I do — think she's the one. It's just I don't know what you were expecting. She reacted the way any stupid girl would have. She fell on her face and acted helpless." The man rubbed his nose again.

"What exactly did you do?"

"I created an earthquake. I thought for sure when she saw her predicament she would try to intercede, or at least prevent those guys from landing on her." Neal said. The man spoke quietly, head down, hands clasped on the table.

"Imbecile. Her powers are dormant. They're controlled by pure emotion. She must feel threatened, fearful, rage even. Must I do everything? Send a child and this is what you get. What am I to tell the Master? That your minor earthquake did nothing more than threaten to expose us?"

Neal stood up; with such force it knocked the chair over making a loud crashing sound on the cement floor.

"Wait! Give me another chance. I was unclear on what I needed to do, but I got it now. I can do it; I'll prove that she is the one." Neal said in a rush, letting his fear show on his face.

"Fine, I will give you one last time to prove yourself, to prove that you have what it takes to be one of us. Master is sending someone of vital importance to see if this girl could really be Sonya. You will wait till then. If what you believe is true, then he will know what the Master wants us to do next."

The man stood up without looking at Neal and walked out. Neal took a deep breath releasing it in a big gust of relief.

"Thank you, Simon." Was the only thing he said as the door shut.

# Chapter 21: Horror Flick

### Alex

I excused myself from the girls so I could take a shower. When I was about to enter the bathroom there was a knock at the door. Paige stood up and on the other side was Ms. Mary. She looked kindly at the two girls and asked if they'd give us a moment alone. The girls obliged and left. Ms. Mary gestured to the bed and then sat in an adjacent desk chair. With nothing else to do, I guess that shower would have to wait. I hobbled over to where she expected me to sit and gingerly lowered myself onto the bed. She looked at me, taking me all in. I felt a sense of calm like when I first encountered Ms. Mary. The smell of salt water and rain returning. With what I learned in the short amount of time since arriving at this *House of Magic* I could conclude that she did indeed have some control over what I could assume was water, and in turn the emotion I felt. I didn't know how, but I knew she must be doing something to soothe the anxieties I've had since missing breakfast this morning — has it only been one day — I feel like it's been weeks since I last left Clara and our overly long road trip.

Her gaze stopped at the ace bandage around my ankle and gestured for me to bring it closer. Out of her apron pocket, she retrieved a small glass bottle. In it was filled with an opaque white liquid and before I could ask what she was doing, she had already unwrapped my brace and was messaging the ointment into my ankle.

The pressure hurt at first, then burned, it was a healing heat searing away the injury. Ms. Mary closed her eyes, mumbling something in a language I couldn't understand. When she was all done, she wiped my ankle with the hem of her apron and told me I could continue on with my shower. I looked down at my ankle. The ankle that just moments ago was three times its rightful size and black and blue from my toes to my shin was healed. It was completely fine.

I looked at her with confusion. My mouth opens ready to rapid fire, the million questions swirling around my brain. But she stopped me before I could.

"You may feel a little tight tomorrow, but other than that, everything should be as it was. Sleep well Alexandra." She turned and walked out of the room without paying me any more attention.

The shower wasn't as relaxing as it could be you know, with all the jumbled thoughts of confusion running around in my head. But it was hot, and I was alone. I stood there as the steam and hot water drenched my face and shoulders and I tried to wrap my mind around the bomb that had just exploded in my face. Ok, so let's say I was a witch or a Mystic or whatever, I've never controlled any elements — that I know of. I mean, I've never tried. Would that mean if I tried, I would? I thought back to all the "incidents" in my past to see if there was a connection I was missing. I've been told if I looked, I would find them. I thought about the context in which certain situations happened, and where my emotions were during the instances. The only thing I could connect was my hope that something would.

Then a bell went off in my brain. No not a bell. A GONG was clanging in my mind. Maybe that's all it took, was the desire to wish for something to happen. You know how the saying goes, "be careful what you wish for". Maybe that was how my "*magic*" works. Maybe I had some kind of power over mind or matter or something like that. What did Nora say, telekinesis or was it telekinetic? I knew I was close to figuring something out. I could see the strings threading through the points I was making in my head, but I didn't know what the conclusion was. I was so in the dark on all this paranormal stuff, I just couldn't see past my ignorance of thinking this was all Hocus Pocus. The girls' said magic was elemental, and if that was true, then what element was I?

A knock outside the bathroom door interrupted my pondering. Somehow, I had forgotten I was even in the shower. I turned off the faucet and wrapped the first towel I could grab around my dripping body. I didn't hear her come in. These damn pocket doors made zero noise, so it was a good thing I had grabbed a towel when I did. I only noticed she had even entered the room because as I turned around to grab my shower tote, we nearly smacked into each other. Dropping my tote, I grabbed her to steady ourselves before we both slipped on the puddle my wet hair created. Before I could make sure she had her footing, she pulled away so fast she just about fell into the tub. Her massive amount of unruly curls were bouncing around her head like they were trying to find safety. The intruder was a small mousy girl, the one who sat at the end of the table talking to herself at dinner the night before. I hadn't seen her since last night. I hadn't noticed if she came to school with us; I hadn't noticed her at all. And now she was in the bathroom clawing at her scalp, muttering frantically to herself.

"Priestess. Spirit Wielder. Trouble. Lost. Hidden. They will find you. You must find them. Before they find you. Restore the Coven. They will find you. Find you. Find you."

I walked closer, hands up in surrender hoping to convey I meant no harm. I needed to hear what she was saying. She wasn't making sense, she was babbling. I couldn't get any closer, because the moment I tried she let out a blood-curdling scream. I jumped back, completely surprised. I covered my ears to block out the terror in her voice. Instantly, the room was buzzing with people. Nora and Paige ran in from one side, with the matrons following soon after. They fluttered around the room, lots of quick talking was happening, everyone was moving in double time. Nora picked up my shower tote, my things splayed out like the aftermath of an explosion; shampoo bottle opened and oozing its content out on the rug, toiletry bag unzipped, its belly empty of the small contents inside, my discarded clothes tossed aside and forgotten. I felt Paige grab my elbow, helping me to my feet, adjusting my towel ensuring it stays put. My hands clutched my ears, fear and shock coursing through me at the thought of being unable to remove her screams from my mind. Ms. Mary in her calm, soothing voice was talking to the girl. Who had shifted from screaming to mumbling her incomplete sentences while Ms. Terra handed her some sort of drink she took without complaint. Together they escorted her out of the bathroom and back down the hall.

What. The. Fuck.

Back in my room, back on my bed, fully dressed and hair almost dry, I simply sat there, staring at nothing and thinking about everything. I can't take this. I want nothing to do with this crazy place or these crazy people. I can't, not anymore. I needed to call Eunice. There had to be somewhere else I could go, there just had to be. This can't be it, there must be another place! None of this makes any sense. My head was going to implode from the ridiculousness I've had to endure in the last 48 hours.

There was a shift of weight on my bed breaking my trance. It was Paige. "Pretty crazy day, huh? New place, new school, earthquake, horror flick in the bathroom. You holding up, okay? I bet you're thinking of all the ways you can get the hell out of here, right? I don't blame you, I tried to myself once. When I first got here, before I knew what this place was — a refuge for lost supernatural kids — Witch kids without a coven. I always knew what I was. My mom grew up in a coven. Her grandmother was a Mystic and taught her everything she knew before the cancer got her. My mom was teaching me a few things too, but she died in a car crash a few years ago and I didn't have anywhere else to go. That's when the Matrons found me. They took me in after they caught me setting fire to an abandoned building in downtown Butte. CPS classified me as an arsonist. The matrons knew otherwise. The matrons always know. My options were either to live here and do community service or spend a year in juvey. You can guess which option I chose so I get it. I do hope you decide to stay, but I get it if you don't. The train station is at the north end of town and runs every 90 minutes. In case you were wondering. And don't be too harsh on Chrissy. She's had it harder than all of us and has been here the longest. But I'll let her, tell you, her story. You might be interested in what she has to say. Just don't touch her, she doesn't like to be touched. Dinner is going to be late tonight."

Paige stood up brushing the creases out of her schoolgirl jumper. Placed her cat eared headphones on her head and spoke. "Her room is the last one on the left. Her bathroom has a plumbing issue, which is why she was in ours. I guess we should have warned you."

Paige didn't say anything else. She continued out of the room, not closing the door behind her, a gesture I think was done on purpose.

# Chapter 22: I'm Not Crazy

**Alex**

I called Eunice; she didn't answer. Somehow, I figured it wasn't because she wasn't near her phone. Normally it's practically glued to her face. Which could mean she's purposefully ignoring my calls. Great. There was no getting out of here and I knew it, but I think I've always known it. There was a part of me that knew I was supposed to be here. Even if I didn't want to be right now, I knew this would be the place where I would find the answers, I didn't know what I was looking for. So, with that, I got up off my bed, took a deep breath and headed down the hall to my left. I needed answers, and I needed them now.

Chrissy's door was cracked, and I could see a singular bed in the middle of the room occupied by the person in question. She was hunched over busying herself with whatever was in front of her. I tapped on her door and the movement opened it wider. I could see she was crocheting, her fingers flying over thin delicate green yarn, concocting some sort of blanket. The pattern was extremely complicated. I cleared my throat.

"Chrissy? Is it okay if I come in?"

I didn't get an answer, but I continued farther into the room. There was a desk chair sitting across from her. I turned it around and sat down. My initial reaction was to reach out to her, but quickly thought against it. She doesn't like to be touched, and I did not want a repeat of the scream queen. So, I opened my mouth to speak again. But she beat me to it.

"I'm not crazy, you know." She looked up at me, pulling her earbuds out of each ear. That's why she didn't hear me. She continued.

"I'm sorry, about earlier. I didn't mean to scare you. I thought the bathroom was empty. My sink doesn't work. And I didn't want to go downstairs just to brush my teeth. I forget sometimes to take my earbuds out, so I didn't hear that you were in there."

"Yeah, I'm sorry too. I didn't mean..."

"I'm clairvoyant. And sometimes when I touch people, it tells me things. About them, about their future. Touching you was too much. Too much." Chrissy rocked back and forth and went back to her crocheting. Muttering to herself again.

"Tell me what you saw. You said something about a Spirit Wielder. What is that?"

I leaned into her, careful to give her space but trying to show how much I needed the answers she might give me. Moments went by that felt like hours. I thought maybe she wouldn't be able to tell me anything. She didn't seem like someone who was consistently working with a full box of crayons. But before I could complete that thought, she began to speak, as clearly as I have ever heard her.

"I don't always see what's going to happen, not exactly anyway. Sometimes I'm wrong. More often than not, I sense what could be or what's meant to be. When you grabbed me, I glimpsed your past lives. And what's in store for your future. You are a Spirit Wielder and from what I can tell, an immensely powerful one. But you're in trouble. There are forces out there that are hunting you. Do you have any idea what or who you are? Because if you don't. You should learn fast, because there are dangerous people who want you."

I felt like the air was being sucked out of the room. My lungs burned; my head was spinning. This was too much. This would be the last brick that pushed me over the edge. People were hunting me. Me. Why? What could I have done or not done to cause all this? I had to get out of this room. I had to get out of this house, out of this state. I needed to call Eunice. She had to come get me." Chrissy spoke again.

"Breathe, Alex, you're going to pass out if you don't."

"You can read my mind?" Not the craziest thing I've heard since I've been here.

"No, but I can read your aura. And you're panicking. Plus, you look like you're about to vomit."

"Auras?"

"Yeah, it's like seeing an energy field around you, only it gauges your spirit essence. I can tell what element someone can wield based on the color of their aura. As well as their emotional state, take Paige, for instance. She is a fire element which usually is a burnt orange color, but she's also, well, always pissed. Which comes out more red. So, she looks like a summer sunset during a forest fire. Muted red and orange with a tint of pink."

"What's my aura?"

"That's how I can confirm what I saw. Your aura is purple. Purple is a royal color. Normally, high priestesses and experienced warlocks are purple. I've never seen it though so I can't confirm it, but I'm almost positive. And you're also a little green, which usually means fear or illness, hence the vomit comment. It's a lot to take in, I understand. But if I were you, I would stop fighting and start listening. You don't have a lot of time."

I was in shock from what she said. I opened my mouth to ask about a million more questions, but then Chrissy put her earbuds back in, signally the universal sign for no more questions. She went back to her crochet, fingers moving as fast as before. But this time she started humming to herself. It sounded like a lullaby, ethereal and a little creepy. I accepted the fact that I would not be getting more answers now, so there was nothing more to do but to go back to my room and wait for dawn. I could smell dinner being cooked downstairs, but my stomach felt like it was made of lead. There was no way I could keep anything down. I gave in and went to bed, hoping tomorrow would be a better day. Somehow, that felt like a long shot. But there's always hope, right? Right?

# Chapter 23: Lots of questions

**Alex**

Breakfast was announced over the loudspeaker. Every sound was magnified, and my head throbbed. The quiet murmurs over pancakes and eggs were live streamed into my eardrums. Forks against ceramic, ice in orange juice glasses, my head was seconds from shattering. Not because of migraines, but because of shock and trauma I still was in due to the thoughts playing loops in my mind. I was reeling from yesterday's educational programming. Mystics, elemental control, clairvoyants... I would need to find a special dictionary to help me with all this new vocabulary, and what is a high priestess, anyway?

"Alex"

I picked my head up from the table to see who was calling me. It was Ms. Terra. She gestured and I followed her. I wasn't eating anyway, just pushing food around my plate, waiting for my appetite to come back. Every pair of eyes followed me out of the room. The day had barely started, and I was already being summoned to the office. I could only imagine what stories they were coming up with in their heads. I bet the minute I left; their minds would fly with all sorts of crazy accusations. All of them looked eager to catch a glimpse as to what it could be. All of them except one. Chrissy only had eyes for her pancakes. I was guessing she already knew what this was about.

I picked up my plate and walked toward the kitchen to deposit my uneaten breakfast, when a leg shot out in my path. I stopped so I wouldn't ram into it. The owner of the leg was Neal. Oh god, just let me through. He cocked his head to the side, leaned back against his chair, arm draped over the back.

"See ya 'round school," he said.

Then, with a wink, he turned back to the table. Nora was sitting across from him, throwing daggers his way with her eyes.

The chair in Ms. Terra's office felt like it was molding to my body. I think I've sat in this chair more often than any other chair in this entire place. I might not have been a straight lace student back in Minneapolis, or St. Paul, or even Bloomington, but if I wasn't careful my stint here would be spent in this chair in this office. Ms. Terra didn't waste any time getting to the nitty gritty.

"Chrissy informed Ms. Mary and I about last night. She was pretty shaken up about it this morning."

"*She* was?" I mumbled under my breath in exasperation. Ms. Terra raised her eyebrows at me.

"I am sure you have more than a few questions."

"Yeah, I've got tons. Where should I start?" Sarcasm right on cue.

"Whatever is most pressing is always the best place to begin."

Replied Ms. Terra, not fazed by my quick tongue. Once again, she was calm and collected. I thought nothing could frazzle the old women. I bit my lower lip, really thinking about her last statement. Everything was pressing.

"Okay. What am I?"

"From what we can gather from Chrissy's intuition. She believes you to be a 'Spirit Wielder' I thought so myself from an earlier easement of your aura and from the things you told me the other day. That is why I gave you The Book. It's extremely old and very powerful. It will only reveal itself to the one who is worthy. When your gifts become clear to you, so will the book. It once belonged to you, and now it has found you again."

*What?!*

I love it when answers bring on more questions. I'll file that little nugget away to deal with later.

"I am sure by now your roommates filled you in on who and what we are, here at the manor. Am I correct?" I nod and she continues. "We refer to ourselves by the name given to us long ago during the formation of the first coven; Mystic Charmed. However, the name has gone out of fashion since The Fall, so the term you might hear most frequently would be Mystics. Chrissy, as you know, is a seer. There are a few others who aren't true mystics but still hold some paranormal abilities, most referred to as fortune tellers, psychics and the like. Their bloodlines are more diluted than that of a true Mystic, making their powers look more like magic tricks than actual casting. But we all have roots from the original coven, the Divine Coven. They were the original Mystics. To trace the actual genealogical tree, however, is rather difficult. Even though the Coven hasn't been in place for some time, we remain true to our traditions by practicing in Charmed Circles. Every coven needs a High Priestess and, well, we haven't had one in quite a number of years. We started to believe that the bloodlines were too diluted to produce any more heirs to the original High Priestess. But from my recent studies, I have been able to understand a bit more, and a prophecy we once thought to be legend, may have more truth than myth."

I had to interrupt her right then. This was a lot of hooey for my liking, and she would need to stop for a moment and back up on the explanations.

"Wait, what are you talking about? I heard Chrissy say that word last night, Priestess, what is that. And what is all this talk about passing down bloodlines? I'm sorry Ms. Terra, if I'm being completely dense, but I'm just not following. What does any of this have to do with me?" I tried to control my breathing. This was too much to take in.

Ms. Terra didn't seem flustered by my outburst; she simply smiled like you would at a frightened animal. She clasped her hands in front of her and started again.

"The bloodlines are passed down from woman to child. North Bound Mystics produce more North Bound Mystics, and so on. Males who are born into our line are as equally powerful as females, however they will only produce paranormal children if they mate with non-Mystics. That's where you'll get your psychics or seers, people with the sight yet cannot harness the true power. The more heirs that are produced from an already diluted bloodline, the fainter the sight becomes. Think of the equivalent of someone having a strong sense of intuition or empaths."

She paused for a moment, making sure I was hearing everything clearly. I simply nodded and waited for her to continue, then a question arose in my mind. "What are you? I mean, what element do you control?" Ms. Terra's politely controlled smile widened, making her face look much younger. She was incredibly beautiful, but you could tell stress and worry made her features harsh, almost cold.

"My Cousin and I are not your average Mystics. I am a North Bound Mystic. I can control earth matter. I can move mountains, uproot trees, grow a field of wildflowers, but my favorite is to simply be in my garden and listen to it speak to me. It tells me what it needs, and it soothes my soul. My cousin Mary is a West Bound Mystic which means she can control water. She can hold a snowflake in the palm of her hand, and it wouldn't melt unless she willed it so. Where the difference is, is that we are part of an elite group of Mystics, called a Logar. Loosely translated, it means 'one who finds. We are the guides who find the souls whose gifts are still pure. The ones with whom the bloodlines are still strong and who may have power they cannot control. Usually, children who've been orphaned and abandoned, the ones where trouble seems to find them."

Ms. Terra gave me a knowing look, head bent forward, eyebrows raised. All that was missing were glasses so she could look over the frame. She continued; I was glued to my seat.

"We find those who've been born with the power, and we help them, train them. Some are children who are still under the care of their mystic parents. We help tutor them, offer them guidance as they grow in their abilities. Sadly, more often than not, we take more permanent roles in the lives of those we come across. Usually because they have been through a tragedy that shatters their lives, car crashes, illness, abandonment. The twins, for instance. I knew their parents very well. They were in our Charmed Circle. A few of us choose to practice the Rites and Rituals of our ancestors. But the traditions we held didn't fully satisfy Derrick, the twin's father. He felt paying homage to Moon Cycles and making Herbal Tonics was too beneath him and his abilities. Mere silhouettes of the power we once held, calling it parlor tricks. He fell into the Dark Arts hoping to find that lost power, but the Dark Arts are a slippery slope. If you call upon it without the proper knowledge, it will control you, instead of you controlling it. Derrick was not strong enough to wield such power, there was a deadly accident killing both him and Jessica, the twins' mother. That's when we took guardianship of the two young ones; they were only 12 when it happened.

"Their story is only one of many, in a long line of Mystics reaching their demise due in part to the Dark Arts. There is another, more powerful Mystic among our kind. He is said to be the Leader of the Dark Arts, and his power is growing. Some believe he is the lost soul of Lord Nicolai. The one who went against our High Priestess and brought on the end of our coven. He has been searching for Mystics who have joined the resistance. And one by one they have suffered tragedy; a car crash, a brutal mugging, fast moving disease.

We will not bow down to him. We only serve White Magic, magic that is pure and good. We have remained hidden here for many years. Mary has done a great job cloaking the valley under a magical fog that protects us from harm.

"We still have hope. We can stop the Dark One once and for all. We're in search of a child. The one we believe is the reincarnation of our lost priestess. *The One Who Is,* she holds the gift of Spirit. We've been searching for years, almost believing the legend simply was a story taught to young Mystics to keep the Magic from dying. We vowed we would make it our destiny to restore our beloved coven. We can defeat the Dark One, and Alex, we think we may have finally found her." She took a controlled breath and pursed her lips together; she said nothing more.

I sat in silence for hours, minutes, maybe it was only seconds. I couldn't believe she was telling me any of this. It was all so unreal, too fanciful. How was I to take her seriously when none of this should be true? I decided for just a moment that I would let go of the unbelievability of it all and lean into her story. If what she was saying was fact, then there were a few –lots– of questions I needed answered.

"How do you know what child you're looking for?" I said, heart racing, head pounding. I could literally feel my blood rushing around my body in a frantic haze. Ms. Terra took a moment before answering me. She looked sad, like she was really going over the words in her head, trying to figure out the best way to explain it to me.

"The story is, a very powerful South Bound Mystic sought out control of our Coven, with plans to kidnap our dear priestess draining her blood to create a new bloodline. Our Priestess, Sonya, was a Spirit Wielder, one of the last of her kind. She foresaw Lord Nicolai's plan of betrayal. He was her most trusted advisor, second only to her. However, he would never lead the coven, and he hated it.

He tried to overthrow her. It is said that she created a spell to transfer her gift of Spirit into a human soul, and they would carry the spirit within them. When the time came to rise, the spirit would find a way to give birth to the new High Priestess. One strong enough to stop Lord Nicolai for all eternity. Others and I have looked everywhere for this mystery human and come up short. With all the years that had gone by, we had almost given up the possibility of finding her. Then you showed up on our radar, and when looking into your past a little more, I had hope once more. Alex, if what Chrissy says is true. You could be her, you could be our salvation, and you could be our future High Priestess.

Oh. My. God.

# Chapter 24: So Much for Sarcasm

### Alex

I was on the bus to school my breakfast discarded, there was no way I was keeping anything down after the conversation with Ms. Terra. All morning I had only one thing on, the goopy mess that used to be my brain, which was, Oh My God.

After Ms. Terra dropped the bomb, no, the nuclear warhead of information, she said it would be completely all right if I wanted to stay at the Manor today. Now, as I sat there on the blasted bus, I was rethinking my plan of going to school. I wanted to pretend my life was normal, at least for a few hours, and going to school seemed like the best way to do that. What better way to pretend nothing happened and to avoid the whole situation altogether, than the regularity of routine. Hell, maybe I'd even try to forget not just last night's events but every event from the last 48 hours. And if we were being fanciful, let's say everything in the last 17 years has been one gigantic cosmic joke. But sadly, that wasn't the case, so here I was on my way to start yet another day of my senior year in high school amidst all the strange and peculiar things that always, always, seem to follow me. I guess I should be used to it by now.

The bench seat shifted, and suddenly Nora was beside me.

"What'd she say?" was spoken in between gum chewing. I gave her a confused look. "Why did Ms. Terra call you into the office last night? Did it have something to do with Neal? You know, because he's just one giant ass. And doesn't mean any harm by his stupid stunts. He likes to dick around with the new kids. Honestly, let's move on from the whole mess. He won't really do anything." Her words were coming at me like bullets from a machine gun.

"Nora, not right now." I snapped at her raising my arms to stop her from pelting me with more rapid-fire explanations. She leaned back in her seat morphing her face into something of anger, maybe even hurt. I felt bad, but at least she stopped talking. I put a hand on her knee and said, "Sorry. I didn't mean anything by it. I'm hanging by a string here. I don't know how much more I can take. I'm trying to get through the day, you know? Ms. Tarra told me told me all about a huge prophecy, birth-rite destiny, big bad evil, you know same old same old. Just your normal run-of-the-mill sort of conversation. I'm trying to wrap my mind around it, sorry I don't mean to be so..."

"Bitchy."

"Well, I was going to say snarky, but ya, I guess that works too." She opened her mouth to say something when suddenly her face went ghost pale and she stammered.

"A... a prophecy? Not the Divine..."

Her voice was a whisper. She sat there fixated on something out the window, as if I was no longer in front of her.

"Nora? What's wrong? Have you heard about it too?"

I asked her, a little afraid of her response because of her sudden catatonic state. She snapped out of whatever hold she was under and grabbed my shoulders with both her hands, so we were now facing each other.

"What did Ms. Terra say to you, exactly?"

I was frightened of her and didn't know whether I should say anything at all. She had such a determined look on her face I felt like there was no getting out of here without telling her something. I gave her the cliff notes of what transpired that morning, keeping to vague recollections. She sat back hard against the tall back of the bench seat. A rush of air escaped her lungs, she shook her head and ringlets bounced with the movement.

"What? What does that mean? Am I some kind of major freak? Why do you look so relieved?" I said. Nora started to giggle, which turned into a full belly laugh. Okay I am totally giving up on making friends. This chick is nuts! Before I could probe her any further as to why she suddenly cracked, we pulled up to the school. She reached for her backpack and turned towards me.

"I sure hope you're the one. I don't see it. But the matrons know their shit. So, for everyone's sake, I sure hope you'll be the one we need." She weaved herself through the sea of bodies that were exiting off the bus. Before I totally lost sight of her, she craned her neck back, and with a little more pep in her tone, said. "See ya 'round school." The odd thing was, Neal said the same thing to me this morning back at the manor. But instead of making me feel reassured, like his sister did, his words made me feel watched.

Every step felt like I was wearing concrete boots. Maybe I should go by the nurse to get more aspirin.

"You look a little green. Breakfast not sitting well?"

Jason.

He came out of nowhere. He jogged up next to me. We were so close, our shoulders brushed up against each other as we walked the last few feet into school.

"I see your ankle isn't broken. From what I saw yesterday, I thought for sure you had some major damage. But I guess you heal fast." He said. A smile slowly showed on my face. The first smile I've had after all the craziness of the last 24 hours.

"Yeah, I guess I'm a fast healer. I'm fine it's —well, it's been a morning."

I didn't know what to say to him; I didn't know what I could say to him.

*Hi. I am part of this elite group called Mystic Charmed, and according to some ancient prophecy I could or could not be the next High Priestess who is supposed to vanquish the evil Lord Nicolai and restore all hope to the once great Divine Coven. You know, right after Cheerleading practice.*

He stumbled over his feet and made a choking sound. It dawned on me then, like a gallon of ice water. He can READ MY MIND! Well, I guess the cat's out of the bag.

"So much for sarcasm. Heh?"

I thought maybe if I made a joke about the situation, it would lighten the mood. But it made it worse. Much worse. I felt him tense up, and he seemed very uncomfortable standing next to me.

"So uh, yeah... how do you do that blocking thing again?"

I tried to laugh, and he tried as well. The whole situation seemed very awkward; we weren't discussing the one thing we both wanted to discuss. Our first class continued with a false nicety feel, forced and stale. We were trying too hard to be friendly. The connection that was so strong yesterday was now fading. The buzz that we found so easily yesterday was now suffocating under a heavy quilt. It reminded me that we were strangers. We didn't know anything about each other. So why then was I so hurt by our distance? It was my fault. I allowed myself to believe that he could be different, that we could be different.

Fortunately, we only had first period together until lunch. I relished those morning classes, because the break allowed our heads, well at least my head, to clear a bit. By lunch, however, I was starting to miss what he had yesterday. We were supposed to meet after school today at some café. Ms. Mary agreed to the night out, but I wondered if it was still going to happen. She was, however, pleased that I had made a friend; I think she was afraid all this crazy stuff was going to make me lose my mind. But hey if I'm able to have an hour away from Neverland Mansion, based on her fear of me needing a padded cell, I'd take it. I wondered again if Jason was going to cancel our plans.

"Are we still on for the café? Or have you had enough crazy for one lifetime, and don't feel like diving into mine?"

I whipped my head around so I could see the face that was behind the voice. Jason was walking up behind me, carrying a small brown bag and slinging a backpack over one shoulder. God, he looked so good. One corner of his mouth went up in a small smile. I need to stop thinking about him, especially in front of him. He sat next to me, sprawled out like he didn't have a care in the world and pulled an apple out of his brown bag.

"You bag your own lunch, how economical of you." I said, hiding a laugh under my breath. He threw an apple at me and opened a bag of chips for us to share.

"I wish I could take credit for the thriftiness of it all, but it's packed for me. My aunt comes by from time to time to make sure my dad and I haven't drowned in dirty laundry, and when she does, she always makes me lunch. I've told her that I have figured out how to use the enormous square white things in my basement, and that I can put peanut butter on bread. But, you know, it makes her feel useful, so what's a boy to do?" I was glad we were back to our easy banter. It felt good.

"Get free fluff and fold and make your aunt happy. Yeah really, you can't say no to that." I laughed.

He was sitting directly beside me; our knees were touching we were so close I thought my heart would stop. Every nerve was on high alert, I thought my skin would catch fire from the heat radiating between us. Jason placed his fingertips on the side of my jaw turning my head towards him. His fingers lingered on my chin longer than was necessary, I was not complaining.

"Close your eyes." He whispered. And in the same tone I heard myself say.

"Why".

"Not that I don't find it flattering to hear all that you have to say, or not say. Everyone is entitled to some privacy; I'm going to attempt to teach you how to block your mind. I'll miss your endearing thoughts, so I'm doing this out of protest." He winked at me, and I blushed major! I think I might have given myself a sunburn from how hot my face was.

"Well, at least I'll still have that." He said as he stared straight into my eyes.

"Hurry and teach me before I decided to put your lunch bag over my head." I told him, completely mortified. A throaty chuckle escaped his lips.

For the remainder of our lunch hour, he tried his best to get me to envision the wall of China around my brain, to get me to put my thoughts behind Fort Knox. I was breaking out in a sweat from all the hard concentrating. I could see now why he chooses to opt out of it all, and just be an "open book". I was making headway. My thoughts weren't as clear as they were this morning. He said he could most closely compare it to hearing someone talk underwater. He knew I was thinking something, but he couldn't make out the exact words unless he concentrated hard. Trying to decipher my static thoughts was more work than it was worth. So, it satisfied us enough and once the bell rang, we went to our next set of classes.

# Chapter 25: Heard of Any Good Prophecies Lately?

### Jason

Jason's head was spinning from Alex's thoughts. He's heard stories over the years about people who could wield magic and cast spells, but it was told as a warning. Something to scare the young ones to keep from leaving the Rez. Dark magic: the bump in the night, steal your soul kind of magic. Alex wasn't like that. She was kind and goofy and sweet, besides, she didn't believe in any of it, he could tell. He needed answers and he knew he couldn't go to his dad. This was probably the exact reason his dad didn't want him to associate with her. Somehow, his dad knew this girl was different, but how? How could he know? The only other person from the tribe who knew the girl was Patrick. *Shit.* That meant he'd have to talk to Patrick. Something he avoided at all costs, but if he wanted answers, he would be the person to have them. Jason turned and instead of heading to class, he hurried down the hall towards the Guidance Counselor's office.

The entire way back to Patrick's office, Jason was trying to decide what he was going to say, and how to control his thoughts. He was never more thankful than right now that he had a better grasp on blocking than most of his pack outside the elders themselves, because if Patrick even gets a hint at what Jason really wanted to know he would be doomed to spend the rest of his senior year on the Rez.

Jason was aware he couldn't come right out and ask, *hey heard of any good prophecy stories lately?* He had to come up with a way where he could protect Alex at all costs.

By the time Jason reached the door of his uncle's office, he thought of a good way to get the answers he needed. Or at least a good place to start. He didn't bother checking in with the ladies at the front desk anymore. They knew who he was, and that he had an open-door policy with his uncle. He let himself in and took the only available seat in his uncle's office. Mikael Patrick was no decorator. His room was void of all Knick knacks aside from one framed jersey of hockey star Wayne Gretzky, Kings fan — who knew. But aside from the blank space he called an office, he was oddly good at his job. He tries to put on a good show of not caring about anything or anybody, but he's made a difference here at the school, in the short time he's been employed. This is a small school and Patrick has called in outside faculty from surrounding colleges to come out and see kids playing their best in whatever sport they're participating in, in hopes of getting them recruited. He implemented a college day for the upperclassman to help them plan a future, he even started a tutoring programming. Jason never thought Patrick liked kids, but then again, maybe there was a reason he majored in education with a degree in social work. Jason thought for the first time how Patrick's life might have been different if it wasn't for the Tribe. Maybe doing something because it is tradition isn't always a good thing.

"What do you want?"

Patrick didn't even look up from his computer before addressing Jason. He knew whatever Jason wanted; it would be irritating.

"What, I can't come sand see my warm and fuzzy uncle? Maybe I had a question about applying for college. Are you really going to turn me away?" Jason kicked up his shoes and placed them on the edge of Patrick's desk, a gesture Jason knew would irritate Patrick.

"I don't have time for this, Jay. What do you want? And besides, aren't you missing an English midterm right now?"

"Oh that, yeah, no big, I've got it handled. No worries."

Jason did indeed not have it handled, he did actually, forget. And was now quickly regretting his rash decision to come and talk to Patrick during this particular period.

"I just wanted to inquire a little about the girl from the other day." The steady staccato of typing coming from Patrick's computer abruptly stopped and Patrick looked at Jason from over his monitor.

"What about the girl?"

"Nothing. Really. You just seem so certain that she was bad news, and you know me, I am an inquisitive boy by nature. You go and tell me something like don't push the red button, and you know I'm bound to—"

"Jason. Don't push the button. Not this time."

"You see, it's situations like that, that get my curiosity peeked. You know she's in like a ton of my classes. We're bound to run into each other from time to time. I just want to know what I'm dealing with, that's all. What kind of alpha would I be—"

"Future alpha."

"Right, *future* alpha would I be if I didn't know every angle of every situation? And I feel like you and pops are keeping something from me and frankly, I don't like it. It might force me to figure things out on my own. And I'm sure you know how much trouble that might be. There might be paperwork involved and bail money. You know we don't want another incident like..."

"Okay. Enough, I get it. Just shut your mouth for a second, will ya? We're not hiding anything from you. There's not a lot we know ourselves. The elders, they've been getting warnings about a disturbance coming. The balance is shifting, darkness is coming. The earth feels it, it's unsettled. We felt it the moment she came to town. Now that's not saying she is whatever could be causing the shift, but there are no coincidences. The elders believe there is a prophecy coming to pass.

"Long ago, when our tribe was young, we weren't the only creatures with paranormal abilities. There were others, beings, who could grow trees with a wave of their hand or bring down the rain during a drought. They were passive nature healers. We called them Charmers because they could charm and control all things within the natural world. We were once in alliance with them. Working together. Building up our lands. Until one day, a shift happened. The elders don't know how or what, but there was a disturbance amongst the Charmers and a darkness crept in. The earth started dying around them. There was a great conflict, a war broke out, lives were lost on both sides. Before it could claim anymore lives, the elders and the shamans used our own abilities, and we locked up our borders and banned the Charmers from entering our lands. We needed to protect the land and our tribe, and so we did. We stopped associating with the outside world unless it was utterly necessary. And so far, it has worked for us. We do what we do, and we let the world do what they do. That is how we've survived for as long as we have." Patrick leaned back in his chair and folded his hands in front of him. Apparently, that was all he was going to say.

"So, what, you just left them? To what? Be killed? Do you even know what happened to them? You say you were allies, yet you hung them to dry. How could the pack do that?" Jason's head was reeling. He didn't know why he was getting so upset, but he knew it was upsetting. He was more confused now than he ever was. But something inside him said Alex was part of the Charmers, and she needed him. She needed help. But he didn't know how, or what.

"Why are you getting so worked up over this? We don't even know if this girl is part of all that. As far as I know, the Elders could be smoking too much peyote. Besides, they would have gotten the pack killed. When there's a disease in the crop, you don't let it stay and fester, you cut it out."

"What like mom? Pull the cancer out. Well, it didn't work, it still killed her."

Jason stood up suddenly, not caring that the force of it knocked his chair across the room, knocking down the framed jersey, cracking the glass. He dashed out, slamming the door behind him. He heard his uncle calling out to him, but he was determined not to look back. The last thing he did was unblock his mind so his uncle could hear his last thought before leaving the office.

*Fuck off.*

# Chapter 26: Don't Lose Consciousness

**Alex**

The last half of my day was very uneventful, thank goodness. It was a welcomed breath of fresh air to have the mundane-ness of regular high school, Spanish, Biology and the like. I thought my life before all this was riddled with the unexplained, but I would rather have pre-prophecy unexplainable than Protector Child for the Masses unexplainable any day. So, it was pleasant, but even that couldn't last for long. Neal was waiting for me next to the door of the girls' locker room, again. I was determined to not let his earthquake freak show rattle my nerves. Whatever he was here to tell me, I wouldn't cower. Besides, if what the Matrons said was true, and I was some sort of Bad Ass Mystic, then I wouldn't allow some teenage punk to play pranks on me.

"What do you want Neal? I'm going to be late."

I said it with as much false bravado as I could muster. I stood straight and looked him right in the eye, well at least I tried, considering how much taller he was than me.

"Oh, C'mon Sug' you ain't sour over a little prank? What, you can't take some innocent fun?"

Even though he had a sexy southern drawl that was slower and sexier than his sisters', more twangy, less high pitched. There was something about him that just made me edgy.

"Yeah, no thanks to you. Those boys could have broken my leg." I was really getting irritated.

"Just messin' with the newbie, no big. What's your specialty? I bet you're a Southie like Paige. I can tell you got a fire inside you." He said, giving me a look like he was undressing me with his eyes. I felt both disgusted and violated.

"Excuse me?" I said. He wasn't one for small talk, leaping into whatever he wants, doesn't he?

"C'mon don't play dumb. I know my sister talked to you, and I know the Hag Duo explained things. What can you do? What element are you?" He said this time with more force and less sleaze. I pressed myself against the door of the gym and tried to put as much distance between us.

"You know your kind of a prick. Not that it's any of your business, no, no one knows what I am. But Ms. Terra seems to believe I'm sort of Wielder of something."

Neal's eyes turned in at the corners and for a second, a weird grin played at his lips. Then he excused himself.

"Ok well, I got to be anywhere but here."

"Yeah, nice talking to you, too." Jerk.

That was weird, but it wasn't the first weird thing that happened today, and most likely wouldn't be the last. But right now, all I had to worry about was getting dressed for Gym and trying not to trip over my own feet. Due to the strange midday earthquake the gym itself was closed but not the lockers. Oddly enough the earthquake didn't cause nearly as much damage as I would expect. Apparently, the only damage was to some floorboards, so until that could be patched up all cases were held in the old auxiliary building. A smaller gym past the baseball fields, and today was calisthenics day. We were asked to pair up and keep score at each different station. Check yes, for possibly pairing up with Jason, check no for having to do strength and flexibilities exercises in front of him.

*Great.*

"What, you aren't up for a little circuit training?" Jason came up behind me. Wall up! I needed to be careful otherwise he would be privy to all my silent conversations.

"You know I'm going to get you a little bell or something. You've got to stop sneaking up on me." I told him.

"Fine, and I'll wear it around my neck if that pleases you." He said jokingly.

"Ok. At least then I'll be able to hear you coming. Hey, I'll even throw in a tag that says, Fido."

Jason raised his eyebrow at me and said something under his breath. It sounded like *fitting*, but I couldn't tell.

Class today was the best class ever. Jason and I were partners, and I swear it seemed like at every opportunity we touched, grazed, bumped and collided. At one point we were so close I thought I was going to faint. I was sitting on the ground, legs stretched out in front of me, heels pressed under this wooden measuring table. I had to reach out over my legs and press my hands on the top of this measuring chart to see how far I could stretch. Jason was hovering over the table so that he could help hold my hands down and read the measurement at the same time. Our two faces were mere inches apart. I could see my reflection in the green of his eyes. I was breathless.

It took everything I had to not close the last few inches separating us and plant my lips on his. Even though I could still feel the wall I had built around my thoughts, my face must have given away all my secrets, because Jason closed the distance leaving only a hairs breath of room between us. But instead of pressing his wonderful lips to mine, he reached over and curled a strand of hair around my ear. I closed my eyes at his touch, willing myself to breathe and not lose consciousness.

"You're beautiful."

His voice was soft and tender. He said it out loud, but I felt it deep in my soul. I couldn't say anything after that. It would have just ruined whatever moment this was, and I wanted to hold on to it for as long as possible.

Like all great things, Coach blew his whistle signaling the end of 6th period.

"We're still on for the café, right?"

Jason was the first one to speak. I nodded in reply, still shaken up by the almost maybe moment we shared in class. We both stood up and walked toward the locker rooms to change out of our gym clothes.

# Chapter 27: You Didn't Deny it.

**Alex**

Later that night, once we were at the café, we found a small table in the back. It was one of those progressive cafés, where everything was mismatched and eccentric, some cultural music was playing overhead, and it was dark and private. Perfect.

The table we sat on wobbled a little and the white-iron garden chairs weren't the most comfortable to sit on, but none of that mattered next to Jason. He ordered some mocha-latte-almond-something for us and leaned back against his chair. He couldn't look more comfortable. I waited a moment, I wanted to start a conversation about abnormal abilities, but didn't know how. I myself was thrown deep into the abnormality and couldn't quite grasp the concept, either. We both opened our mouths to say something then closed them to let the other speak. Jason took the lead. His words came out slowly, but with confidence behind them.

"My family and I, my circle of friends, we're different from everyone else here in town. Yes, I can read thoughts. Normally it's limited to the people in my 'community', so the fact that you can too is a little strange. I've never come across someone who can *hear* me who wasn't a part of our pack." I sat back against the chair; my head began to spin.

"You're different? What does that mean, exactly?" I asked him. I thought maybe there was a chance he was like me, maybe he was a

136

Mystic as well. There was a long pause. He was staring at the mosaic tiles glued to the table. He spoke calmly and carefully.

"You're different too, aren't you? What kind of different are you? What happened in Econ to Moira, wasn't by chance. Was it?" My breath caught in my throat, and I almost choked on the brown sugary liquid I was sipping.

"Excuse me? What did I do exactly? Or what do you think I did? I didn't do anything. I didn't do anything on purpose. I don't know what you're talking about."

"You're doing that thing again."

"What thing?"

"That thing where you babble endlessly, because you're utterly flustered. It's cute."

"Cute?! Cute? Are you flirting with me right now? This is so not the time to be flirty."

'My mind felt like it was filling up with honey. Nothing but sticky murky thoughts were running through my brain. *I* barely knew what happened to Moira. How could he claim to know? How could he think I had anything to do with Queen Bitch face? I mean, hell, I didn't know I could do anything until I sat down with Ms. Terra. And that was only after it was all said and done. What could he possibly think I can do? In my random avalanche of thoughts, I let part of my wall slip because he answered my unsaid conversation.

"Are you unaware of the ability you possess? I saw you. Your eyes were distant, and your thoughts were shadowed, not evil shadow but like a cloud was covering your brain. You were in a trance, so I kicked you. Then everything went back to normal. Which is why yes, I know you had something to do with it. Shit, I don't blame you. Moira's a bitch she got what she deserved. It's just incredibly odd that you don't know this." The whole time he was speaking, all I could think was, he knew.

I was happy for the early lesson in mind blocking, because until I got more answers from him, I wasn't ready to give up all my secrets. Let's collect some facts for just a minute. He thinks I can do things. I knew he could read minds. We both knew that there was nothing normal about either of us. Yet I didn't know what type of abnormal he was, and it sounds like he didn't know what type of abnormal I was. Okay. I can work with that. Maybe he was a Mystic. Isn't that how the saying goes, 'takes one to know one'? But neither Terra nor Mary has said anything about mind reading, but maybe we just haven't gotten to that part of the educational lesson. I mean, for all I know, tomorrow I'm going to find out that I can fly.

That would be pretty cool. Focus Alex. Not the right time.

Maybe that's why I feel so connected to him, because he's like me. I couldn't help but want to tell him everything I knew, everything I was. He would understand. He would help me get through this. Maybe I was supposed to find him, like I was supposed to find Terra and Mary. Maybe he was a different kind of guide. Could I handle this without him? What if I didn't want to? A smile crept up on my face, thinking about him and me, in this crazy mess together. I felt my whole body warm as if the sun was shining directly on me. Right then I could feel the wall I built peel back like a curtain. It was just enough to reveal a glimpse of what I was thinking, and I didn't care. I was falling for Jason; I didn't want to hide anything from him.

He was sitting across from me and moved from his devil may care slouch and was now leaning onto the table. He looked right at me, there was nowhere for me to go but stay locked in his gaze. He wasn't staring, wasn't judging, simply waiting. Waiting for me to say something. Anything. I was unaware of anybody else in the café. I opened my mouth, yet I had no idea what I was going to say. He broke the silence first.

"You know, there are explanations for things like that." I knew all too well about the many explanations there could be. He carried on not waiting to see if I would respond. "You know, like... paranormal things."

"What like monsters and witches?" I said, my voice coming out with a strained laugh, trying to make light of the situation. Then a new thought encroached on my thinking: what if he wasn't like me? What if he was one of those gifted psychics like Terra was saying? Parlor tricks. And if I told him I was some, almost-could-be-High-Priestess he might freak out. My head was going to split open all over this poor wobbly garden table. I was definitely not caffeinated enough for this conversation.

"Don't tell me you think I'm some sort of lab baby science experiment that has gone wrong? Someone who fell into a chemical reactor and can control things with her mind." I said not so jokingly.

He just shrugged his shoulders. I tried to wall up my thoughts again, putting imaginary spackle in the holes of my mind-wall. It was slowly crumbling away, but I thought better of it, so I built it back up. I decided I would just lie through my teeth until I found out more about him. I couldn't allow myself to be blinded by my emotions or else I might end up being blindsided but something I wasn't prepared for.

"It could be worse." He said.

Yeah, worse, what could be worse than what I already was, an untrained Mystic with the weight of our existence on my shoulders.

"You could be green."

I whipped my head up from the coffee I was swirling and looked at him with shock.

"Hey, I thought you said you weren't going to decider my fuzzy thoughts!"

"I did. I'm not. I mean. I'm trying not to. It's just you're having a hard time keeping the wall up. I know it's wrong, but I want to understand what you are, and how I can help you."

*I want to help you.*

This time I heard him in my head. The non-voice that I felt in my soul. His thoughts penetrated my mind even though I was blocking my thoughts. Interesting fact. And with that, I remembered why I wanted to meet him here. This wasn't just about me, he had to start answering some of my questions. I couldn't take any more surprises or secrets. I had to get some answers, otherwise what was I doing here? Jason stood up and paid for our drinks. He told me to wait there so he could bring his motorcycle around from the back of the café. He also promised to answer some of my questions but thought a change of scenery would be nice.

We stood on the curb next to his bike. The easy confidence that he usually carried was gone now. And in its place was an awkwardness I didn't think he could even possess. Jason was stalling. That much I could tell. He kicked loose gravel under his feet, scratched the back of his head, readjusted the mirror on his bike. If it was going to be this hard, he didn't have to tell me anything.

"No, well yeah, it is hard, but no, I want to tell you. It's only hard because I have never told anyone before. It goes against everything I've been taught. And just so you know you aren't blocking me anymore, or at least not as much." He mumbled.

"Nice change of subject, but ugh, why can't I get this?"

"When your emotions are heightened, it gets harder to hold the block. At least that has been my experience."

"Are you saying my emotions are heightened?" A small laugh escaped his lips. His perfect lips. I was falling for Jason, so my will to control my thoughts was collapsing.

"I mean, you are rather charming." I gave him what I hoped was my most flirty smile. I think it worked, because he gave me a smile back, one that could set my hair on fire.

"You pay me too much credit. But you deserve some answers. I'm just afraid once you get the answers, you won't look at me the same." He said, his voice losing all the charm from earlier, it was now somber almost sad. He tucked his chin in toward his chest and he looked at me through hooded eyelids.

"Alexandra, promise me you'll stay. Promise me you won't leave. I don't think I could handle it if you did. I know you don't know me, but you can't deny that you feel something for me, too. I'm afraid that once you hear the truth..." He let out a deep sigh. "Stay with me Alexandra."

Hearing my full name on his lips killed me. It was a song only he could sing. He sounded so lost. I didn't want him to be alone, I didn't want to be alone. I extended my hand toward his face, and I ran my fingers down the side of his beautiful check bone. His cheek pressed into my hand and his eyes closed. He placed a gentle kiss on the inside of my palm.

"It's ok Jason, tell me. I'm here. I'm not going anywhere." Without looking at me, he spoke. "Have you ever heard of Skin Walkers?" I knew it was a question I wasn't expected to answer.

"My pack, we're not your average tribe. We're known as Skin Walkers. We transform. Into animals."

My stomach hit the floor. I had to physically touch my jaw to make sure that it wasn't hanging opened gapping at this beautiful boy and his wild tale. Is he for real? Did he just say what I think I heard him say? Animal? Like legit true animals? Now I really must have stepped into some type of science fiction novel. This can't be real. This can't be what he's about to tell me. This is a cosmic joke he's playing on the new girl. But then I looked at him. My eyes met his green jade ones, and there was no humor in them. Only sadness and vulnerability. He was opening up to me; he was taking a jump he didn't know he could land. I knew right then that he was telling me the truth, and it scared him. I took his hands in mine and planted my feet even firmer into the pavement, determined to show him I wasn't going anywhere. I gave him a look I hoped would convey as much. It did. A hint of a smile touched his sad eyes. He took a long blink and spoke again.

"Not everyone in the tribe can Spirit Walk, just a select few. I can't explain it as well as the elders can, but it comes down to who's been touched with the gift. We believe that our Spirit Gods create every soul, they are the deciders of our fate. It's through their divine decisions of who will be gifted as shamans, workers, leaders, etc. But their greatest decision is who will be Walkers. As Walkers, our spirits need to be strong, and it's within that strength that determines what form our Spirit Animal — or Spirit Guide will take. Our Spirit Animal determines our place in the pack, the powerful Alpha Wolf, the wise majestic Eagle, the loyal Beaver, the worker Fox, every animal plays a role in our pack. Every position is just as important as the next. It's what brings balance to our pack and to the tribe."

He leaned against his bike, hands in pocket, waiting for whatever I was about to say next. What was I going to say? What could I say? My mind couldn't process what he was telling me. The logistics and realism of it just couldn't be probable. But my heart was telling me to believe. With everything I've heard so far since arriving in this crazy town, what was a little shape shifting to add to the mix? A war was going on in my head, two ends of a magnet trying to fight for dominance, and I didn't know which end would come out victorious. I squeezed my eyelids together, took a deep breath and tried formulating words to ask him the many questions coursing through my brain.

"So, what are you? I mean, what's your Spirit Animal?"

My voice sounded harsher than I intended, but this was literally about to make my brain explode. It was all too much.

"In my native language, it's called a Cheete. You would know it as a wolf."

"You're serious? You're seriously telling me you turn into a wolf? Like a wolf wolf? Full howl at the moon wolf? Killed by a silver bullet sort of wolf? Next, you're going to tell me you're not just a wolf but the Alpha wolf. Wouldn't that just be my luck? Not only do I land in this mysterious town where I come to find out my destiny is to save some dying breed of Mystics, but that I'm also falling for the alpha wolf himself."

I hadn't realized I started pacing around. My ranting in full force now, just an endless stream of words spilling out of me. I guess I finally snapped with all the heavy hitting news stories pilling up on me. Then it dawned on me. While I've been babbling, he hasn't interrupted me. He didn't correct me. I called him the alpha, and he didn't deny it. I stopped my feet. I almost tumbled over them with the abruptness of it.

"You didn't deny it."

"Deny what?"

"The alpha joke. You're not saying you are...?"

"Well, you see..."

"Oh, my god! What does that mean? Like leader? Like boss? Like you're the one in charge?! Of course, of course. Not only do I stumble into this fairytale world of monsters and Mystics, but I have befriended the king monster himself." I not only saw, but I felt him wince at the last part. I was being mean. I knew it. But I couldn't help it. It was just one crazy thing after another I was going to snap.

"But do you believe me?" He gave me a sideways look. "I half expected you to take off in a dead sprint."

"You know what Jason, honestly with all that has happened to me in the last 24, no 48 hours, I am willing to believe just about anything at this point. You're telling me you're some kind of alpha wolf. Well, isn't that just great! It fits right in with everything else I've learned since coming to the crazy town. So why wouldn't it be true? Yes, Jason. I believe you. But I don't know how to process this information." He grimaced for just a second.

"You sound mad. Are you mad?" I took a deep breath and tried to calm my erratic nerves. I lifted my hands and grabbed his elbows; I slid my hands up and down his biceps. Feeling his body under his black canvas jacket was like therapy, it helped sooth my nerves.

"I'm sorry, I... I've been through an awful lot since moving here. If I'm coming off a little bitchy, I apologize. I'm here Jason, I'm not going anywhere." He reached out and wrapped his arms around me, my small body tucked inside his powerful arms. I felt so protected, so wanted. I completely dropped my wall and silently told him.

*Don't let me go.*

# Chapter 28: Rip Its Way Out.

### Jason

"You went to go see that girl tonight, didn't you? What have I told you?" Joseph said.

"Dad, she goes to my school. How am I not supposed to see her?" Jason replied in fully teenage insolence.

"That wasn't what I was referring to!"

"Yeah, I know you have your goon's constantly watching me like I was a simple child."

"You may be my son, but you are still a child. Until you're Alpha, I can have the whole pack watching you if I so choose. I want you to stay away from her. You will have nothing to do with her." It wasn't exactly an order, but it wasn't something he could deny.

"Since when are my associations ever in question? If you have it your way, I'll be Alpha shortly. And I would hope that my progression as your son and future Alpha would warrant a little more respect than just being some child!" Jason stood a little taller now, not cowering to his father as he should have. As the respect of the Alpha required. But deep in his veins ran Alpha blood as well, and when it came to Alex he couldn't, he wouldn't back down.

"Jason."

Jason's dad had a very weary tone to his words. This wasn't the first conflict of interest they were disputing over. Raising a teenage son without the help of a mother can tax even the most involved father. But Jason's dad, being in the position he was in, wasn't always able to be there for him in the capacity Joseph wanted. Which means often times Joseph needed to put his foot down not just as dad, but as Alpha as well. And that's when things would get heated.

Jason sat in his favorite chair. His dad paced the small galley kitchen that overlooked the living room.

"Do you have any idea how dangerous that girl could be? Our family has been protecting these lands for hundreds of years. We have seen our fair share of adversaries and nothing as powerful as her kind. That girl can unleash an evil our kind has not seen since the Great War." Joseph was trying to control his exasperation.

"Dad, I really think you're overreacting. She barely found out who she was, and honestly, I don't think she believes it. If she doesn't know what she is, how in the hell do you know?" Jason sat there, thumbing through an old comic book, tying to sound uninterested when really he couldn't be more intrigued.

"Are you telling me the girl is clueless about her heritage? How does she not know?" His father stopped pacing and went to sit across from Jason in the beat-up love seat.

"They abandoned her as a baby, and she has no knowledge of her family. What gives you the impression she's evil? You don't even know her. From what I've seen, she's just a normal teenage girl. Well, as normal as you can be when you have telekinetic abilities."

Jason put down the dog-eared comic book and reached for the bag of potato chips that was sitting on the table. He was not about to tell his father all that he knew about her, even though he didn't quite understand what that was exactly. His dad was deep in his own thoughts, leg twitching aimlessly was a tell-tell sign he was somewhere else. Jason was grateful for his years of practice at blocking his thoughts. He was also thankful that his dad seemed too preoccupied to try and see through the block. Something that both relieved him and alarmed him.

"Dad, why do you look so worried about some girl?" Jason was growing concerned over his father's uneasiness.

Jospeh stood up in a big rush, knocking over Jason's half empty soda can, spilling brown liquid all over the coffee table and Jason's favorite comic book. Jason quickly grabbed for it. Thankfully, only the cover was damaged. He shook the book spraying sugary soda all over the coffee table, which by now was just a sticky mess. He'll have to clean that up later. Jason followed his father into the back room where he had stormed off.

Jospeh was standing in the small room at the back of the house. Which doubled as a den/office when Jason's father had his "colleagues" a.k.a. goon-patrol pack members over to discuss, "official business" — which Jason had been previously kept from until he had his first shift, two years ago.

"Dad?" His father's back was to Jason.

"For as long as I can remember, we have been protecting our land from what outsiders would call fairy tales. Hell, even ourselves would be classified as make believe. But it has been our duty to keep the evil at bay." Jason shifted his weight uneasily, feeling the anxiety his father was exuding.

"What does that have to do with Alex? She's not evil, hell she's not even a rival Tribe member. So really, how evil can one telekinetic girl be?" Jason was leaning on the door frame. The tension in the room was too thick to enter. He felt safer somehow, just on the outskirts of the room.

"You said that earlier. That she was telekinetic. Do you mean she can move things with her mind?" His father turned toward him now, a large leather book in his hands, his brows furrowed, waiting for Jason to answer.

"I don't know, maybe. Something weird happened in class on her first day. And I know she can hear my thoughts, at least when I push them out to her. As far as I know, that's the extent of it."

"She can what? Wait... when you what? Jay. Are you're telling me you've...we've no time for that right now. But believe me, we'll circle back to that." Jason shrugged his shoulders in a *what do you expect,* sort of way and his dad pushed through that minor revelation and continued with his thought. He was sitting in the office chair by his desk, fingers pressing the bridge of his nose, eyes shut tight.

"Do you know anything about this book?" He picked up his head to look at Jason, the book resting on his lap.

"Yeah, that's the Old Book. It's about our history," Jason replied.

"Correct. Long time ago, the Kootenai and the Charmers, the call themselves Mystics, were once equals, both working together to fend off the evil who would harm us while protecting the Commoners who occupied the surrounding lands, and together we kept our presence a secret. But that wasn't enough for some. There was division among our kind and among the Mystics. The Kootenai split, creating new Tribes, and separate territories. The new Alphas were hungry for power, power to be Alpha and control the population. Our family kept the name and what lands we could and have been gaining it back ever since. We are the original tribe, and one day I hope to see us all united again. That is why it is so important that you take your spot as Alpha when the time comes. But of course, you knew all that. It has been instilled in you ever since your spirit animal chose you, and you had your first shift.

"What you haven't been told is what became of the Charmers. The story you know is about the Metee-kolen-ol the race of evil Charmers with hearts of ice. Only they weren't always evil. They were once Charmers, just like your little friend." Jason dared to glance over to his father.

"You may be my son, but I am still Alpha, and your thoughts are never completely shielded from me. I saw the girl inadvertently tell you who she was." His father informed him and then continued.

"Some Charmers fall into temptation over the Dark Arts, and when the temptation turns into an addiction, the Metee-kolen-ol spirit takes over and the Dark Arts are in control. Charmers did not divide over land and territory like our brethren had. They fell apart at the hands of one individual. This Charmer wasn't only power hungry, he wanted control over everything. Commoners, Charmers and the Kootenai. He tried to defeat his own High Priestess. Our book doesn't explain what happened, for that is not our history to tell. What it does say is, one day a new High Priestess will be born, and she will have the power to restore or destroy. Ever since then, the Charmers have not been trusted. A following has gathered under the new leader of the Metee-kolen-ol, and they are out to destroy and capture anything that gets in their way. They gain strength by drawing out the life energy of their victims. Like leaches, they grab hold of the innocent and bleed everything out of them until there is nothing left but the shell of their human body."

Jason was feeling overwhelmed by this discovery. He couldn't imagine Alex destroying anything on purpose. He couldn't reveal how much this story was affecting him, so instead of asking the millions of questions rolling in his head, he simply rolled his eyes and said.

"What like vampires? Come on." The small vein in his father's temple throbbed, tell-tell sign that his father did not think his antics were amusing.

"Where do you think the Commoners derived all their legends from? You know that all myths and legends started out as having a grain of truth. But the bigger issue here is if those, 'Vampires' as you call them, if they locate the girl who carries the High Priestess' spirit, then all is lost."

Jason was hanging on to every word his father was saying, waiting for some good news to come out of this instead of, 'your

Hopefully-Wanna-Be-Girlfriend is in peril'. But his father said nothing else, simply sat in his chair, completely still.

"They will find a way to corrupt her. They will bring her an inch from death only to promise to save her once she swears her allegiance to them. And if she does, they will be unstoppable. Free to behoove as much havoc and chaos as they see fit." Now Jason didn't think this was a joke anymore, not a joke at all, but very real, too real.

"How do we stop them? How do we prevent this from happening? They can't take her. I won't let it happen." His Dad was beginning to see how much this girl meant to him. He didn't need to read his thoughts to know what was written all over his face. This saddened Joseph because he knew a relationship between the two of them would never work. But he also knew his son. For he was just as stubborn as he was. In a defeated tone, he said.

"We can't, Jason, only she can stop them. She is the only one who could summon enough power to destroy them." He looked away, not wanting to meet his son's eyes.

"Dad, what aren't you telling me?" There was pain in Jason's voice. But even more in his fathers.

"Yes, she has the ability, but if she doesn't fully understand it, or has control of it, destroying the evil could destroy her as well."

His father looked tired, he rubbed his chin, trying to contemplate what this girl could mean to the future of his tribe. The lines around his father's eyes were more defined than ever before. His brown skin looked pale instead of golden. It almost seemed like his hair was graying right before Jason's eyes. Jason stood up to his full height, determined not to let fear control him. His father was a pillar of strength not just to him, but to the entire tribe. He has never seen his father falter or be unsure of any situation that came to pass. Not until tonight.

"Dad, how do you know about this girl? How do you know Alex is this one you are talking about?" Jason felt like a child, young and naïve. His Dad looked at him and in a soft voice answered.

"Because we have also been tracking the girl." A shot of confusion blindsided Jason.

"What?! Is that why you and Patrick have told me to stay away from her? Because you think she's some evil doer in the making? You don't even know her! Why haven't I heard about this before? What good does it do to tell me now? She's not like that. She's not evil, she's strong. She's good."

Jason looked more like a wolf now than ever before. He paced back and forth in the small hallway; his lupin body lean and sleek shivered under the surface of his skin. It was itching to be released.

"I have done everything you've asked. I run patrols; I help keep order amongst our pack. I'm stepping up to be Alpha. I've even defeated my fair share of mystical foe beings. I have never questioned you or gone against your authority. Ever. But this time, this time, I don't think I can stay away." Jason's eyes were pleading. His fathers were stoic.

"This girl, I feel something for her. It's the first time since... since mom died that I've allowed my heart to open. Dad, I can't, you just have to trust me. Trust that I might know a little more about her than you do. She is not evil. She doesn't want to harm us or expose us; I know it."

Jason stood there, hands pressed against the wall of the hallway, his forehead leaning against the cool paint. He was trying hard to push down the urge to shift into his wolf. The wolf wanted it. He wanted to escape and run off the energy that was coursing through Jason's veins. It was clawing at him from within. Trying to rip its way out, Jason could feel his muscles and bones responding to the welcomed pain of the transformation that was sure to happen. His wolf was sensing the fear and tension of the situation and was growing anxious. It needed to be freed; it needs to run. He felt his bones tense in anticipation.

"Jason, you have an obligation to your pack, to your family. Your alliance goes deeper than some high school crush. If the others knew you were consorting with a Charmer, they wouldn't trust you. They don't want their future leader to be seduced by dark magic, it puts us in jeopardy. I'm sorry son, it can't happen. This girl could end us. She could end our history. You need to stay away from her. The family and your rightful place depend on it. She has no place here."

His father's words were harsh and full of authority. Yet it still lacked the vibrato of an official Alpha command. Once Alpha's words pressed upon you, you had no choice but to respond and act in duty. To disobey would tear you from the pack. Jason's father was not ready to use such force. Was it from fear of having his son disobey an official order or sadness over Jason's wayward heart? He didn't know. But for now, it was a warning, not a command.

Before Jason even registered the last few words of his Father's speech, he was already out of the house. He didn't need to be there physically to hear his Father, he would have heard regardless either vocally or internally. Whatever the case, Jason was gone. Down the hall, out the door, flying leap off the porch, four large, padded paws thumping straight for open woods. Shreds of clothes littering the stoop, the only thing left to mark Jason's presence. The cry of a wolf rang out somewhere in the distance. Baying and pained.

# Chapter 29: I'm a Realist

**Alex**

My first weekend at the Manor was full of fun, hallmark moments and girl bonding. Oh wait, that's what would have happened in a made for T.V. Saturday special. My life was more like an episode of the Twilight Zone, all horror and Sci-Fi all the time. The Matrons take the weekends to teach us self-reliance and life skills, so the weekend is full of house chores, small do it yourself projects and a few basic Elemental Magic 101 lectures. I didn't mind the sweeping and folding laundry, Ms. Mary said by during our tasks without complaint is how we earn our freedom for any after-school activities or weekend plans. So yeah, if me doing some gardening gets me to maybe possibly go see a movie with Jason later. Then so be it. I'll do my fair share. This place, the Manor, it was kind of... fantastic.

All my other group homes were so awful. They placed me in over crowed overwhelmed families who didn't want me to begin with. Which was fine by me. I never stayed in a home for over a year anyway, so it was only a matter of time before they placed me in a different over crowed underfunded group home. But this place was different. It was like a home, a weird, supernaturally gifted family. Sure, everyone had their minor problems, Nora was still borrowing clothes from Paige's closet without asking. Chrissy was working on social issues with Ms. Terra, trying to be more engaged, more involved in a social setting. And Neal had gone missing, Nora was not taking it well. Sometimes she was fine, completely self-involved and assured that Neal was just blowing off steam for being reprimanded. At other times she was inconsolably certain that Neal had gone searching for Lord Nicolai. Who I have just recently found out through my first Mystic 101 lecture was the guy I saw in my vision. The one responsible for the fall of the coven. Great!

Jason and I had plans to grab a bite later, and I was a little afraid it might be awkward after our conversation the night before outside the café. It was so charged, full of unspoken emotions and long kept secrets. But after Jason told me what he told me, everything seemed so — easy. Almost familiar. Like I've known him my whole life. After our conversation, Jason squeezed a motorcycle helmet over my head and took me home on the bike. It was thrilling being on the back of his bike, feeling the road underneath us and clinging to the warmth of him, his body a wall of protection.

Before Jason came to pick me up for your date. I made sure to change out of my top and jeans I'd been wearing to "clean" the manor. Then brushed and re-brushed my hair. It was never quite right, either it was too big, or it lacked any kind of bounce, but today was a decently good hair day. I was thankful now that I took a shower this morning instead of waiting for tonight. It was just pizza after all, so why was I freaking out. Oh, that's right, it's because this would be my first, *First Date*. And not just a meet-and-greet to swap fantastical stories of unbelievable magical creatures that the pair of us were.

Paige and I were alone in our room and we both seemed to be busy getting ready for pre-approved plans. If I wasn't mistaken, was Paige humming? "You seem less cynical tonight, almost giddy. What? You have, some kind of hot date?" Paige was sitting on her lower bunk applying another layer of mascara on her already mascara covered eyelashes. Nails painted a fresh coat of black and her bangs had a new pink stripe running off one side.

"I'm not a cynic, I'm a realist, and for your information, I do. I do have plans for tonight." She shot me a look that read, Do Not Disturb. I was not going to let her weird Emo attitude damper my good mood.

"Really? Do tell. What are these hot plans you have maybe we can compare?"

"You know, the usual. Going down to the Promenade, debating whether I'll let Tyler Johnston get to second base or if I wanna see Meet Me in Central Park for like the third time. Wait, did you say you have a date? Like an actual date with an actual person? Wow, you're faster than I am, not even a full week under your belt, and you're already breaking hearts. Good going, my hats off to you." She turned her attention back to her trilling cell phone and was lost once again to her text messages.

"No, it's not like that. Jason's not just some boy. And I take my relationships a little more seriously than you're implying."

What relationships, I thought secretly to myself. I've never had any to take seriously. She suddenly sat straight up, nearly hitting her head on the top bunk. I think she swallowed her gum.

"Excuse me. Did you say Jason? You don't mean Jason Alder, do you? He's possibly one of the hottest guys at our school! He hasn't shown any interest in any girl since he enrolled last year. How the hell did you snag a date with him? No offense, of course, but he's been in a walking coma ever sense his mom died." I smiled sweetly at her for her backhanded comment.

"You know when someone says, 'no offense' they actually mean all the offense possible."

She was staring at me like a deer caught in headlights. I didn't, however, have any idea what she was talking about? I didn't even know his mom had died. He never mentioned it, nor did he seem to be in any kind of coma. I was, once again, reminded of how very little I knew about him. I mean, I knew possibly the biggest secret one could know about Jason Alder. But other than knowing what he was, I knew nothing about *who* he was. I had to check my emotions again, needed to reign in my over fluttering heart whenever he was near. I needed to get to know him first, before I let my heart get all gooey at the thought of him.

Before I could get all worked up over Paige's "shocked" comment (I'll be offended about that later) I made myself believe that's what first dates are all about. For getting to know someone, that was the whole point. Right? Nothing would ruin this night. I chose my black matchstick pants with my teal faux cashmere sweater Clara had given me for Christmas last year. It was a little worn at the sleeves, but it hugged my frame nicely making my boyish figure look a little more womanly. I hoped the pizza place had some outdoor seating, though, so I wouldn't sweat through this thick, poly-blended sweater. Which would have been a more appropriate label than 'imitation cashmere' call it what it is, T.J. Maxx, polyester.

While I was getting ready, Jason texted to confirm pizza was still what we wanted to do. I gave him a quick reply and finished putting my makeup on. As I finished putting everything away, my phone rang, this time an actual phone call and not just a text.

"You ready to go?"

I heard him say the second I swiped the talk button on my phone, which reminded me I would need to find a way to keep up my phone bill. It would be a hard commute to continue my job back at the ice cream parlor.

"Hello Alex, how are you? Hello Jason, I'm fine, thank you. Would you like to accompany me to the pizza parlor tonight? Yes, I would love to go to the pizza parlor with you. Are you ready now or do you need another few minutes? No, I am ready. Let me grab my jacket."

I continued my one-sided conversation over the phone all the way down the stairs to the front door. When he interjected, finally done listening to me having a conversation for the both of us.

"Hello dear Alexandra, I hope ye well this twilight moon, the weather is splendidly lovely this time of year would not you say? My driver and I, for I am nary without one, are on our way to your front door. I will have him ring the Misses to let them know of my arrival." I opened the front door and Jason, who was standing just beyond the little walkway, gave a sweeping bow that would rival any Emily Dickens novel.

"Hardy har-har, all I'm saying is that a little refinement is never lost." I said into the phone.

"All right, I caught the hint." He hung up.

I was so excited. I could never have a few hours to hang with my friends back in Minnesota, all the Foster Moms were way too strict to leave me unsupervised, and I didn't really have a lot of friends to hang out with, anyway. So, this, being able to leave the house without adult supervision and being able to be out on the town with a friend was a whole new experience. Not to mention doing all this with a totally hot guy, Double New Experience.

I was about to close the door but remembered I had left my purse in the kitchen earlier when I was talking to Ms. Mary about where I was going and with who. I called out to Jason letting him know I'd be right back and turned around to grab my bag.

# Chapter 30: Depressing First Date Conversations.

**Alex**

I paused before opening the front door back to Jason, checking the wall I constructed around my thoughts. Yup, still there. I took a second to gather my wits and opened the door to the outside. There was Jason, standing at the end of the lane, perched against his motorcycle. If it was at all possible for Jason to look even hotter than he normally did, he surpassed it. He showed no signs that he noticed I was approaching him. I slowed my steps just a little. I wanted to drink up the sight of him, to linger my gaze on his easy stance against his cycle. He was always so courteous when I was around him, always had an air of confidence, yet never cocky. I wanted to be around him. I wanted to get as close to him as the laws of physics would allow. As I came towards him, I noticed his body language was worlds apart from what I had grown accustomed to seeing. His head hung low on his shoulders his arms crossed over his chest. He looked sad, lost in his contemplation alone in a world all by himself, and right then I picked up my step. I didn't want him to be lost anymore. I wanted to shoulder his worry for him, no matter what it was.

Jason's head popped up at the sound of my steps on the pebbled walkway. He stood up straighter and tucked his arms in the pockets of his distressed denim jeans.

"Hey gorgeous, you look great." His eyes looked over my appearance. I was very glad I wore the teal sweater. "You ready to go?" He tossed a helmet at me and reached for the other one balancing on his handlebars.

"Are you ok? I noticed you looked a little, not all here?" He gave me a solid nod and helped me with my helmet. I did notice that he didn't actually answer my question.

I've only ever been on a motorcycle once and that was when Jason gave me a ride home from the café. It was an amazing experience, but I was still so caught up in what we had just been discussing that I couldn't take any of it in, not really. But now, being on the back of his bike as the sun was setting, and we were whisking down streets and around corners, it was exhilarating. I could feel the cold air kissing my skin through my clothes, my ankles, my wrist, my neck, anywhere my clothes didn't reach. Thankful for the afterthought of grabbing my bigger coat. The wind was like tiny shards of ice licking at my skin, freezing it upon touch. It was intoxicating.

Nothing could have cooled my core; it was a fire burning deep within like a sleeping volcano. I had a hold on Jason that was so tight it could have broken ribs. My arms gripped his waist, my hands buried into the pockets of his jacket. Thighs gripped the outside of his legs, vibrating to the roar of the engine I was straddling. My chest pressed hard against his back. No light or wind or ice could have penetrated. There was no telling where he stopped, and I began. Every move he made, I made. Every lean we took, we took it together. We moved as one.

We pulled into the center of town and slowed to a crawl through the main streets. It seemed like everyone showed up in town tonight. Winter was fading and you could feel that spring was coming. The nights were getting shorter and the crisp, cool air was slowly warming. He parked the bike along the strip of shops that made up the main square of town. We attached our helmets to the back of his bike and started walking down the sidewalk. We were only on the bike for about 15 minutes, but my legs were so unstable they wobbled. Jason held on to my arm to steady me. Oh god did he smell good! I wanted to wrap myself up in it, to be surrounded by the scent of pine and soap. He moved his hand down my arm, slowly tracing my elbow and forearm, leaving a trail of goose bumps in his wake. He stopped at my hand and held on tightly. We held hands all the way to the pizza shop.

My wish was granted and there was outside seating on the veranda behind the restaurant and it was open mic-night, and if the other acts were as good as the duo singing a folksy song with a guitar and tambourine, I was here for it. Halfway through our large sausage and mushroom pizza, most of which was eaten by Jason, along with two cherry coke refills later, our night was turning out to be perfect. Jason and I talked about everything, well everything normal teenagers talk about, favorite hobbies, schools, television programs, just about everything, well almost. The more we talked, the more we connected, the more it was harder to keep my emotions at bay.

Even with all the talking, the comment Paige had made earlier was still bugging me, and Jason had yet to say anything about his mom. Everything was going so well, and so far we've been nothing but open with each other, so I figured I'd come out and ask him about it.

"Well so you told me about your dad. He's the Chief of your tribe and your family has been the leaders of it for as long as you can remember. That makes you like a prince, huh? But you haven't said anything about your mom?" He absentmindedly picked at a cold piece of pizza in front of him. I looked down at my plate, feeling the tension in the room that wasn't there just a moment ago.

"My mom, she... she died a few years ago." That much I knew, but hearing it from him was so final.

"I'm sorry, that's awful." It was a pathetic thing to say, but what do you say to someone who's lost a parent? He inhaled deeply, and I wanted to tell him to stop, to not explain. I didn't want him to drudge up old memories that still stung. I didn't want him to feel pain, not anymore, not now that I was here for him. My wall was up. That much I knew; it was becoming very easy to have it always in place. It wasn't hard at all. It felt comforting, like having a heavy quilt over you in the cold months. It was reassuring. My face, my face though, always gave away what I was thinking. He reached out and placed a hand on my arm. He was about to tell me about a painful memory, yet here he was comforting me. He was too unreal to be real.

"It was two years ago. I had just turned 15. The boys in my pack, once they hit a certain age our Shaman, Hokama, takes us on a guided journey up the mountain to see if a spirit animal will choose us; the warrior within that guides us for the rest of our lives. He communicates with our ancestors to know which one of us is destined for a Spirit Guide. There's a manhood ceremony we must perform with the men and elders of our tribe. It will determine if we're ready to receive our totem. But even though the elders communicate with the spirits, they aren't always right and there are times when a boy will take the journey and come back empty. If we've been found worthy, the next full moon after our journey we'll take on our animal form and have our first shift. The first shift is a very scary thing. It's frantic and chaotic. Your bones and muscles are contorting in ways they weren't made to rotate. It's painful and numbing. It's dangerous. You're in and out of rationality; your human mind is trying to regain its composure while your inner animal instinct is registering survival and fear."

Jason was replaying the story for me, and while he was talking, he was being transported back to when it all happened. He was reliving the events of two years ago. I could see it, in his brow line, his far-away eyes, the hunch in his shoulders and the cold clamminess of his hands that I held in my own. I tried to tell him to stop, but he was too far gone. He couldn't hear anything I said.

"Surrounded by the men and boys of those who have changed before me is an honor. It's a ritual of a boy becoming a man. There have been many who have not made it through the change. It was too much for them. Their human bodies weren't strong enough to carry the spirit within, and they lost the fight to contain both. There was a lot of pressure on me, being the Alpha's son, to see what our Ancestors thought my warrior animal should be. My father is a Wolf, the Alpha, proud and fearless like a leader should be. There was an importance riding on my shoulders that the other boys didn't have, because the elders and other men in attendance knew they would be witnessing the 'birth' of their new Alpha." Jason was no longer in front of me. He was back in those woods, back to that day. I wasn't here; the café wasn't here. It was only Jason and his memory.

"There was a roar of hoots and hollers when Hokama handed me my Totem. It was the Wolf. The wolf represents loyalty and is a Great Communicator and holds in his heart compassion and intelligence. The rightful fit for the future Alpha. My father was very proud. I don't remember much from the actual change. There was a lot of pain and trauma. I was slipping in and out of cognizance. My senses were multiplying. I could suddenly hear the heartbeats of the surrounding men. I could smell moss and decay of the forest; it weaved around me telling me the stories of the men and animals who roamed the woods in times past. I saw every path; I could read every decision that was being made here in the woods. It was awful, but wonderful, both confusing and exhilarating. My head was splitting in two from the overload of new senses, and my body was being ripped in half by the animal trying to escape. Pain, pain was all I could feel.

"Then there was pandemonium. Confusion. In the middle of my drunken haze screams of alarm were blaring in my ears, the sound heightened by the wolf within. I unexpectedly smelled blood, lots of blood. Distantly, I remembered a few of the others bleed from where the skin hadn't stretched in time for the bone to maneuver. But this blood was different, it wasn't my blood. Somehow, I knew it wasn't mine. Then, as suddenly as it had started, I felt teeth around my neck, fangs on my haunches, a mixture of arms and paws, and wings groping at me, prying me away from whatever was in front of me. I didn't know what was going on. The animal within was angry, was maddened by the hamper of violence it craved. Silence, a deathly silence, cut through my animal rage like a Mac truck. I was full wolf now, not the twisted half human I've been fighting. My body was aching, but it wasn't painful, it was a welcomed ache. I made it, I made it through my first shift. But as I looked around at my pack something was wrong. Now through my wolf's eyes I picked up every detail, as if it was daylight and not the full moon of night.

"There in a crumpled heap was blood and destruction, flesh ripped from bone and clothes shredded like paper. I sauntered over to it, my blood pumping like a thunderstorm in my ears. Slowly my eyes took in a familiar color of cloth, green like apples. Green like the apron my mother always wore. My mother...there on the ground in a pool of blood was my mother. The blood I had smelled was hers, and it was all over my muzzle, my paws. I retched, heaved the contents of my stomach all over the ground in front of me. I hurled until there was nothing left. The surrounding people were approaching me, hands up in defeat. Trying to signify there was no danger here, except I was the danger. Me, I was dangerous. I couldn't understand, I wouldn't. I ran, I ran into the woods, I ran till my paws were bloody and sore. I deserved to keep running until my body gave out. But I didn't know where to go, where could I go to escape what've done?"

He stopped talking. He had tears in his eyes, I reached out to touch his cheek catching a tear that had fallen. In a flash, he grabbed my wrist hard, yanking it away from his face. His eyes shined like reflections in a mirror, and a growl escaped from under his teeth.

"Jason, you're hurting me." He snapped out of it, dropping my wrist and turning away from me. In a low, gruff voice, I heard him say.

"Oh god, Alexandra, I'm so sorry. I didn't mean..."

"Stop, it's okay. I'm fine. That story was... I really don't know what to say to that without it sounding, well stupid." I rubbed my wrist under the table, the sting of his fingers lingered, and a bruise was forming.

"My father, after running through the night, found me near Canada, still in my wolf form. He told me my mom was alive. Her leg was badly destroyed but she would live. The others were able to separate me from her and they saved her. She was alive. Only when an Alpha bites an enemy, they release a toxin into the bloodstream, a toxin that's fatal. Since I wasn't a full alpha yet, I didn't carry the same level of toxins in my bite. There was hope the Shamans could cleanse my mom and free her from the toxin. But when that didn't work, my dad took her to doctors hoping Western medicine could cure her. They diagnosed her with a rare cancer, and that was the story. She was attacked in the woods by a rabid dog and developed some sort of cancer. But the chemo only did so much, she died six months later, because of me. I killed her. She made sure to tell me this wasn't my fault. That I didn't know how to control my wolf, that a new Walker is never more dangerous than that first night. She forgave me and told me she would always love me. The first few shifts our animal instincts are so strong our natural fight-or-flight takes over."

He didn't look at me. I looked down at my wrist under the table. There were bruises blooming where his fingers had grabbed me. I pulled my sleeve low over my hand, hoping to hide it.

"They said no one saw her coming, but somehow, I feel like they're leaving something out. Why was she there? What did she need? She knew how dangerous this ceremony was, she had to have some reason for being out there that night. My mother did nothing that wasn't planned."

I tugged on my sleeve again. This was Jason. He would never intentionally hurt me. He was legitimately emotional. I understood that more than anybody. Look what happened to the poor girls (and sometimes dogs) when I get overly emotional. I never thought about what would happen if that power was turned back on me. Listen to me, I sounded like a Lifetime T.V. special, making excuses for my battered relationship. I was not in a battered relationship, hell I was barely even in a relationship. Before I got too deep into my own thoughts, Jason interrupted me.

"Alexandra? Are you okay? I really can't tell you how horrified I am at myself for grabbing you like that. I normally have more control, I...I don't know what came over me, please forgive me-"

"Jason it's okay really, I get it. Please let's just move on, okay. It's getting late. I should probably be going, anyway." Jason sank his head in his hands over the table, looking completely defeated.

"This is not how I thought our first date would go. I had no intention of releasing all my trauma on you in one night, I was hoping to at least save that for out next date." A half smile crept up on his face as he attempted to lighten the mood. "Let me at least buy you an ice cream. I hear ice cream makes up for anything. Maybe it would work on overly depressing first date conversation and the accidental infliction of pain."

His smile was back, the smoldering I know I look too amazing, smile. And we were back, as if the awkward moment beforehand never even happened. However, it did. Jason inadvertently killed his mother. How was I going to deal with that?

# Chapter 31: Mundane Banter

### Alex

We ate our ice cream outside. It was too hot and crowded inside the tiny ice cream parlor. Our ice cream would have melted before it made it to our mouths. Even though we were back to our easy banter, I couldn't help but feel like there was a weight over my shoulders from the news of his mom. I mean, how do you process such a tragedy?

"Are you going to try out for any school sports?" Jason's attempt at small talk. I laced my fingers with his as we strolled back to his motorcycle. I felt him ease up a bit. His form became more relaxed. We both subconsciously or not decided we weren't going to talk any more about our past or paranormal things tonight.

Our conversation fell back into mundane type banter; what's your favorite movie, what shouldn't be on pizza, if you could travel anywhere where would you go? When Harry Met Sally; Mushrooms; Egypt. Until finally we were back at his motorcycle and my curfew was approaching. A sense of relief washed over me for the excuse to go home. I didn't want to upset the Matrons on my first night of being out, and I also needed to go home to process everything that had transpired this evening. Not just the fact that Jason's transition led to the death of his mother, but the fact that he can transition at all, the whole situation was so unbelievable. But really, at this point, with all the talk of mystics and dark arts, is an

167

animal transformation that much of a jump? I needed to call Clara, not to ask her to come pick me up, but to ask whether she knew. How much of my history was she aware of? How did she find this place for me? What was she keeping from me?

Back on the bike, weaving and gliding through small country roads to the manor, didn't feel as thrilling as it had earlier. Now it felt dangerous and cold. The wind forced its way in and around my ankles and jacket like it was trying to pull me off the bike. It took everything I had to hold on to Jason so I wouldn't fall off. Holding on to Jason felt both safe and wearisome. I started to doubt what his transitions and temper could mean. My wrist still hurt under my jacket, where he grabbed me. Could he lose his temper again, in a more ultimate way? I shook the thought out of my head. I was tired and overwhelmed and it was doing me no good to spin my thoughts right now. I needed to get home, get warm, and call Clara. I didn't care what time it was. I needed to hear her voice.

Jason helped me off the bike, steadying me so I didn't crash into the ground. I refused to think about the worries that were trying to surface. Jason was here with me, and this felt right. We stood next to his bike merely inches apart. I looked up at him. His deep green eyes were glassy, as if he was holding back tears. I reached up to caress his cheek, eyes closing with the touch of my hand a shaky breath escaping his lips. I couldn't look away, I couldn't move. I needed him to know I was here. A voice rumbled around me, the feeling reverberating throughout my entire body.

*Alexandra*

I felt Jason's voice in my head, tinted with despair. I shook my head, wanting to stop him from saying anything else. I didn't want him to say anything he couldn't take back. Not yet. Not right now. Not until after we've had some time to sort out the revelations, we both uncovered tonight. Instead, we stared at each other, unspoken words sparking and swirling around us like the charged air before a thunderstorm. I could feel the impregnated energy swelling around us. Then suddenly everything stopped. No one moved, no one breathed.

We froze in time until Jason took my chin in his hand and ever so gently leaned down to press his lips to mine. Hesitantly at first, almost cautiously wondering if I'd accept his advancement. I responded by leaning into him, grabbing the open zipper of his jacket and clinging to him as if my life depended on it. He was the beacon that was going to get me through this storm. Jason answering my call pressed his lips in hunger against mine, and then we were kissing. Kissing was breathing to us. We needed it to survive. It was beautiful and dangerous. There was a desperation to it, like he was trying to drink me in before I faded into nothing. Then, just a quick as it started, he pulled away. A breath catching on my own lips in a salient cry of finality. I didn't want it to stop. I didn't ever want it to stop. Jason pressed his forehead against mine. His skin was hot, almost too hot. No one said anything. But ultimately, Jason broke the silence.

"You should go. Back inside." He said each word like they pained him.

I wanted to take that pain. I wanted him to feel peace. But I knew he was right. The matrons would be waiting for me, and I didn't want to give them any reason to come out and look for me. I didn't say anything. I nodded in agreement and walked up to the house. I didn't look back. I was afraid if I did, he wouldn't be there. Or that he would be. And I didn't know which one was worse.

# Chapter 32: Some Kind of Freak

**Alex**

"Alex, is that you? It's one in the morning. Is everything okay? What happened?"

Clara's voice was thick with sleep. For a quick second I regretted my brash decision to call her now, not taking into account the time difference, when I should have waited for the morning. But then I remember why I needed to talk to her now and not later.

"Did you know?"

"Know what?"

Her voice was becoming clearer. She was slowly starting to wake up. I could tell she was putting on her Case Worker voice. She was hiding something.

"Know who or what I am? That something was different about me? Did you know? Because if you did, why didn't you tell me? How could you keep that from me?! I mean, don't you think I had the right to know that what everyone always said about me was true? That I really was some kind of freak?"

"Alex, take a breath." I could almost hear her forehead furrow and the subsequent hand rub that followed.

"You're not a freak. No, I didn't know. I mean, not really. I had my suspicions. It wasn't until I was researching alternative places for you, I even came across the Matrons. I don't even know how it happened. One day, while I was looking into different places, an email showed up in my inbox. An advertisement about the manor. I don't know where it came from or how I got on the email list, but as I was reading through the pamphlet, everything clicked. The pamphlet was all about kids who needed a second chance, ones who found themselves in situations that defied the odds. I took a shot and called the Matrons."

A memory jogged my mind suddenly. Paige telling me how she came to be in this place when she said, *the matrons always know.* They knew. They knew back then — three states away. How is that possible? Clara continued.

"Terra was the one I spoke to first, and it was as if she was waiting for my call. I don't know how to explain it, but I just knew that this was the place for you. I didn't know why. It wasn't until we arrived that she told me my suspicions were true. You were special, you could do special things. But most importantly, you would be safe. Alex, that's all I wanted for you. Was a place for you to be safe. Protected. A place you could finally call home."

"Special? You thought I was special? What does that even mean?" I interrupted her.

I was getting angry. I felt like she had betrayed me. She thought I was special. Was that just a nice way of saying she thought I was a freak like everyone else did? I was pacing now, back and forth in the dark kitchen. I didn't want to wake anyone up with my late phone call, so I called Clara from the kitchen. But in my haste to call her, I didn't bother to turn on the lights and now I was too angry to care. I continued to circle the kitchen in the dark, the dim glow of the oven hood light the only thing illuminating my path.

"Why didn't you tell me? How long did you think I was '*special*' or whatever friendly word you're trying to say? Do you have any idea the things I've heard in the last week? The stories they want me to believe about who or what I am? And you don't think that I could have used a little head up? 'Hey, I'm going to take you to some magical freak school because you might be some sort of demoniacal being. And there's a huge possibility that you have indeed caused all the destruction and devastation all the angry neighbors have blamed you for, for your entire life. And now I can just dump you off'."

"Hey, wait a minute, that's not fair! Alex—" I cut her off with a, "oh ya?"

I knew Clara didn't deserve the rage I was flinging at her, but I had so much pent up aggression about everything that has happened to me, and not just this last week with the matrons or even with Jason but for my entire life. Every terrible accident, every horrible mishap or unexplained occurrence was because of me. Because of my unchecked magical ability and an overload of emotions, I didn't know how to control. I couldn't help thinking that all those foster homes, all those burned bridges and terrified faces... were justified, were warranted. I was to be feared. I was the problem.

"Alexandra!"

My attention went back to the phone. I must have zoned out, spiraling into the depressive, dark thoughts of my past and hadn't realized I was still on the phone and Clara was trying to snap me out of it. I turned my attention back to Clara in Illinois.

"Alex. You're not a freak. You truly are special, and I've known it ever since I've met you. Not because you may or may not have certain abilities, but because of who you are. You are an amazing individual even without the abilities. I've never known anyone with so much compassion and care for others. You know what it's like to be on the outside. Use that. You are strong. You deserve this. Don't let this rob you of anything. You deserve it all. I know it. Listen to the matrons. Learn from them. I have always known something destined you for great things, and this is it. Here we are Alexandra. All you have to do now is accept it. I am always here for you, you know that. But you need to lean on the matrons now. You are where you belong. Finally. Now wash your face and get to bed."

Before hanging up, I heard her say.

"I forgive you for waking me up at such a god-awful time to yell at me. I know you're stressed, and I won't hold it against you. But Alex, you do this again and I will drive through the night to kick your ass, you hear me?"

"Sorry, I just..."

"I know. I love you."

"Clara?"

"Mm-hm?"

"Thank you."

I heard the phone click off. She was never one for goodbyes. I felt exhausted. Like I had run a triathlon through mud in a snowstorm. Completely spent of everything I had. I didn't realize how much I was holding onto until it all came flooding out all over Clara. I made a mental note to write her a postcard. She was one of the few who still loved getting snail mail. But I know she understands and wouldn't hold anything against me. I mean, this isn't the first time I've called her in the middle of the night because of the situation in my group home. However, this would be the first time I didn't expect her to be arriving the next morning. This was it. I wasn't going anywhere. And I think I've finally come to accept that I really am home. And I wasn't going anywhere.

# Chapter 33: Replaced With Resentment

*Alex*

Apparently, we had a free day off of school. On Monday, when I had started the ritual of getting ready for the day. Paige and Norah informed me there was no school because of an in-service teacher development something or another. This was news to me, but like everything else, I am always the last to know. The girls also told me that the matrons would be gone for most of the day. Something about important errands outside of town, so we were on our own for the day.

Immediately, I thought about calling Jason, but then something stopped me. We haven't talked since Saturday night. I wanted more than anything else to see him again. I knew if we could see each other in the light of day, everything would be okay. And if that kiss at the end of the night was any indication of how his feelings were, I will say I think he felt the same way I did. As if on cue, my phone trilled behind me. I fumbled with the pocket of my jeans to pull it out before I missed the call. It was Jason. Of course, it was.

"How far away does that mind reading power go?"

"Dropping pleasantries this morning, are we? Hi how are you? I'm fine, thank you."

"No, you're right. I gave you a hard time. I should practice what I preach. Yes, hello Jason, how are you? Good? Good. How far away does the mind reading work?" I heard him chuckle on the other side.

I loved that chuckle. It was throaty and oh so sexy. He answered my question.

"Well, I guess that depends. When I'm in my wolf's form, I can hear my pack a few miles away, maybe ten. When I'm in human form, it gets knocked down to maybe a few yards a mile at most. It depends on how well I know the person I'm listening to. Why? You weren't thinking about me right before I called you, were you?"

I could hear that devil may care smile in his voice and I was so glad he couldn't see me because my face was a very unattractive red at the moment.

"Aren't we a little full of ourselves today? I was just wondering, that's all. But I am glad you called. I didn't know if you — if after the other night — I'm just glad you called." Thankfully Jason interrupted my would be prattle and saved me the embarrassment.

"Ya, well, I'm glad you answered. I was wondering, today is a no school day. Are you able to get out and do something in town? I thought maybe you might want a tour in the daylight. And it gives me an excuse to see you again, and hopefully leave you with a better core memory of our date."

"Are you asking me out on a day date?"

"If the answer is yes, then I am. If it's no, then I guess all that's left for me to do is cry into a pillow and listen to R.E.M's *Losing My Religion* on an endless loop."

"Well, we can't have you doing that now, can we? When did you want to go?" I asked him as I started to mentally plan what I should wear.

"I was sort of thinking, now? I'm in the driveway."

What?! Oh my god I couldn't believe that he was here. Now! I still had bed head hair and pre-coffee reflects. I wasn't ready. What was he thinking? But of course, I didn't want him to go away, so I decided I could take a quick army shower and pull myself together. But he was going to pay for this. He was going to have to wait until

I was good and ready. I wouldn't make him wait long, just long enough.

After the quickest shower of my life, I plaited my hair in a simple side braid. Threw on some mascara and lip gloss and turned towards my much need-of-an-update wardrobe. I could tell by looking out the window it had frosted over a little during the night. A sprinkling of sugar dusted the land in crystalized heaps. I opted for my heavier pair of jeans for warmth, and one of the few thicker long-sleeved thermals I owned that didn't look like long underwear. It was a deep purple color with small white hearts zigzagging down the sleeves. I was thankful for Clara, who bought me the best Christmas present a few years back, a pair of black Doc Martin's. I finally got them to a point where they were worn like butter and kept my toesies toasty warm.

Once outside, my eyes immediately locked onto Jason. He was indeed right outside, leaning against his bike, scrolling his phone. Today's attire was a red wool scarf which he had poking out of a heavy leather jacket, and dark blue jeans cuffed over his worn black boots. I guess he dressed for the weather as well. For just a minute, I felt a little bad for making him wait out in the cold. But then my wet hair thumped against my cheek as I turned to close the front door and remembered how his surprise arrival denied me a meeting with my blow dryer. And I was suddenly glad he had to stand out in the cold.

"I like the scarf. It softens the whole bad boy on a motorcycle look you've got going on." I teased him as I walked closer to him and his bike.

"Actually, I brought it for you. It's a lot colder than it was last time, and I didn't want you to freeze."

Jason unwound the scarf from around his neck and came over to wrap it around my own. It was warm and smelled like winter air and soap. Once the scarf was tucked away under my jacket and our helmets were on, we mounted the bike and headed into town. He was right. It was a lot colder this time around than it had been the other night. I was glad I went with my heavier jeans and large coat, but I took note to purchase myself some long wool socks that would cover my ankles and calves and some gloves. My wrist became open airways for the freezing wind to wrap its icy fingers along my exposed skin. Jason stopped the bike in front of the café where we had met that first night.

"I thought we would start with a hot cup of coffee,"

"Yes please. I can't believe how cold it is. I thought spring would be here by now."

"Ya, that's Montana for you. It doesn't want to let go of the ice and snow."

"What do you do in the snow? You can't ride your motorcycle in the snow, can you?" As we discussed the ins and outs of the snow, we walked into the café and ordered very large and very hot coffees and a couple of cream cheese Danishes. My favorite.

"When the roads are undrivable, I drive my mom's car if I have to. But I prefer the bike. There's something about the open road of freedom the bike gives me. I don't like being confined in the frame of a car. I like the openness of the bike."

"And it looks pretty bad ass." I said in between bites of warm buttery Danish.

"Ya and it's pretty bad ass." He chuckled as he sipped his coffee.

We left the café and started walking down the street into the heart of downtown. It was still a little early, and the shops were just now opening up, doors were slowly being unlocked, signs switching from close to open. The sidewalks were steadily gaining more traffic as people came out for brunch and or to peruse the farmers' market. This town was so sweet, a small town hallmark sort of town. A far cry from the hustle and bustle of the cold shoulder city I came from.

Before I could get too lost in the serenity that was this little town, a familiar face came into view.

"Well, well, look who's out and about. You enjoyin' some mountain air?"

Neal was standing inside a veranda of one of the restaurants in the main part of town. A scrawny man was sitting at a table across from him dressed in an expensive suit.

"Hello Neal. You haven't been at the Manor in a few days. You know your sister's pretty worried about you."

"Aw, she ain't worried. She's just a big Ol' Drama Queen." I blatantly rolled my eyes at him. He obviously didn't care about his sister. Which was quite sad because on some days she was nearly inconsolable.

I gave Jason's hand a tight squeeze, and we walked a little faster so we could pass him that much quicker. We were nearly past the restaurant when Neal ran up to us and reached his hand out, grabbing my upper arm. I spun towards him, shocked at the audacity of his embrace. Jason tensed up, free hand in a fist, about ready to clock him across the face. Neal's dining companion stood up still at his table on the veranda of the restaurant, waved a hand in the air towards Jason. Then suddenly Jason doubled over, his hands clenching the sides of his head, a strangled groan leaving his lips. I tried to reach for him, but Neal's hand was still holding on to my arm, making me immobile.

"Let go of me! What are you doing to Jason?" I tried yelling, but no sound came out.

I hadn't realized we had walked towards the end of the street where there was just an empty park. It was too cold and too early for anybody to be out using it. We were alone. Neal's lips were right at my ear. I could feel his hot breath on the side of my face. His voice was a rough, fierce whisper.

"You could be great Alex. Powerful. Think about it. You don't have to do anything you don't want too, and everything you do. There would be no one to stop you. You could have it all. You are the one who holds the key." I couldn't believe this was happening. I was standing on the street, being held against my will by a guy who thoroughly frightened me. I couldn't do anything. I froze, watching Jason hunched over in agony.

Without warning, I was dragged to somewhere else, in a world someplace else. I was having another vision. But this one wasn't like the one I had at the manor. This one felt dark and thick. It was wrong. I didn't want to be here. I wanted nothing to do with this vision. This time, instead of me watching it unfold, I was the one living through it firsthand. In this vision, I was someone to be respected, worshiped, even feared. I had whatever my heart (or better yet) my pride wanted. No, this isn't right. Where am I? What is going on? I had to get out of here; this is not what I wanted. I tried to pull myself out of the fog; I tried to picture the vision spilling away like water over the side of a basin, carried over like a stream down river. It was working. I could see the sides of my vision blurring. The shops and the street where I was standing was slowly coming back in focus.

I was me again back in front of the restaurant, back again with Jason. Who was still fighting the pain in his head. I gathered my senses, pulled whatever strength I had and focused. I focused on the surrounding things. If everything that Ms. Terra told me was indeed true, then in theory, I should be able to use my gifts to get us the hell out of this situation. I steadied my feet to take a leap of faith; in myself. I was going to move things with my mind. On purpose. I had no idea where to start, or what I was doing, but I tried to make something happen. My first attempt was completely fruitless, I had no idea what I was even trying to do. All the other times when I had supposedly done things, it was completely without my knowledge. I felt the vision trying to take me over once more, the dark inky feeling of fingers clawing up my back, trying to drag me down.

*That's it! Enough!* I thought to myself.

I had to get control over this. I had to start believing in myself. The edges of my vision were darkening. I was losing this fight and quickly. I had to think; I had to act. I thought back to those other times when things had happened around me. Moria and her voice, Charlotte and the lockers. What was the connection? *Think, Alex think!* The pressure of the darkness was making it hard to concentrate, I had to push through. Then it hit me. The similarities between those incidences were emotion. Pure, unadulterated emotions. Sadness towards charlotte for trying to take away the only boy who showed me even an ounce of kindness. Embarrassment towards Moria, who decided to single me out on my first day of class. I had to harness my emotions and use it to make my will be done. And If I knew anything, I knew that at this very moment the emotion I had plenty of, was rage.

I squeezed my eyes shut and took in a deep breath. I imagined my rage was a swirling entity encompassing my space, a physical force I could condense into a brilliantly glowing ball of bright light. Once I had all that emotion bundled into a sphere of pure power. I opened my eyes and through my blurred vision I found Neal's partner still standing on the deck of the restaurant, waving his hand in Jason's direction. I hurled the ball of light straight at him. The force of it colliding straight into his chest, knocking him off his feet, smashing him through the restaurant window. Trail of broken glass and window frames in his wake. Then I turned my attention to Neal, who still had my arm clutched in his grip. One look at him and I knew he was regretting his decision, but I didn't give him a chance to take it back. I could still see my power rippling around me like gossamer lace, alive and weaving its way around me. I envisioned that same lacy string looping its way around every one of Neal's grubby finger around my arm and in one instantaneous pull, all four fingers flung backwards in an ungodly manner, leaving behind the satisfied sounds of bones breaking.

Neal shrieked in agony, grasping his mangled hand and stormed off down the street, his partner long forgotten. The man he was with had fled the scene as well, refusing the offers of help from the poor restaurant patrons. I could slightly hear their concerned conversation. They thought he might have been drunk and wanted to flee the scene. The minute our two assailants were out of commission, whatever spell Jason was under no longer had any effect. He was on the ground on all fours, looking a little worse for wear. His breathing was labored, he had beads of sweats accumulating on his forehead. I ran over to him.

"Jason! Jason, are you okay?"

He staggered to his feet, and we clumsily made our way back to his bike. He was still holding his head, but at least his breathing was more normal. We stopped, and I looked up at him, trying to assess how he was doing. I had no idea why any of that happened or how. I especially didn't know who that guy was with Neal. Jason finally stood up straighter, the color coming back to his face. He looked at me slowly. I couldn't quite decipher the expression in his eyes, but it almost looked, like fear.

"Stay...stay away from me."

He stammered, taking a few steps back knocking into the handlebars of his bike in the process.

"What? Jason, are you okay? What are you saying? What happened to you?"

He was mumbling something under his breath. I couldn't catch any of the words he was saying, but he looked angry and confused.

"Jason."

My voice was nothing but a breeze in the wind; I didn't have the strength for anything more. What was he saying? How could he look at me like this? I didn't dare take a step closer to him. My heart was crushed. I pressed my hand into chest as if I had to physically hold my heart from falling apart, and prayed to whoever was listening that this had to be a mistake.

In a hoarse whisper, trying to keep the tears out of my voice, I reached out to Jason to try to resolve whatever had gone so horribly wrong.

"Jason, please, I don't know what happened. Or who that guy was. Neal's been missing from the manor for days. I didn't know he'd be here now. I didn't mean to drag you into this crazy mess. I... I don't know what to say."

My endless babble poured off my lips like word vomit trying to fill the painful silence he was giving me. I had no idea what could have happened in the short period to make him look at me like this. Could he really be this upset at me because of the two douche bags who attacked us? Or was it because he got caught in the middle of my crazy Mystic mess? I mean, he was a Walker, for crying out loud. He had to be used to paranormal stuff, right?

I dared to take one small step closer to him, but he put a hand up to stop me. Which was followed by the cruelest look he could have given me. It kicked the air out of my lungs. I stepped back.

"Don't Alex. I saw — everything. It was you, or someone who looked like you. There were others, other Charmers, and the horrible things you all did — or someone who looked like you did. I can't... I can't be here right now. I need to get back. I'll take you home, but I can't — be here — with you." His words were clipped and cold.

"What are you talking about? I didn't *do* anything. I've been here with you this whole time. They attacked me! I'm sure you're mistaken. What did you see Jason, what did you see?"

I tried again to reach a handout to him, but my body was stuck in a viscous sludge that was drowning my movements. What could he have seen that was so horrible? What could I have done? I was so confused, so hurt, so utterly lost like I've never been before. I wanted it to stop. I wanted time to stop, to slow down so at least I could make some kind of sense out of the anger I saw in his eyes.

"Jason, please." I was crying now. I didn't know when the tears started to flow, but here they were, and I couldn't stop them.

"Jason, talk to me, please I don't know what happened. I don't know what you saw, but please." He looked despondent now. He adjusted his jacket on his shoulders and spoke. I could tell it took all he had to keep what restraint he was possessing.

"I'm going to take you home now."

"No, it's ok, I'll walk. We're not that far."

"I said I'll take you home." He snapped at me, a small roar coming out from behind his words. I flinched. His eyes softened for a second. They looked regretful, like the Jason I knew. I looked again, trying to hold on to a glimmer of hope, but it was gone. Replaced with resentment. There was nothing I could do but take the helmet from Jason's outstretch hand and fit it on my head. Jason did not help me with the buckle this time.

The ride home was awkward. The thrill of hugging Jason's body to mine was no longer there. Now it was replaced with stiffness and hostility. I needed to hold on to him for safety and for my bearings. I tried to keep as much distance as I could safely muster between us. Our movements now weren't so fluid, but stiff. Either he seemed colder, or the air had turned bitter. I couldn't tell the difference.

We reached the manor. He tilted the bike and stood up to give me enough room to slide off the back. I handed him the helmet, and he attached it back onto its peg. He waited till I was a few steps down the lane before taking off in a cloud of dust and gravel. My walk home was long, cold, and very lonely.

# Chapter 34: It Was Inevitable

### Jason

There was a rush of noise as Jason came barreling into his cub-house. A rickety old bunk house made up of crude materials they had gathered or pilfered as boys long ago. Such as; discarded drywall sheets, 2x4 wooden planks, plastic roofing and an old French door with a stained glass window they had found on a demolition site about to be crushed. He and his buddies had built the bunk themselves deep in the woods on tribal territory. They deemed it fitting to call it "Cub" House instead of a clubhouse. Now it was more of a forgotten hangout of times past. Old comic books and empty cartons of chocolate chips cookies lay in corners under mismatched kitchen chairs that have seen better days. Sleeping bags and blankets lay in piles on the pair of matching couches they paid Old Man Lehi 50 bucks for. It seemed like a good price, even though there were a few broken springs, and one had a missing cushion. Lost memories of boyhood in simpler times lay dormant to teenage revelries.

Jason, caught in his rage, was thrashing through the small house, which seemed smaller now that his stormy fury was in full force. He picked up a chair and hurled it across the room. Fist went flying. Knick knacks were like shrapnel whizzing around the cabin. The only thing that broke his blind frenzy was a knock on the open door. A baseball went flying toward the sound. A hand as fast as lightning shot up and caught the ball in a seamless motion, almost as if expecting it.

"Dude, your aim is getting better, but you still throw like a girl." Said the intruder.

"Fuck off Austin, I'm not in the mood for it right now." Jason said.

"No really? You mean you're not destroying our Boys Club for shit in giggles?"

Jason turned from Austin and leaped out the open window on the other side of the cabin. Austin followed him but used the door instead. Austin was Jason's best friend. He was a few inches shorter than Jason and even though he was also 17; he hadn't quite grown out of his baby fat. His face was a littler rounder, and he carried a few extra pounds in the middle. He had a mop of brown hair that grew out in curls, which always got caught in his eyes. Jason couldn't count how many fights Austin and his mom had over his hair. With the moppy hair and his big, round, brown eyes, Austin always looked more like an adorable puppy dog than the Ram that lived inside him.

"Should I even ask what's wrong?" Austin asked Jason, sticking his hands in his pockets, afraid Jason would turn his wrath on him.

"Why even bother asking when all you have to do is just look for yourself?" Jason's sullen mood was calming. Austin always had that effect on him, especially these last few years with his moms passing. He has been Jason's calming force through it all.

"Come on, give me a little credit. You know I have more respect for you than prying into your private life. But with the way you're carrying on, it seems to me I might have to. You haven't been this pissed since, well, since your-"

"Shut it, Austin." Jason interrupted Austin, not wanting to hear the end of his statement. He ran his fingers through his hair, trying to calm himself down. He needed to make sense of the last few hours.

"I saw it. I saw why my mom was there that night. I can't explain it, but it would have happened no matter what. Somehow it would have happened."

He was pacing around the forest, half talking to himself, half talking to Austin. Austin reached out and grabbed Jason by the shoulders to keep him from moving. Jason wasn't making any sense.

"Whoa dude, slow down. What in the hell are you even talking about right now? See what? What did you see? And you know damn well what happened with your mom was just a horrible freak accident. No one blames you for what happened."

"No Austin, you're not listening to me. I saw it! I had like a vision or something. Something happened to me — I don't know — something." Jason broke free from Austin's grip and continued to pace and babble.

"What are you talking about?" Austin was growing incredibly frustrated with Jason's lack of focus on his end of the conversation.

"Just listen, okay?! I'm trying to explain it. This morning I was, I was — with a girl — and we were walking and then some dude came up to us and he grabbed her. I made a move for him and suddenly I was lost in darkness and an incredible pain shot through my head like the world's worst headache! Right before I thought I was gonna pass out from the pain, images appeared in front of me like I was watching a movie on a large projector screen. I saw Chief Etu, and he was being tortured. A Charmer, a powerful one, was torturing him. He was in so much pain. I tried to look away, but the vision was everywhere. There was nowhere for me to look where I wouldn't see his broken body. The Charmer was putting a curse on him. One that would follow him for generations. My Grandfather, Chief of our tribe, he looked at me pain evident in his eyes and began to speak to me through Spirit Talking. He told me the curse would start a blood war between my father and me. The death of an innocent would begin the rift that would split our tribe. My mom, was the innocent death. It was inevitable."

Jason was standing in the forest talking to Austin. But he wasn't. He was miles away talking to himself; in a state of shock and fear from hearing the words out loud about the vision that was still so fresh in his memory. It was then that Austin chose to breach Jason's mind like only a Walker can and see for himself what Jason was talking about. The minute Austin saw Jason's vision, he was speechless. He saw Chief Etu, who was Jason's Great Grandfather and who was one of the most revered elders to the Kootenai Tribe. Jason never meets his great grandfather. A Walker's life span is triple to that of a typical human. But he passed away before Jason was born and lived to be the oldest Tribe member of their kind.

Austin continued to evade Jason's mind and watch the vision unfold on a loop in Jason's head. There was a woman, the one who was torturing Chief Etu, who was speaking in a language he couldn't understand. Austin had a feeling that what Jason said earlier was true. This woman was speaking an evil curse over the bound and broken body of their revered Chief. He shook his head to remove himself from Jason's vision and get back to reality.

"Jason, you have to tell your father. Maybe he doesn't know about this or maybe he does, but either way, you need to say something. This woman. What if she's still alive or has a following of evil creepers like herself and they're planning on wreaking havoc or something as equally dangerous, and we know nothing about it? Who was she, anyway? Was she a demon or just some crazy, powerful Charmer?" Now it was Austin's turn to pace frantically around the forest.

"I don't know, maybe. This whole thing is just insane. I met this girl. She is amazing. I mean, I know I just met her, but I can't explain how she makes me feel. It's like she woke up something inside of me. Something I thought had died along with my mother. I can see myself with her, see her in my life. And the crazy thing is, I think my mom knew I would find this girl. Before she died, she told me.

*There will be a day when your heart will lead you into the unknown. You will find someone who will make you question everything you thought you knew. She will push you, and strengthen you, and together you two will be a great and powerful force. Don't be so closed and broken that you won't listen to your heart when she comes for you. Let her warm your soul. You'll know it when she comes. Listen Jay, listen to your spirit. It will never steer you wrong.*

I can't explain it, but that's how this girl makes me feel. Like I have found the water source to quench the thirst I've been buried under."

Jason looked at Austin, tears in his eyes, completely vulnerable, completely unaware of what to do next. He slumped down against the side of a tree, arms resting on his raised knees, his shoulders going slack. Everything was running in overdrive, and it had drained all the life from him. His voice now was just a strained whisper.

"The girl, she looks a lot like the woman in the vision. A younger one, but the resemblance is there. It was uncanny." Jason laid his head in his hands, concealing his face.

"What are you saying Jay, that this girl's ancestor is the woman you saw, or that she *is* the woman you saw? How can that be?" Austin was crouched in front of him, close enough to catch the confused, almost sad expression on Jason's slumped shoulders.

"I don't know. I have to go talk to my father."

# Chapter 35: First-Class Jerk

**Alex**

Jason never came to class. In a sense I was relieved. I didn't know if I could handle having to sit next to him for an entire hour after how he reacted on our day date. Instead, I gave in to the drone of the day. I needed distractions. I took notes and read textbooks, pretended to be a normal typical high school student. If I kept this up, maybe I'll pass my classes this semester.

Of course, I couldn't escape entirely from thinking about Jason. During one of my classes, our assignment was to read to yourself. I couldn't, for the life of me, get into the *Tale of Two Cities*, so naturally my thoughts drifted to Jason and the ups and major downs of our relationship. If I can even call it a relationship. He made me feel seen. I felt for once that things weren't as crazy as they seemed, because there were crazier things out there other than me. The first half of our date was fantastic. It couldn't have gone any better. I had someone who understood this ridiculous world I was now a part of. I thought for sure he would be the one person who might understand. But then Neal happened. I still don't know what Jason saw or what that man did to him, but the way he looked at me because of it... I can never forget that. He looked at me with such hatred. How do I begin to process what happened when he won't even talk to me?

He wasn't there all week, no strike that, he wasn't in the classes we shared all week. But he was there. I would see him weaving

189

through the crowd of students, avoiding my gaze, ducking around corners. He never looked my way or made any attempt to approach me or talk to me. Fine. He wanted to play that game. We can play. I avoided him as well and went on with my days. But they all went by in a gray blur. I attended my classes; Lissa and I studied together in the library. I did my chores at the Manor, listened to the lectures on Elemental magic. I did everything normal teenagers do. I was going through the motions, walking, talking, but not present, not really anyway. How could I? For a moment, just a fleeting hint of time, I had something — someone — who I thought cared about me. But now, I was alone. I've always been alone, but now I know what it's like to be in the company of someone who makes me happy. Someone who makes me forget about all the awful things that have ever happened. Being alone has never felt so isolating.

By Friday, however, I was done being the jilted female. I was going to talk to him. If he didn't let me talk to him in person, then there were other ways to get through to him. But I was going to say something. He finally came to P.E. yesterday but avoided me for the entire period. If he is in gym again today or even in our first period class, I was going to make him talk to me.

As I walked to my first class of the day, I thought about the morning when everything went to shit. I have thought about nothing but that morning and the events that led up to Neal and his jackass friend holding us hostage. I don't know if the vision I saw was the same one Jason saw but after talking to the Matrons about Neal (who by the way has still not come back to the manor and has completely gone over to the dark side) and his so-called partner. The type of vision they threw at me, I've been told, is one that can be manipulated. To create something of their own making. Visions can be used as weapons to control and convince people what you want them to see. It's possible to learn and gain the skills needed to be able to understand what visions have been manipulated so you can decipher which ones are true. But it is something that must be mastered. The Matrons have assured me that with time, I will have these skills. But today, I didn't.

I have been on the business end of those visions. I know how debilitating and completely freaky they can be. They can transfer you to a time and place you can't control. I've concluded that the *me* he thinks he saw, might have been Sonya. It just has to be. I've seen her in my visions, and we look strikingly similar, so it must be. Unless he saw something in the future, a possibly manipulated awful event. The future is so subjective. Jason needs to know the truth about visions and how they can be fabricated. He really can't be mad at something he thinks I could maybe someday do.

I took a detour to my locker, hoping the elephant-flies in my belly would calm down long enough for me to keep my resolve so I can talk to Jason. Just as I was about to gather the books I would need for class, a voice sounded behind me.

"It wasn't you."

I closed my eyes and let out the faintest breath. Hearing his words was music to my ears. My body ached for him. It was no surprise that I felt his presence like a welcomed rainfall over an arid wasteland. I closed my locker door, not removing my eyes from the rusted tin of the locker front. I thought about what he said. *It wasn't me.* My elation of just having him close, just having him talking to me again, was quickly fading. I was determined to keep my resolve. He put us in this awkward exchange by choosing not to talk to me. Jason was the one who freaked out on me. He was the one that wouldn't look me in the eye, who avoided me for an entire week!

*I know, not my best move.*

His voice was in my head. Wall up! Ugh, he was in my head, of course he was. After a week of not needing to hide my thoughts, I had forgotten to use the trick he taught me in those early days to prevent him from incidentally reading my thoughts. Well, that little freebie was over. I put up such a wall it would be harder to penetrate it than Fort Knox.

My temper was rising. I've been wishing all week that we could put everything behind us so we could start new again with that same connection we once had. But then I remembered how he made me feel that morning. How the look of hatred was so easily written on his face without even trying to understand or talk to me about it. It didn't matter that the look he was giving me now was a beautiful look of honesty and humility. He looked like someone had carved him from a tree for generations to marvel at. I answered him in the best way I knew how, full of snark and sass.

"I didn't do what exactly? Turn into some evil sorceress that you're going to maul to death?"

"Okay, I deserve that. And no, I'm not going to maul you. Besides, I don't care too much for human flesh. They're too gamey for me. I might maim a little, but definitely not maul." He said in return. I raised my eyebrows at him.

"Okay, bad joke." He snickered a little. I rolled my eyes.

"I have no plans to maim you. But by the look in your eyes, I can't say the same for you." We were face to face, and worlds apart.

"You don't talk to me for a week and now you're Mr. Funnyman? Well, sue me if I don't find your satire amusing, I thought, out of everyone, you would be the one who wouldn't make me feel like a freak." I walked away then. I wanted to confront him, but now having the opportunity, I realized I was just to hurt to listen to him make sarcastic jokes. But before I could move more than two feet away, he grabbed my elbow, firm yet gentle.

"Alexandra wait. I'm sorry, I really freaked out back there; all jokes aside, you deserve an apology, and I didn't know how to give you one without sounding like such a dirt bag for bailing on you. I can't believe I let myself treat you that way. I was so sure you'd want nothing to do with me, and I wouldn't blame you if that was true."

My resolve was crumbling. I wanted to go to him to be in his arms again, but things seemed different now. He was still holding my arm like a life raft in the middle of a capsized vessel, me the anchor surrounded by the debris of our almost relationship. He didn't let go but readjusted his grip. No longer holding on with desperation, his hold was now more of an embrace.

"That's not true. Yes, you were a first-class jerk, but I never wanted to have nothing to do with you. But what makes you think, that whatever or whoever you saw wasn't me?"

"I talked to my dad. He knows more about all this stuff than I do. We can talk about it later."

"We can. But not right now."

He let go then. A small smile inched up one side of his face. He didn't say anything else. I felt him settle back on his heals as he released a shaky breath. The bell rang and I turned to go to class not waiting to see if he would stop me. He didn't.

I took my seat in class and when I thought Jason was going to be a no show; he slipped in right before the late bell rang. I wanted to still be mad. Although nothing was resolved in the hallway, at least he apologized for overreacting. I'll be interested to hear what his dad had to say that made him change his mind about me. I didn't want to break whatever small connection we finally found. It was a bubble floating on a breeze, I didn't want it to pop. We sat in class together. Every now and again we would glance in each other's direction, and he would smile at me, and I would smile at him. We passed a couple notes, small talk in writing. I was glad that we were talking again, that we were doing anything again, but it seemed different, it seemed awkward or forced.

We sat together during lunch as well, and it seemed we picked up where we left off. The banter, the shared lunch from his aunt, it was nice. Being near him was amazing. The sense of comfort and familiarity soothed my soul like a balm on a burn. I wanted to be nowhere but there on that grassy knoll with Jason. And even though he was smiling at me, and casually found ways to touch my hand, or move a strand of hair behind my ear. There was something behind his eyes, in his face, that was saying something else. Something sad.

# Chapter 36: Never Once Looking Back

**Alex**

To my pleasant surprise, Coach Jenson was not in attendance for today's gym class. In his place was a scrawny young man who looked like he wanted to be anywhere but here. Instead of gathering in the auxiliary gym like we have been, we headed outside toward the track. If I could have asked for anything to do for my gym hour, running would be it. That's the one sporting event I can do. Run. Like writing, it's a solo skill. There's just something about your feet hitting pavement. Once you find that rhythmic pat-pat-pat of your feet, it sings in tunes with your breath and your heart and it's a dance. Just you and the wind and the freeness of your thoughts bouncing in step to the sounds of the streets. Methodical, constant. The thump, thump, thump sound of the blood coursing through your heart in your head is hypnotic. I love the burn in my muscles after pushing myself to run one more mile, 50 more yards, 5 more minutes. Running was the one thing I really needed to do. Maybe I could run off the frustration of it all.

We were given our instructions to do one of the many track and field options that were spread around the course. I of course, chose to focus on the long-distance running. I was going to enjoy this. Of course, you had the usual groups take up their usual spots. The pretty girls made their way up to the bleachers to sit and gab amongst themselves. I am sure the substitute would not give them a second glance. The bigger boys went directly to the shot-put balls and diskettes. A few went to the long jump, so on and so forth. I couldn't care less, I wanted to run.

I took a few jumps, shook out my arms and legs, made sure everything was nice and loose. Then I ran. I round the last bend of my first lap, I was enjoying the sound of the wind as it rushed through my hair, when I sensed another runner coming up fast on my left. I hugged the right side of my lane to give the new runner some space, but instead of passing me, they were following in stride with me. I snuck a glance out of my peripheral. It was Jason. I picked up my pace. So did he. I wasn't in the mood to have another awkward moment with him, nor did I have the strength to take any bad news, which for whatever reason I felt certain I was about to hear. I ran faster.

"Ok I deserve that too," Jason said to my back as I put more distance between us.

"Yeah, you do." I couldn't resist.

I was running fast now, nearly in a full sprint, and it wasn't fazing him. He kept right on with me. But I knew I couldn't keep up this pace for much longer, there was no way I could compete with his animal endurance.

"You can run like this all you want, but you're either going to tire out or go into cardiac arrest. But either way, I'm not going away until you talk to me."

I lowered my head and slowed down... a bit. He took my slower stride to mean I gave him clearance to speak. I focused on my running, trying not to seem too interested in what he was about to say. I looked over at him for a moment and I swear I saw him mock punch the air. But I'm sure it was just the natural rhythm of his arm moving while he ran. I slowed my stride to a walk. I needed to stop anyway and catch my breath.

"Okay talk." I said in between breaths. I didn't know what he was going to say, but it did not prepare me for what he said. He kicked at the chalky dirt under our feet and mumbled.

"It's later."

"Come again?" It completely confused me about where he was going with this.

"You said we could talk about it later. It's later."

He stopped, and a part of me wanted to keep on walking and leave him in my dust. But I wanted answers. I wanted to repair whatever broke the fledgling connection we were forming. I stopped my feet, took a deep breath and turned to look at him. He took that as my acceptance that I would listen to him. We continued our walk as he continued to talk.

"I know it wasn't you. I don't know much but I have an idea of what happened, and about your story and I'm sorry, but it still makes things complicated." I picked up my pace. He was so infuriating sometimes. Why was he being so cryptic?

*Why won't you just tell me?*

I thought loudly in my head in the space between us, not checking to see if my wall was still up.

*Because it would change everything if I did.*

He answered me back, his unspoken words echoed in my head and even though there were no vocalized words, the emotion behind his statement came out loud and clear.

*You don't know that. Jason, I can't lose you.* I replied.

It seemed a little funny having a conversation with someone in my head. But with Jason, it felt so natural, like I've been doing it for years. It was the most natural thing I could be doing.

*I don't want to let you go.* He replied back to me.

There was such a sense of sadness behind his words, I felt my emotions bubble up behind my eyes, and I couldn't let it take over. I needed to leave the conversation because I was afraid it would close a door that I never expected to be open. I wasn't ready for any conversation that would end what we had barely started.

For the remainder of the class, running was the only thing I did. No more talking, no more silent conversations, no more confusing emotions. I just ran. I needed to push myself. I needed to feel something other than emotional confusion. I knew my legs would hate me in the morning. But at least it would be a physical pain, and not an eternal one. His last words to me were echoing in my head like the sound of a car horn in a tunnel.

He didn't want to let me go. What does that mean?

P.E. was over, so there was nothing more to do but hit the showers and change back into my school clothes. My hair was still damp from the shower, and it stuck to my shirt. I was pleased to have gym as my last class. At least my hair wouldn't frizz while at school. The bus ride, however, would be a different story, which was why I was glad my school day was ending. I was about to walk to my locker — alone — when I thought about waiting for Jason by the gym doors. That's what we used to do, before everything went wonky between us. But I didn't. The walk to my locker was strange, it seemed as if everything was moving at warped speed, and I was stuck in slow motion. Students whizzed by me rushing to their lockers. The buzz of the approaching weekend was palpable. But I was walking uphill, through the mud, in a windstorm. My feet felt heavy, as if my shoes suddenly weighed 10 pounds each. I made it to and from my locker, bagging up the books I would need for homework that waited for me. When suddenly I felt something deep inside me telling me to turn around. Turn around and go out the back doors. Don't go forward, turn around. I wished I would have listened to the voice.

Jason was there, leaning against the door frame. A barrier between me and the waiting buses, and for the first time, I wasn't happy to see him. My heart didn't skip a beat, it ached. He didn't see me yet, or if he did, he didn't look up. It wasn't until I was a few feet in front of him that he picked up his head to look at me. His eyes, his beautiful green eyes, had a shine to them, and a deeper green than I have ever noticed before. I was going to say something, but I thought better of it. I bit my lips, unsure what would have come out had I chosen to speak. He looked at me then, really looked at me, into my eyes, my soul. He took a slow breath in.

"Alex, I'm sorry. But we can't do this, we can't see each other anymore. I know you don't understand, but I must do what's right, even if at the moment it doesn't feel right. I'm sorry, but I have to go."

His words were saying one thing, but his actions were saying something completely different. He didn't make any effort to leave. He stood there, feet planted in front of me, daring me to say something, to dispute his remark. But how could I? My eyes shifted all around me. I couldn't focus on any one thing. How could this be happening? Was it all because of that guy? The guy at the restaurant? Because of some stupid vision that was probably all full of shit!

He was right. I didn't understand. How could I understand something he wasn't willing to explain to me? I was furious, heartbroken, confused, everything all at once and yet nothing at all. I finally looked up at him, my eyes filling fast with tears I knew were seconds from bursting down my face. I heard myself say something, but it was as if I was having an out-of-body experience. I was a shell of some girl who found the one person who made her whole world change for the better yet was being rejected for something she couldn't control. When words came out of my mouth, my voice was stronger than I thought was possible.

"Why?"

He reached up and caressed the side of my cheek with his fingers, tracing a line from my temple to my jaw. In that way he does so very well. I leaned into his hand as the fresh scent of soap and cedar rushed over me. I closed my eyes, unable to prevent the tears from slipping down my checks. I felt a light kiss on my temple where his hand had just been. He leaned in and whispered in my ear.

"I'm sorry Alexendra, things are beyond my control."

He turned and walked away. My eyes followed him out the door, down the steps, and to his motorcycle. He rode away, never once looking back.

# Chapter 37: Fuzzy Around the Edges

**Alex**

The late morning sun was filtering in through the curtained window, causing a blinding stripe right across my pillow. I blinked a few times, trying to get my eyes to adjust to the light. It was way past morning; I slept through half the day. I laid in bed, still in a sleepy fog. It was another weekend at the Manor and this time I didn't have the prospect of going to see Jason. I've loved the weekends we've been able to spend together, the stolen moments, the stolen kisses, the easy conversations, but now to not see him was torture. I showered and dressed and was brushing my hair when I heard the door open. It was Nora who came in in a big rush.

"What did you do? This is all your fault! They're going to transfer us! Things were fine before you got here. You made all this happen!"

Then the walls trembled. I heard the windows whine in complaint. My feet fumbled, trying to find balance. I tried to focus but I was bouncing so much I saw two Nora's instead of one. I wanted to talk to her, get her to calm down. I was bracing myself against my desk, trying to figure out what I could say before our ceiling fell on top of us. Nora looked furious. Her powder blue eyes were now midnight blue, almost black. Her blonde ringlets were flying behind her in rage.

"Nora. Nora! You have to listen to me." I struggled to say above the noise. I had to yell over the sound of our room wobbling underneath our feet. Where were the Matrons? There's no way they couldn't hear the noise.

"Nora, what are you talking about? He attacked me. I was trying to defend myself. Nora, you have to believe me! Please, Nora stop!"

Something hit my head, hard. I felt warm fluid seep through my hair above my temple, blood. I looked down at my feet, and a chunk of dry wall lay in pieces. That was part of my ceiling! Okay, this crazy bitch was out of her mind. If she wasn't going to calm down so we could discuss this rationally, so help me god I was not responsible for any reciprocating actions. I closed my eyes and concentrated on my Spirit. I've been practicing lately in an attempt to take my mind off of my Jason troubles and now accessing Spirit was almost as easy as breathing. It truly was a part of me. I could feel the buzz in my head that came with calling upon my gift. It was kind of cool how easy it was getting. I envisioned the spirit like it was a glowing ball I could manipulate, as I braced myself against my bouncing desk, I held my spirit ball in my two hands and pushed it towards Nora.

The ball of energy I manifested pushed her out of the open door and she landed right on her ass. Her head hit the wall behind her. As soon as her concentration broke, the room stopped shaking. Everything went still. Nora was sitting against the wall, looking a little dazed. Her eyes were back to powder blue and her hair looked like she lost a bet with a blow dryer. She raised a hand to the back of her head, but I think she was fine. I carefully walked over to her in case she was going to open the ground underneath me. Right away, I heard footsteps on the stairs and voices calling up. The first one to approach us was one of the guys from the Manor, the tall blonde and handsome one, Ryan. Right behind him was Ms. Mary, who was the first one to speak up.

"Nora James, what have you done?"

Nora sat there with daggers in her eyes. She was looking at me but spoke to Ms. Mary; the words coming out through her teeth like poison.

"Neal's gone because of her. He was doing so well until she showed up. He hasn't been back in two weeks, and I know he is using dark magic. I can feel it."

I was getting angry with this chick. Who was she to blame me for her psychotic brother's behavior? What had I done? Yet here she was saying *I* was the one who made *him* leave. I was about to open my mouth to protest when Ryan beat me to it.

"He attacked her Nora. Face it. He's crossed over. He's been talking to Lord Nicolai's goons, and he's bailed on me for the past month. Not to mention I saw him follow a man into The Rusty Nail. That place is chock full of dark magic users. You know he's been slipping for a while; he's not going to just stand idle while we try to restore the coven. He's not a follower, never has been. You know that better than anyone. There was nothing we could have done, and you know just as well as we do, Alex could be the one."

Ryan didn't say much to me since I arrived at the manor, outside of the normal, nice pleasantries. He once asked for my notes from Chem last week, he missed the class because of a sinus infection. When he did talk to me, his words came out with such confidence you would have thought we were old friends.

We were all scurried into the kitchen. The brightness of the sun filtering into the room made my eyes squint, and the pain behind them was excruciating. I was sitting on a bar stool at the breakfast counter while the Matrons circled around me with a washcloth and strong smelling ointments. I felt like a baby monkey being groomed. They were talking above me, as if I wasn't siting there at all. I tried to follow as best as my muddled mind could. But between the blow to the head and the adrenaline that was now leaving my body, not to mention the use of magic so early in the morning. Everything was a little fuzzy around the edges. Their voices were hushed and swift, but I caught a few words.

"The Dark Coven is getting stronger and without a High Priestess, we stand no chance against them. It won't end well if we can't find Neal."

"We don't know for sure Neal was involved."

"Terra, do you think? Could he have—?"

"No, Mary, you shouldn't say it. We have no proof."

"Lord Nicolai, I know he was here. I felt the wards, they've been tampered. And Neal, he's always been so troubled."

"Hush Mary."

The last thing I remembered was Mary telling me to drink an opaque liquid. She poured it into a small crystal glass and told me to lay down on one of the fainting couches in the living room. I couldn't go to my room since part of the ceiling was taking up residence on my bed. But after whatever ointment the matrons had lathered on my forehead, the cut that was caused from the drywall slamming into me was sure enough knitting itself back together and the pain was no longer as evident. They should sell whatever this stuff was they would make a killing! It truly was magic, but I guess that's what my life was now. Magic. It took all my strength and effort to walk the ten paces to the couch from the kitchen before my eyes became too heavy to keep open. What did they just have me drink? Whatever it was, it was strong. I was asleep before I hit the couch.

# Chapter 38: You Were Chasing Me Down

*Alex*

After what seemed like the longest nap of my life, amazingly, the gash in my forehead was nearly healed. All that remained from being the object of Nora's wrath was a small pink raised line where the new skin had knitted itself back together, nothing some well placed bangs couldn't hide. I'm telling you; they should sell that stuff. Once the matrons gave me the all clear and deemed me concussion free, they told me to take it easy for the rest of the afternoon. So, of course, that meant I needed to lace up my running shoes.

There really is something therapeutic about running. As I ran, I kept replaying the conversation the Matrons had this morning, a conversation I was most likely not supposed to hear. The conversation they did make me privy to was full of more pep talks, telling me things like destiny and purpose and responsibilities. But they didn't once ask me what I thought.

I was so disconnected from this world I now found myself in, this mythical world I was such a crucial part of. Ms. Mary tried her best to explain more about the prophecy. About how, even though I can't fully understand the gravity of what's happening right now, I needed to have faith that when the time came, I would know what to do. Okay Yoda. I nodded and hmm-mm'd at all the appropriate spots, but I still had my doubts. Lots of them.

I was hitting a good stride now. My heartbeat was up and my breathing was steady. I didn't want to get lost, so I made sure to keep an eye out for landmarks and street signs. I didn't have my ear buds in, but I still managed to get lost in my head and block out the outside world. Which is why when I was joined suddenly by another runner, I let out a sharp yelp.

"Hey, sorry, I didn't mean to startle you. I've been calling your name for like two blocks. You must really be in the zone."

It was Ryan. He was wearing an athletic shirt from our high school and somehow, he managed to fill it out in all the best ways. He also had on those break away pants that I normally find ridicules, but now, not so much. I started to blush, and I turned my head before he noticed.

"Uh, sorry, I was just thinking." I mumbled in reply.

"Yeah, that was some pretty heavy stuff back there, huh? Kind of sucks it all lands on your shoulders, but you shouldn't let it burry you. Take it in slowly, focus on building up your gifts. That's really all you can do, you know. I don't know all of what the Matrons have been telling you, but I'm sure they're saying how important everything is, blah blah blah. But how do you feel about all this?"

Ryan was keeping pace with me but started to slow down, so I slowed down as well. I was kind of blown away by him. No one has ever asked me my opinion before. They all just assumed I would handle and take anything on that came my way. Which I guess I will, since it looks like I have zero choice in the matter. But it's awfully nice to at least be asked how I feel about saving a dying race of Mystics, rather just assume everything is all's well. His concern threw me off a bit.

"You can really run, you know. I've been trying to catch up with you for like the last five minutes." He laughed at himself, and it was sort of endearing. "Man, if I would have known, I would have stretched before chasing you down. I'm afraid it might have looked like I *was* chasing you. I don't know if I should be thankful the cops haven't been called yet or concerned that no one tried to help you." Again, there was a laugh behind his voice.

"You were chasing me down? What did I do to hold up an Am/Pm?"

Ryan was the last person I would expect to come follow me. I thought for sure he was more interested in girls like Nora. Plus, other than today, he hasn't said one word to me since I arrived, so why now?

"Nah, I just thought maybe you'd want some company. I know if I was just given the fate of all mankind, I would want someone by my side."

"It's not like I am going to be saving the planet from global warming or anything. You make it seem like it's a life and death situation."

*God, I hope it wasn't.*

He gave me a funny look. Please tell me we weren't in dire straits yet, but true to form, I tried to break the awkwardness with more awkwardness. "Besides, why would someone like you want to hang out with a nobody like me?" He reached out and grabbed my arm and we both stopped in a hurry.

"What is that supposed to mean? You don't think I want to spend time with you?" I looked down at my scuffed shoes. I would have to buy new ones soon. I had gotten these at a secondhand store, and they looked a little warn then. Now they just look sad and pathetic. Especially in comparison to his brand new looking running shoes.

"I don't know, it's just, we haven't talked much, and I always see you hanging out with Nora. I just thought the two of you were something of an item." He laughed now, loud and full.

"Nora? You thought I was dating Nora, the drama queen? If you haven't already noticed, she's a bit high maintenance. No, I just hang out with her because she and Neal are like attached at the hip. I guess being twins does that. And well, Neal used to be cool until he went all power hungry. No, me and Nora, that's not going to happen. Even though I think she wishes it was different."

I suddenly felt relief. Why? I liked Jason, or I did. I mean I do. Even if he doesn't like me anymore. It shocked me that I thought I felt something toward Ryan. I didn't like Ryan. It must just be confusion and heartache that was making me loopy, or better yet desperate to think I was feeling anything for him. I mean, sure, he was good looking. I mean, if you like that tall, muscular football build, sort of hot. But that was an obvious sort of hot, not like Jason. Jason was rugged and natural. There was something so organic about his wind tossed hair and sun kissed skin.

Now there was more drama inside my head to crash around. Between my longing thoughts for Jason and my confused thoughts about Ryan, I felt like I was going to explode. I started running again. Ryan was right behind me, catching my stride. He didn't make any comment about my lack of conversation, and we just ran together. It was nice. It felt like he didn't want or need anything from me. We just ran. We turned the corner and headed back to the Manor. It was getting close to dinnertime, and I couldn't wait for this day to be over.

Over it was. I was glad for the uneventful unfolding of the rest of my weekend. I studied with Paige, and helped Ms. Marry pull weeds from the garden, I even baked cookies with Chrissy. We burnt them but they were edible, sort of. Nora moved out of our room. She's been staying in one of the empty rooms along the hall. I haven't seen much of her, and I have to admit, it's been nice. The Matrons did their witchy thing, and our ceiling was patched up lickety-split. Sometimes magic really did have its benefits.

Like my weekend, the next few weeks were just as ordinary. Except, for a little thing called Ryan. Ryan's original Chemistry partner moved out of state, so we've been partners ever since. It was nice. Having someone to talk to, work with, it was easy. Our partnership was easy, and it didn't hurt that he was also easy to look at. But it was complicated. My heart still very much belonged to Jason, even though I hadn't really seen him since that day. He hasn't been to school since he left. I saw him once at the store, when I went to run errands with Ms. Terra. He looked at me, I thought he might have started to walk towards me. My heart stopped, but then he turned around. I watched him turn around and leave the store. He wants to talk to me, I know it, I can feel it. I wish I knew what was keeping him from doing it. I needed to find answers, I just didn't know how.

When I wasn't dealing with my complicated feelings for Jason, complicated feelings for Ryan were emerging. Ryan was here. In my school. In my house. In my head. Why was it so difficult to turn your feelings off when you didn't want to deal with them? Maybe that's what that book is about, the one I have yet to read for class, Sense and Sensibility. Doesn't the main character have to decide between falling in love with her heart's desire or trying to love a match that was practical? Maybe I should catch up on my reading and learn something.

I t was the weekend, and Paige, Ryan, and even Chrissy decided to go to the café. The Matrons were going to be holding a Charmed Circle with a few other adult Mystics since it was a New Moon. They were determined to hold on to whatever traditions they could, with or without their High Priestess. Which meant we had a free night to be teenagers, regular teenagers who go to movies and eat fast food. So, my housemates thought it would be a good idea to go out for dinner, to give the adults some space. Even Chrissy seemed a little excited. She's been working on some blocking spells herself, so now being out in public wasn't as dramatically overwhelming as it once was. I didn't want to stay in and be by myself or be alone with Nora. So, I braced myself to spend an evening out, in a café I've only been to once before, with Jason.

# Chapter 39: I Didn't Resist

**Alex**

We took the city bus to the café; they play live music on the weekends, so when we got there, the place was packed. We found a table outside, up against the wall of the building. We could hear the band but couldn't see the band, we didn't mind. The table was out of the way, so at least we didn't have people surrounding us trying to get a peek.

We ordered our food; juicy hamburgers and mile high fries, it was greasy and great. The band was great too, the vibe, the company, the whole thing. This would have been a great night out; except I didn't notice. I have been trying to get Jason out of my mind, trying and failing. I just couldn't understand how one minute he could be a jerk, then the next minute be apologizing for being said jerk. Then another minute telling me he doesn't want to leave me, then he leaves me. Were all the boys so confusing? Or just boys who turn into wolves? My head was spinning from all this change. Which is why I agreed to go out so I could get my mind off of Jason, and here I was – out—and my mind was not off of Jason. Instead, it was on Jason, very much on Jason.

"Hey, you need to get out of your head. Come dance with me."

Before I could give Ryan an answer, he pulled my hand, getting me off my chair. We pushed our way through the crowd of people and found an open spot amongst the other dancers. The band was loud and reverberating, the kind of sound you feel in your bones. The atmosphere was deafening and electric. It was fantastic and numbing, exactly what I needed. We danced, we danced until the room spun.

"I'm glad you're finally having fun. I was getting a little worried there." Ryan had to shout over the noise. We were standing so close together, yet I still had to strain to hear him.

"Yeah, I guess it just took some loud music and two glasses of coke to give me a confidence booster." It felt weird to shout at someone who stood right in front of me, but that was the only way for anybody to hear anything.

"You look really good tonight. I wanted to tell you that since we got here." He was shouting at me and, of course, the band chose that very moment to stop. Everyone within 50 feet heard his loud declaration. My cheeks burned with embarrassment. Ryan, however, did not look fazed one bit, he looked almost pleased with himself.

"I'm going to get something from the café. You want anything?" I didn't trust myself to speak, so I nodded in reply. My body was still buzzing from the adrenaline of dancing, and Ryan's declaration threw me for a loop. I followed him back inside the café. Now that it was getting later, there weren't as many people in the dining room of the café. I guess coffee isn't as popular of a drink at night. The dining area felt very large compared to the crowded veranda outside.

"What do you want?" Said a scantily clad woman behind the bar.

"Uhm, I'll have water with lemon and a chocolate chip cookie." I told her, trying not to stare at the even scantier clad pin-up girl tattooed across her neck. Ryan ordered what sounded like an overly complicated overly sweat hot coffee and a lemon scone.

The lady disappeared into the back and a younger woman took her place, reading off the receipt list to catch up on the orders. The younger barista scurried between the espresso machines and the incoming customers, she seemed incredibly overwhelmed. I offered to pay for our order, but before I could even get my wallet out, Ryan had already handed her cash. We moved away from the register to wait for our drinks, but the flustered look on the barista's face made me think we'd be waiting a while.

Once we received our drinks and sweets, we found some open sitting near a large picture window. We sat on a small ornate couch barely large enough to accommodate us both. But in fear of making an awkward situation even more awkward, I stayed put and let out a relaxing breath, trying to calm my thumping heart.

"What *do* you really think about all this, the Covens, the Mystics, all of it? You never did give me an answer." He took a long sip of his coffee.

I furrowed my brow, thinking about his question. It was nice to have someone to talk to again. With Jason icing me out, and Nora going completely catatonic and locked in her room, the only conversationalist I've had has been Paige. Who on her best days merely tolerates me and Chrissy. Crissy who, had a spell go wrong and it died her hair blue, has now gone headfirst into her spell studies. Determined to never have a spell go wrong again. So, Ryan coming along was a breath of fresh air. Here he was simply wondering how I was handling things. He wanted to know what my opinion was on the whole matter instead of assuming he already knew the answer. It wasn't about whether I would declare my allegiance or not, he just wanted to know me.

Everyone else at the Manor seemed to look at me like I would have all the answers they needed to hear. But I guess if I am what they say I am, a High Priestess incarnate — so to speak — maybe I do have all the answers. I just don't know them yet. Right now, however, all I feel like is a normal teenage girl struggling with boy issues, and that was fine by me. It was a pleasant change of pace to be with someone who seemed to have my interest at heart. I thought Jason had my interest at heart. I thought he had my heart.

I was about to answer him when the barista made her way over to us to ask if there was anything more we needed. We politely thanked her as she gathered our cups and plates from our table. When she reached for the mug, it made me shift backwards. But the tight quarters shifted my hips making my knees pressed against Ryan. I thought about repositioning myself, but the look of warmth and stability on Ryan's face was intoxicating. I stayed as I was. I was glad for my decision because I wanted to let go. Let go of Jason, let go of the hurt, let go of the unknown.

"I bet you're pretty freaked out, huh?" He relax into the sofa, arm draped across the armrest.

"It's pretty heavy stuff, White Covens, Dark Covens, destruction, it's a lot to take in." I found a loose string on the sweater dress I was wearing and pulled aimlessly at it rather than meeting Ryan's stare. I tried not to fidget; I tried to look comfortable, and I tried to not think about Jason.

"Well, for what it's worth, you're handling yourself pretty well. The Matrons haven't locked you up in a padded room yet." His smile was as bright as a thousand stars.

"They have a padded room?" My eyes almost jumped out of my head.

"You never know. I mean, have you seen the inside of Nora's room?" He winked.

There it is again, that smile, that confident, almost cocky smile that was too perfected to be genuine. But after getting to know Ryan these last few weeks I knew that it was. Genuine. He was a genuinely nice and decent guy. Ryans wasn't just a hot jock like he portrays himself to be, he's also been a good friend. I wasn't used to receiving attention from guys. Especially guys like Ryan. I wasn't model gorgeous, but I wasn't plain either, but pretty enough to be noticed, and when you have roommates like Nora, it's hard to not compare yourself to those whose beauty seems effortless. It was still hard to believe that Ryan preferred my company over any of the other girls in school. Apparently, my Guy-Vibe was broken due to the complete miss judgment of Jason. It must be the altitude.

I wanted to keep our easy banter going so I asked him the one thing I've been dying to know. "How did you end up at the Manor?"

"It was pretty cut and dry. My mother belonged to the White Coven. I grew up not far from here. My mom and the Matrons were always researching and trying to find the One Who Is, the one who would mend the broken circle." He looked up at me from the water glass the barista had handed him after taking away his coffee mug. The movement for him was effortless. Before speaking again, he licked his lips, perfection, again.

"When I was eleven my mother died in a building fire. Her office went up in a blaze because of bad wiring, or so they say. I had no other family. The Matrons took me in. I was their first ward, then came the twins two years later. They've been bringing others in ever since. Helping when they could. Trying to set things right bit by bit."

"I'm so sorry. What about your dad?" I couldn't help but ask, as noisy as it seemed. I had an undeniable urge to reach out and touch him, but I clenched my hands together instead. I refused to fall for another boy who could eventually break my heart.

"I don't know him. My mom never mentioned him, and I never asked. We were close, so there was probably a good reason she never mentioned him. I do, however; believe her death was no accident. I think someone set that building on fire. I remember her being extra protective right before she died. She kept talking about the feeling of being watched. Her office was a brand new build. Having a fire start because of faulty wires made no sense. I think someone set the fire. I think someone meant to kill her." The way he said it, there was no room for doubt. Ryan didn't seem like his cool have everything together self anymore. He had a faraway look in his eyes, and his shoulders were tense.

"You think someone murdered her? Why? What would be the reason?"

I was leaning in now, completely engrossed in his unfortunate story. Instinctively, I reached out towards him. I had to. He looked so defeated, so deflated. I touched the hand that was resting on his knee. He looked at me. It was a gentle look, not at all like the Ryan I've been talking to all night. If I knew any better, I would have thought there might be something brewing between the two of us, something other than lab partners. I dismissed the thought. I thought I wanted to give in, to put down my guard and allow myself to move on. But I couldn't, my heart and my head couldn't agree. Ryan continued.

"The report says it was a textbook case. It happened during winter when the central heating was on and working harder during the colder months of the year. The Fire Marshall said there was evidence of bad wiring. What made no sense was that the building had an inspection not too long before the fire. The landlord was renewing its lease, so they needed to do a building check for insurance purposes, and nothing came back as faulty. The fire started in the front of the building and a filling cabinet fell, blocking the only fire exist. Trapping my mom inside. She was burned alive. I know because I've been digging into old flies and reports through the years, there had to be an explanation. I need to know. I need to find answers. But I always come up empty-handed, full of dead ends and closed doors. Somewhere someone has to know something.

"My mom was the most careful, economically minded person I knew. She would never have overused the heater or left it on after hours. Mom barely used it as it was. She worked for a small company and tried to save costs wherever she could. I remember always asking her to turn the heat up when I had to be there after school, and she would always tell me to go put my coat on, we'd be leave soon. There should have been no reason a perfectly fine, practically new system would go up in smoke. It made no sense. There had to be more to the story and the Matrons agree with me."

I didn't know what to say. His story was so terrible, so unnecessary. His poor mom, what an awful thing to live through at such a young age. He hunched over, arms across his knees. He seemed exhausted from carrying the weight of his tragedy. He was normally the happy-go-lucky guy. But he wasn't tonight. It really makes you think about what people have going on deep inside themselves, even when they seem so happy and put together. How many of us feel isolated and alone, even if we're surrounded by people? I inched closer towards him and put my hand on his back, caressing the taut muscles that lay under his polo shirt. I wanted him to know I was here for him, one orphan to another.

He turned his head in my direction and laid an arm over my leg. We locked eyes. I was extremely aware of the fact that we were face to face, so close that I could smell the coffee coming from his lips. His plump, slightly parted lips were my entire view. The space between us was diminishing. Our heads leveled and our noses brushed. His lips skimmed over mine softly at first, a whisper spoken in secret. The touch of his lips was so slight, yet it felt like they were yelling their presence all the same. The pressure grew stronger. Our lips moved with purpose. I don't know who gave in first. Was it him giving into the sadness of losing his mom, or was it me wanting to get lost in someone who made me feel seen without explanation? Either way, our kisses grew deeper. There was a hunger for them. A hand found the back of my neck pressing me tighter against him while another one was on the small of my back, flirting with the hem of my shirt. My hands gripped both sides of his head, my fingers tangling in his shaggy hair, steading him, steading me. All I wanted was to feel, to touch, to taste. I didn't resist.

Like a thunderbolt to my chest, my thoughts went straight to Jason. Jason, who I thought truly cared for me yet dumped me for some unknown bogus reason he wouldn't even explain. It filled every corner of my mind. I was suffocating. I shouldn't be here. I pushed Ryan away, his lips red and swollen from our kisses, his eyes big and glossy. He gave me a look of confusion. I needed to get out of here. I needed to get away from him. I didn't want to hurt Ryan and I didn't know what this meant or what it was. I stood up, toppling the chess pieces off the adjacent table next to us. I was gasping for a moment trying to locate my purse, my gravity, my breath.

"What happened? Where are you going?" Ryan caught my arm. He didn't look confident anymore. He looked bewildered, confused. Hurt.

"I have to go. I'm sorry. I just — I need to go." He dropped my arm.

"Hold on, let me get the others. We'll walk to the bus stop together." Ryan stood up, making sure we weren't leaving anything behind. I put my hand out to stop him.

"No. I mean, no thank you, it's okay. I want to walk, we're not that far. Tell the girls I'll see them back at the Manor. I just need to get some air, clear my head a bit. Thank you, Ryan. I had an enjoyable time, really. I truly did, and I'm sorry. I'll see you back at the manor."

I gazed into his hazel eyes one last time, just long enough not to get lost in them, but hopefully long enough to convey that I had a good time. A better time than I deserved. He deserves better than some messed up head case like me. I hoped he wouldn't press the issue anymore. I might have said yes if he asked again. So, before he could say anything more, I walked out of the café.

# Chapter 40: Like One of Those Nightmares

**Alex**

Halfway home, I feared I might have taken a wrong turn somewhere. The town wasn't very large. No matter where you went, the roads eventually spit you back out into the center of town like a big grid. The focal point being the town's giant water tower that served like a beacon to all its visitors. If I kept the tower in my sight, and stayed away from the less populated neighborhoods, I should find my way. I would end up back at the promenade and be able to retrace my steps back to the Manor. *Right?* I mean, my thinking seemed so logical. Or so I thought.

I was walking for a good 35 minutes. I should have ended up at the promenade 10 minutes ago. I had been making steady right turns toward the center of town; I must have turned when I wasn't supposed to. Frustrated, I stopped my feet for just a second to see if I could gather my bearings, see where I went wrong. Nothing around me looked familiar. The late winter sky has been staying lighter and lighter with each passing day as spring slowly arrived. But that just means it goes from dusk to pitch black in a matter of minutes. Now it was pitch black. We must have been at the café longer than I thought.

I felt my heart speed up. I think my nerves were getting the best of me, making all the boogie men and ghost stories come to life. My feet picked up their pace. Walking faster than my normal stride, panic grew with every step. I had to be close now. Any minute, I should see the familiar loom of the cement high school building. Or the converted gas lampstands that lined the promenade — something — something should look familiar. I begged it to look familiar.

Empty store fronts that have long been forgotten peppered the streets. Paint chipped and pealing, store signs half gone. I didn't want to be here. I needed to turn around. I needed to retrace my steps. How did I get so lost? How did I not think the town was this big? Where did I go wrong, with my route, with my life? The few lights that worked were dim. Why didn't I let Ryan walk me home? Why was I always so stubborn? These questions and so many more were swimming around in my over reactive brain. I was going to have a panic attack if I didn't get my heart to calm down.

Finally, I heard the customary sounds of adult revelry. Muffled tones of garage-band percussion mixed with the buzz of bantering voices and clinking of glasses. A restaurant was lively with people coming and going, or at least it looked like a restaurant, but I think a bar would've been a better description for it. Every nerve in my body froze. I thought about using my phone to call someone, but then remembered quickly that my battery was dead. Of course, my absentness to remember to charge my phone would kick me in the ass now. But even if it was working, the only number I had programmed into it was Jasons. And I didn't know if he would answer my call. When the sign to the bar came into view, I couldn't believe it actually said The Rusty Nail, like something right out of the Wild West days. Who knows, maybe it was. I could see people inside the dimly lit bar, a few stragglers standing outside having a smoke. Right next to the bar, I could see a very seedy tattoo parlor. Yeah, let's get drunk, then get some ink on my body that I'm going to regret in the morning. Good financial plan.

I crossed over to the other side of the street hoping to avoid any direct path with the revelers at either joint. Once I was out of the way of the two places, I let out a big breath, still walking at a hurried pace but not too fast as to draw attention to myself. I relaxed a little. I felt a slight relief because the surroundings up a head looked familiar again. I tightened my jacket around my neck in a feeble attempt to block out the chill that was creeping up around me. The sudden chill and the climbing fear of my situation made my blood run cold.

I thought maybe I might have heard footsteps behind me. I stopped to listen. The soft shuffling of steps stopped as well. I assumed it was someone who must have come out of the bar stumbling their way back to where they needed to go. I hoped where they need to go was an Uber and not the alternative. I continued to move forward. I could see the end of the block and it indeed looked familiar. It took all that I had not to take off at a run, but I really did not want to draw any undue attention to myself. A girl running down the street in a green sweater dress and ballet flats might be seen as odd.

The footsteps continued and were sounding steadier and more purposeful. I was panicking. I quickly looked from left to right, I was hoping to find something — anything — that would get me off the street, a friendly store clerk, a cop on his beat, a time machine. But there was nothing. The stores had closed hours ago, only the ghostly pale security lights remained illuminated inside. My tail was right on my heels now. I could hear his breath behind me. I didn't bother to look back. I just ran.

My muscles complained, the adrenaline of the moment and my run this morning was creating a terrible combination on my joints and sore muscles. I cursed myself now for pushing myself so hard. The unwelcome yet familiar burn in my thighs was weighing me down. I felt every stride with such heat, my muscles felt as if they would melt off my bones, rendering my legs completely useless. My ballet flats weren't helping matters, either. I had to work twice as hard to keep the shoes on my feet. I debated whether to ditch them and run to freedom barefoot. Behind me, I heard every heavy step. I was thankful now that he wasn't wearing tennis shoes; the soft sound of rubber would have been lost to the wind. At least now I could track the distance between us by the beat of his steps hitting the ground.

There was no mistaking now this person was after me. No attempt to call out to me or get my attention to prove they were a friend. There was only the chase. I felt like I was stuck in a nightmare, the one where you're running down a corridor that grows longer with every step never coming to an end. It would only be a matter of seconds before they closed the gap between us. What would the papers say tomorrow, *"Teen Girl Found Dead in the Streets."* Would there even be a story? Would the Matrons know to look for me, or would they think I was just another runaway teen escaping a bad situation? What would Jason think? would he come looking for me? Would he care?

That was the last thought I allowed myself to have before my resolute kicked in. I won't allow some maniac pervert to get the best of me. I was a High Freaking Priestess it was time now to put that theory to the test. I no longer needed to fear anybody. I had resources at my fingertips, literally. My bravado got the best of me, and I stumbled, nearly crashing my knees into the pavement below my feet. Which allowed for whoever it was behind me to reach out and grab the back of my jacket. The teeth of the zipper gouged into my throat from the sheer force of my collar being yanked away from my neck, leaving my skin raw. I glimpsed the person behind me and from that nanosecond glance, I could see all I needed to see. Despite the dark baseball hat and oversized jacket, I knew without a doubt of who it was. I also knew fear was written all over my face — so much for that ass kicking attitude I thought I had.

He threw me against the building behind us, my head hitting the wall with a wet crack. I felt a hot pain from the connection and an oozing sensation of warm liquid instantly coating my hair. Why did it seem like my head was always the first thing to get damaged in any altercations I came across? I was surely going to have irreparable brain damage before I was even legal to do any damage for myself. My attacker, who I could clearly see now, was Neal, seized ahold of my neck and constricted my throat under his fingers. Not enough to cut off my breathing but enough to make every inhalation burn like cut glass imbedded in the back of my mouth. My mind was running a million miles a minute trying to find some way out of this, some way to get freed.

His other hand was slowly and roughly running down the side of my body, first my shoulders, then the outer side of my breast. His fingers ran down my ribs and over my hips, all the way down to the hem of my dress. His fingers dug into the fatty part of my thigh. It burned like acid. His hand slid up my leg grabbing hold of my hipbone, the night air biting at my exposed skin. Every touch, every fumbled caress was painful, horrifically unbearable. I was frozen, I couldn't move. I was going to remember this day forever. Nothing would be the same anymore. I needed to do something I needed to fight. Tears streaked my face, but not from despair, from anger and rage. He brought his lips close to my ear.

"You're her, The One. The all-powerful Mystic who is going to destroy the Dark Coven. But how can you? You seem to me like just some scared little bitch." His words dripped out of him with pleasure and venom. "We can't have anyone ruining what we have been working towards for so long. Can't have anyone rebuilding the White Coven, especially now since we're nearly restored."

I wasn't going to just stand here while this creep groped me like some victim. I was no victim. Quickly, I regained my senses, determined to fight back however I could. I was not now nor ever will be a victim. Today wouldn't be the day that changed that. I brought my knee up quick and made contact and caught him completely off guard; he hunched away from me, trying to catch the breath I just knocked out of him. I side stepped, putting distance between us and ran.

I needed to manifest something I could hurl at this creep and blast him to the other side of town. I took a deep breath, which was hard to do at a full sprint, but I needed to focus myself. Channeling Spirit from nothing has gotten easier to do but I've been practicing when I've been calm. I was frantic, out of breath, I needed to calm myself. I was too worked up; my adrenaline was too high. Ms. Terra told me anything can be manipulated if I could see its energy. Everything has energy. So, I tried, in my frantic state I tried to see energy around me. It happened slowly at first, then all at once, I saw the things around me not as they are but as their energy form made them to be. Trash cans glimmered and vibrated. Streetlamps that were once dimmed and burned out buzzed and whirled as the energy from the electoral wires within them sang with power and spirit. Everything was energy, "non-spatial" as Ms. Merry told me. Energy which can be manipulated and shaped by our will. Neal and his earthquakes, Page and her fire, me and the vocal abilities of the head cheerleader. If you can harness the energy, you can use it, and suddenly for me, everything was energy. I could see it, which means I could use it.

I was in a laser light show. Everything around me was resonating in a wide range of neon colors like a thousand glow sticks in the shapes of everyday ordinary items. I stopped running; I needed to concentrate. I pulled energy from the various items around me to create the biggest ball of light I've ever seen. I moved my arms and hands in a circular motion to condense the ball of light. I was turning energy into something tangible, something solid. Yet I wasn't holding anything at all. It hovered in the air in front of me, turning and forming with every wave of my hand. It felt heavy and weightless all at once. I haven't done anything quite like this before, other than the brief exertion of my own energy I threw at Nora. This was different. This was powerful. I didn't know if I had the strength to control it, but Neal, having recovered from a sharp knee to his groin, was gaining speed and closing the distance between him and me. It was now or never.

With no more deliberation, I flung the glowing orb straight at Neal and, with satisfaction, it hit my target square in the belly. Pushing him back against a building, the sizzling sound and the scent of burning flesh filled the street. I could only imagine what his skin looked like under the glowing ball. The orb had faded and was slowly disintegrating back into the energy from once it came from.

"Bitch!"

Was all I heard him say while he hunched over, pawing at his stomach. I focused my eyes in disbelief, I couldn't believe what happened.

His face was shaded from the light because of the brim of his hat, but it was tinted red with anger. The front of his jacket and shirt were completely singed, and black pieces of cotton stuck to his skin. I turned on my heel and ran. I got maybe three strides into a dead sprint when my face hit the pavement, hard. My chin burst open. I hope I didn't fracture my jawbone. Blood filled my mouth, I must of bit my tongue, my cheek, I didn't know. I spit out whatever blood I could to prevent swallowing too much of it. Did I trip? Before I could answer my own question, the ground underneath me quivered. I lifted my body up on my arms. Everything felt shaky. My vision was doubling.

I was sure I had a concussion, what number is this now, three? The ground moved again. It was nearly impossible to maneuver myself onto my feet. I was in the middle of a rumbling earthquake. Dammit Neal. I tried to steady myself, but the ground was unrelenting. I felt like I was on a tiny boat in a really wavy ocean. I fell again. My elbows took the brunt of the fall, this time gravel and dirt embedding itself into the thin cloth of my jacket. Sharp pain zinged down both sides of my arms. I shook the daze out of my head and tried to stay present. I needed to fight back. I needed to defend myself. But how could I do any of that if I couldn't even get up off the ground?

"No point in running if you can't find your feet?" I heard him say. It was disgusting how self-assured his voice sounded, his bravado coming back after the blow to the gut. His entire midsection looked like melted rubber; he would feel that in the morning for sure.

I braced myself on a nearby wall, using it to claw myself into an upward position. I was determined to fight back. I would fight till there was no more fight left in me. I was woozy from the loss of blood and banged up pretty bad, but I was going to get this bastard. I felt like I was on a carnival fun house floor. But it was okay. I was up and I was standing, I had a perfect shot at the creep. I gathered up my strength and concentrated on forming another lightning ball. I had it. It wasn't as large as the first, but it crackled all the same. I braced myself against the wall, ready to throw the energy at Neal. I wound up and threw it right at him, but instead of hitting my target; it slammed against the brick wall, throwing dust and debris all over the sidewalk Neal had dodged it just in time.

I was gearing up to try again, but before I could, something large came barreling out of a side alley and hit Neal like a freight train hitting wooden crates. Two figures grappled on the floor. I couldn't make out what was going on, who was who or what was what. I was squinting, my eyes trying to see through the darkness and dizziness that was slowing overtaking me. I couldn't make out what was going on. All I could tell was that it was large and gray, and what looked to be *fur*. Was it a dog? The two figures had wrestled their way around and into the adjoining ally. I slowly made my way to where I could see the two figures fighting. If I forced myself to focus, I could make out arms, legs, a tail...?

I could see that one figure had four legs, and since I was just chased by Neal on his two legs, I knew it wasn't him. I heard snapping, grunting and snarling with some — er, a lot of — expletives thrown in there. The two were locked in a fierce battle. Then I heard a whimper, like the sound dogs make when they're hurt. Which answered my suspicions. There was a dog-like creature kicking Neals' ass. A piece of something large fell on the creature. Rubble, maybe stone. I looked up above the two fighting figures and saw a fissure running up along the building, straight into a missing chunk of the old building. I thought about trying to help by zapping Neal, but my aim wasn't the greatest and I didn't want to risk hitting whatever had come to my rescue. I saw one of Neal's legs clamped inside the dog's jaw. There was a lot of ripping and protest from Neal. He kicked the dog in the face with his free leg and freed his mangled appendage.

A scream — no, a squeal of tires on pavement—broke through the night. A car came at us fast. Everything halted as if someone had pulled the plug on our little action flick. All heads turned; one freaked out girl, one creepy attacker, and one dog all stopped in mid-whatever-survival mode they were in and turned toward the car. A black Lincoln Sudan skidded to a stop and there was the man who was with Neal that morning. The tall, thin looking one, he stuck his head out the open car window, pointing some kind of weird gun at us. I may not be a gunsmith by any means, but I have seen a few animal control shows, and I think what he was wielding was a tranquilizer gun. I thought to myself, what an odd choice of defense weapon to just have on hand.

But regardless as to why this guy was pointing a very large tranquilizer at us was beside the point. Before anything else could register, I heard a soft *WHUMP* of the gun being fired, I saw Neal hobbling his broken body over to the car, dragging a nasty-looking leg behind him. Neal got into the car, which spun around and drove out the way it came in, but not before I glimpsed someone's head in the back window. A head with a mountain of brown curls and big wide brown eyes that were silently screaming at me. An angry welt developing across her cheek. Chrissy! The bastards had Chrissy! Then the car was gone.

Leaving me alone, bloodied, bruised and terribly frightened and with what I could see in the faint glow of the streetlight, was not a dog at all, but a wolf.

# Chapter 41: Other Random Boy Stuff

### Alex

Too late did I think about trying to get a license plate number or find some type of identifying markers of the car, the people inside, anything I could use. Everything happened so fast. The only thing left to remember this horrible night was the hot pain in my chin and a feeling of being spun around in an industrial dryer. I immediately remembered the wolf. The wolf who had saved my life and could be terribly injured. The wolf who was... no longer there. I whipped my head around scanning for the wolf, a dog, a man in a wool sweater, anything. But there was nothing.

I instantly regretted the whipping of the head when a blazing heat burned the sides of my jawbone, the pain making my vision double. If Neal broke my jaw, I was going to kill him. First, I was going to find him, then I was going to kill him. Through the pain in my jaw and my double vision, I did make out a shape, a figure hiding in the shadows. It wasn't a wolf, or a man in a wool sweater, but someone *was* sitting beyond the building. A young man, his body was cloaked in shadow, he stayed just outside the light of the streetlamp. He was hunched over, bracing himself on his arms, fingers splayed out to hold his weight he was taking short, labored breaths. The sidewalk below was spotted with blood. His hair fell over his face, covering his eyes, but the profile was unmistakable. I knew immediately who the figure was.

My eyes must have been deceiving me because it looked like he wasn't wearing any clothes. With complete embarrassment, I looked again, and it was clear that yes, he was naked, naked and injured. He shifted his weight and let out a painful groan. Without even thinking, my feet took off across the street. I hurried to his side; afraid he was more injured than he looked. He brought his legs in tighter against his side, a movement that brought attention to the fact he didn't have a stitch of clothing on.

I went into nurse mode because the body of this beautiful naked boy, whose every muscle was defined and perfectly placed like a sculpted piece of earthen clay still warm from the kiln, had no effect on my nerves. My only thought was how he was injured and how can I help him. I needed to make sure he wasn't going to bleed out and die here on the streets in front of me. I looked around hoping to find anything to use to help stop the bleeding. When I came up short, I thought the best thing I could do was at least to apply pressure with my hand. That's what they say right? Apply pressure. I reached my hand towards the first gash I could see, when he moved away from me, speaking in a gruff and unsteady tone.

"My backpack."

"What? Your what?" I tried to catch what he was saying, but it was so faint and gravelly.

"My backpack, it's behind those pallets. I need my backpack."

This time, his words were a little more fluid, more resonance in his voice. I looked over to where he was gesturing, and a few yards down was a pile of pallets stacked behind one of the stores. I ran over to retrieve the backpack and quickly returned it to Jason. He reached for it and unzipped the main compartment, pulling out a wad of clothes, a pair of jeans and a blue cotton T-shirt. I turned my head to the side, averting my gaze while he pulled his pants on. I heard him groan, and I forgot whatever courtesy I was giving him. He sounded like he was in a lot of pain. Luckily, his pants were completely on now, but he was struggling to maneuver his shirt over his head. I helped him with his shirt, shimming it around and down past his shoulders and chest.

"Thanks."

"Don't thank me. You're the one who saved me. Who knew what would have happened if you didn't show up? Oh God, I can't even start to think about— "Jason interrupted me before I could finish the statement.

"I'm here. Nothing is going to happen to you."

He sounded stronger than he looked. There was an intensity behind his eyes, leaving no room for doubt. I believed what he was saying. I felt safe, protected. He, however, was hurt, and I could tell it was worse than he was letting on. His skin, which was normally so warm and vibrant, was now pale, resembling the color of muddy water. Blood was seeping through the shoulder of his shirt.

"Jason, you're hurt. We need to get you to the hospital. Come on, I'll help you up."

"No. No hospitals. In my bag, there's a jar. Can you hand it to me?"

"You don't need a jar. You need a doctor."

"I'm fine. I'll be fine, just give me the jar. Please."

I dug around in his backpack, underneath the schoolbooks, lost pens, wads of paper, and other random boy stuff was indeed a small jar just big enough to fit snuggly in the palm of my hand. I unscrewed the cap to reveal some sort of glossy ointment. it resembled the consistency of Vaseline but had a strong sent of pine. I handed it to him. He nodded his thanks and reached for the jar.

"What is it?" My curiosity getting the better of me.

He struggled to release one arm from his t-shirt. I reached to help him, but he subtly deflected my help. Once his shoulder was exposed, I could get a better look at the furious gash across his rotator cuff. It was wet and gnarly. He attempted to rub the ointment into his wound. But I could tell how much of a struggle it was, I took it from him and continued to rub it into the wound and surrounding area. Now that I was up close and personal to whatever it was, I was rubbing all over this beautiful yet injured boy, I grew suddenly intoxicated by the scent of this cream. It was more than just pine. It was also minty, and sweet like oranges. It was the weirdest combination of aromas, but it was the most pleasantly smelling thing I have ever experienced. I believed it was healing my own ailments just by taking in the scent of it. Instantly I saw relief on his face from whatever this was. I guess it was one of those fast-acting creams. What is with this town and their crazy magical creams?

"It's yarrow." I heard him say weakly.

"It's what?"

I was so glad that he was talking. I didn't mind that I had forgotten to block my thoughts, and he was once again answering questions I had yet to ask.

"Yarrow. It's a plant that promotes healing. It helps stop the bleeding, along with a bunch of other things I don't remember right now. It's from our Akbaalia, a healer in my village. My body heals itself quickly naturally, but this speeds it along and makes it less painful and guards against infections. And they say it keeps the evil from entering my body through the open wound."

He mumbled the last part, as if he didn't believe in the theories of his village. Well, the cream and his magical healing abilties must be working because he looked fully recovered. The color was back in his cheeks and his breathing was finally steady. He moved his shoulder around a bit, apparently feeling loads better. He took the jar from me so he could recap the lid. Jason was the first to say what was both in the back of our minds.

"There was a girl in the car." There was an unasked question behind his statement.

"She's from the Manor. I don't know what Neal and his goon friend want with her. This was my fault. I knew it. He wanted me. He was going to use her to get to me." My mind was reeling. Chrissy could be in real trouble. I had a sickening feeling that I was right. She was in that car because of me.

"Goon friend?" Jason broke my frantic suspicions.

"Yeah, that's what I call him." Jason gave me an unexpected smile. I missed his smile. It was nice to see it again, that even though a building just fell on top of him, and I was almost maybe killed by some crazed loser, he could still smile at me like that. Not to mention one of my housemates might have been kidnapped. But that smile lasted only seconds, for the gravity of the situation quickly descended on us. I had to find Chrissy. I had to make sure Jason was okay. I had to get out of this damn alley!

### *Chapter: 42 My Body Needed to Heal*
#### Alex

Jason and I were frozen where we were in that dimly lit alley. It seemed like there was so much to do, but we had no idea what to do first. I wanted to make sure he was okay, but maybe I didn't need to, because right then he was up and moving around. But how? There was so much blood on the sidewalk under our feet. It looked like every inch of his body was covered in bruises. I didn't understand.

"I told you; my body naturally heals itself. Plus, the Yarrow helps speeds things up. Are you okay? You look a little worse for wear yourself." He leaned over to put a hand on my shoulder, but at the last minute, thought better of it. Maybe he thought I wouldn't take it well after all that happened. And honestly, I didn't know if I would have. This was all just so much, the attack, the wolf, Jason; I didn't know what I was thinking. Maybe I was just in shock. I forgot he could hear my every thought, because he looked away after that and gave us a wider berth. I think I was in shock, shock that he was moving and talking, and not bleeding out and broken.

"My head hurts really bad and my chin, too." I could talk without too much discomfort, which probably meant my jaw wasn't broken. My face would surely show signs of trauma in the morning. Jason, having heard my unspoken unsure thoughts about him, must have wanted to keep his distance because he stretched out his arm to hand me the jar of Yarrow. I guess that was his subtle sign for me to rub it on myself instead of visa-versa. Note taken.

I managed to gingerly rub the earthly smell of this luscious cream on my chin and jawline and the cooling sensation magically staunched the fire and pain that, up to that moment, was overwhelmingly taking over all my senses. The blow to my head would have to wait, for there would be no way for me to even know where the wound was, but at least I could tell the bleeding had stopped.

Now that the pain in my face was fading to nothing. I could start processing the fact that not only had I defended myself with mythical balls of energy against a manmade earthquake, but I also witnessed someone turn into a very large dog, or wolf, or whatever. And that large canine creature could not only survive but walk away from having pounds of concrete fall from the sky. I shook my head, to physically get over the disbelief I was in and to kick myself back into gear. We needed to get moving.

My mind was still open to Jason, because he grabbed his backpack and started walking down the street towards what I hoped was civilization. He didn't need to check that I was following because, of course, he could hear in my thoughts that I was. To which I heard him chuckle under his breath. Okay, back up the wall goes. I needed to build the wall because I didn't want him in my head. I didn't know what he would hear... I didn't know what thoughts I would think. I needed my head to be a place that only I was in. At least for now. I don't know what was going on between us. I thought he didn't want to be around me. Yet here he was, saving me. Again. How did he know where I was? Better question was, where were we going now? My questions were answered shortly because, after going one block down a side street, we reached his motorcycle.

"Wait, we can't get on that. What if you have like broken ribs or something? That can't be safe. No, there has to be another way. Maybe we could—"

I think the adrenaline and shock were finally wearing off. Or maybe the idea of mounting a motorcycle after all the events that happened in the last hour finally made my brain snap because I panicked. I felt my heart speed up, my breathing became erratic, and I could no longer control it. Things looked fuzzy. My head felt dizzy. I kept trying to catch my breath. I didn't feel right. I could feel the wall I was erecting in my brain crumble and crash and all the thoughts that ran through my head during the last few hours flooded every space of my brain. I thought the force of them all would crush me. My body gave up the fight, and I felt myself break. Tears fell uninhibitedly from my eyes, washing away everything I was holding on to; from tonight, from last week, last year, to the last decade. My body wept.

"Alexandra, you're having a panic attack. You need to sit down, try to control your breathing. You're going to be okay. I'm here. You're not alone."

Jason was there, but he wasn't. He left. He left me. I was alone. Neal found me and I was alone. His words weren't penetrating the uncontrolled heaves of my shoulders, the sobs that came in waves. It felt like I would never stop crying, that I would cry tears until every drop of water squeezed out of my body and it left me an empty shell, numb to everything. I would never heal. I wanted to lie down; I wanted to sleep; my body needed to sleep.

"Jason."

Was the only thing I said before I felt my legs give out.

# Chapter 43: Zombie for Brains

### Jason

"Alexandra, I'm here. I'm right here."

Jason caught her before her head hit the ground. He needed to get her to his village. Takoda, the Akbaalia, the healer, would know what to do. But how, how could he get an unconscious girl to his land on a motorcycle? His mind was reeling. He felt as if this was his fault. If only he would have gotten there sooner. If only he wasn't so worried about what his father or his tribe would have to say, if only he would have been with her tonight. Then maybe he could have prevented this from happening. But he got there too late. Her attacker got there first. Movement from the lifeless girl in his arms brought him back to the now Alex was waking up. He cradled her carefully and watched as she opened her eyes and tried to gather her bearings.

"How do you feel?" He muttered, trying not to startle her already fragile body. Alex sat up on her own. A hand going directly to her forehead, rubbing her eyes into focus.

"Ow. I feel... awful." She said in a hushed and wobbly voice.

"Eloquently put, and I'd agree you don't look so great." Jason said in a more sarcastic voice. He teased her, trying to regain some of that connection they used to have.

"Cut me some slack, you're not the one covered in blood." There was a faint laugh behind her words, like a mirage of their easy banter.

Jason felt his heart pull towards her. His heart was craving the connection they once had. He wanted her; he needed her.

"True. You do look like you've had zombie brains for dinner." Jason smirked the half smile he knew Alex couldn't resist and gestured to the front of her gray jacket; it was covered in blood from her bleeding chin. Alex followed his gaze and confirmed that yes, indeed, she was covered in her own dried blood. It was red, vibrant blood, a screaming reminder of the trauma that took place tonight.

"Let's go. I need to get you to my village. You need to see Takoda. We need to find your roommate, and we better hurry." Jason made sure Alex was carefully secured on his bike and drove off toward his father's land.

# Chapter 44: Dawn Had Broke

### Alex

I vaguely remember the motorcycle ride to Jason's land. My head was still pounding from the falling debris of the building. But at least the helmet made it feel like it wouldn't crack into a thousand pieces like Humpty Dumpty. Without the helmet, I thought for sure all my gooey brain matter would fall right out. One good thing was, I texted Paige to tell her about Chrissy. I wanted to see if what I saw was really her. Luckily for me, the longest train in history stopped our commute for a solid six minutes and, in that time, I received a stream of frantic text all about Christy.

Apparently, the group got separated at the coffee shop on their way to catch the bus home. A random car and mafia looking goons came out of nowhere and grabbed Chrissy throwing her in the back. They haven't been able to get ahold of the matrons and didn't know if they should call the authorities given, they're not the average citizens. So, they headed back to the manor to come up with a plan B. I didn't know what the plan was because that was when the train cleared our intersection. Jason continued down the road. I did *not* trust myself in my current condition to text while being on the back of a moving motorcycle.

Somehow, I knew the moment we crossed into Jason's land. I felt it. As if I entered a state of peace that had physically manifested itself around me, like a weighted blanket grounding me to the earth.

There was a definite sense of separation. A veil that boarded this land, a constant reminder that we were now on private land, sacred land. I noticed my senses were a little hazy, a little duller. I didn't mind at all because with the dulling of my senses came the much needed relief from the pain I was in. For just a second, I joked to myself that his village must be pumping some type of invisible pain killer into the air, but that was too nuts to be true. It had to be the concussion talking and the last of the shock wearing off. But it was a little confusing to be slightly numb and not in complete control of myself.

When we dismounted the bike, I heard Jason say. "Are you in a lot of pain? Do you want to see the healer?" There was so much concern laced into every word.

"No, I'm fine. We need to find Chrissy." Too much time had already passed, and we needed to find her. We needed to find her before anything could happen.

Now that I released my head from the helmet, I could take in my surroundings in full. This place, this land, was nothing I could have imagined. It was magical. There was a deep, spicy smell of pine and a heady smell of smoke and dirt that transformed me to a place of security and pride. Everywhere I looked lay cabins and houses and shelters; some made of logs and bricks, some made of cedar and stone, none were the same and all of them were perfect. The forest floor made natural pathways of moss and ferns weaving in and around the structures and community areas. Footpaths formed from dirt and gravel acted like colorful markers of places to go.

There was a wide open area in the middle that looked to be the site of a recent bonfire. Even though it was night outside, the strings of lights hanging from posts and strung to trees illuminated the nearby porches and walkways covering everything in a glowy-soft romantic ambiance. It felt like I stepped into a fairytale story. I couldn't believe this place was real.

"Alexandra."

*Put up your wall. While you're here, I need you to have your wall up and be as strong as you can make it. We'll be able to talk in private later. But I need you to do it now.*

Jason's words in my head no longer startled me like they once did. It felt like something we did all the time, when in reality I tried very hard to not communicate with him like this. I wanted to be the only one in my head. But listening to his hurried words and feeling the urgency behind them, I understood how useful this skill could be. So, before I followed his directions, I answered back.

*Alright, but I'm going to have a lot of explanations coming my way.*

I erected the thickest wall around my mind I could. Imagining walls built of concrete and metal with rivets and padlocks crisscrossing around the whole damn thing. It felt impenetrable. I hope it was. I looked over at Jason to see if it worked. The only answer he gave me was a wink that would have brought me to my knees if I weren't leaning against his motorcycle. I turned away from him to hide some of the blush I'm sure was giving away all my secrets. I didn't want him to know he still affected me. I caught my breath, because man, he was too gorgeous for his own good.

My face was back to its original color, I pushed away from the cycle and heard Jason calling me from somewhere up ahead. I hadn't realized he had walked away while I was trying to desperately to control the blush on my face. My eyes had to adjust to the dim lighting, but once they did, it was such a natural thing. Unlike reading in low light where your eyes strained to stay in focus, this felt right. This was a place that needed to be treated with respect and delicacy. I hurried out of my revere and caught up to Jason. He was heading toward a peculiar-looking cabin. Unlike the cottages that occupied most of this area, this cabin was round, or somewhat round. It had a thatched style roof made of dried reeds and moss. Which was so odd, considering there was smoke trailing out the middle of the building. My mind couldn't comprehend how the roof could be made of tinder yet not catch fire? This was definitely something you didn't see every day.

Jason stopped before entering onto the footpath that led to the small round dwelling.

"This is the home of our Elder, Hokama. He can help us locate Chrissy. He'll know what to do." He held my hand, and I welcomed the embrace. The touch grounded me. It was the first time he openly reached for me, where it wasn't essential for my safety. Hand in hand, we walked the short distance to the door. Even from out here, an overwhelming scent of sage and cedar wafted over me. It was so strong, my eyes watered. Jason knocked on the door, and an old man walked out. He wasn't a tall man, but his presence was substantial. He was sun kissed and wind burned, his dark eyes were onyx stones in his harsh face. He wore a white leather tunic with intricate beading of a finely threaded silhouette design of an eagle in flight. The old man nodded once at Jason and turned and disappeared back into the house. I guess that was the okay sign for us to continue up the walkway.

Jason, still holding on to me, continued forward into the house. Then something extremely strange happened. Jason walked into the house just fine, trailing me behind him, when suddenly I couldn't move anymore. Something was preventing me from crossing the threshold. It felt like a piece of plexiglass blocking me. The movement made Jason and I break free from the hold we had. Jason looked back; confusion written all over his face. He looked around, trying to figure out what the blockade could be. His eyes scanned the doorjamb, and there, hanging just outside the door, was a small, dried bouquet of something I didn't recognize. Jason swiftly reached up and yanked the flowers off the door and stuck them in his pocket. Instantaneously, the invisible wall was gone, leaving me to practically fall into the house. I looked up to Jason searching for answers, but the only thing I found in his beautiful green eyes was a plea to stay quiet. I silenced the words that were forming on my tongue. This all happened in a matter of seconds, and we both looked around to see if anybody else noticed what happened. We didn't see anyone. Hopefully, it went without notice. I was, however, going to ask Jason what that was all about the minute I had a chance.

There were men sitting in an open circle around the room, a small fire pit made of mud and rock. A young man was stoking the small flames, coaxing them to grow. Jason looked at the Elders in the room. His shoulders were firm, and his face was unreadable. He maintained a wide distance between the both of us, but he was careful enough to make sure the distance wasn't too great so that I wouldn't feel secluded. I could tell we had entered a serious place, a somber place. A place that wasn't the most welcoming, to outsiders like me. My nerves were telling me to turn around, to get out of this house. But if this guy could help us find Chrissy, I had to do everything I could to make sure that happened. She was in trouble, and it was all because of me.

Hokama, the man who had answered the door, never took his eyes off me. It wasn't a glaring stare, but a watchful one. I couldn't meet his gaze. I didn't know whether it was from fear or shame, but either way I had couldn't return his stare. Jason glanced at me for just a moment and gave me a comforting nod and gestured to a small wooden stool covered in animal hide and adorned with feathers. It looked more like a piece of art than a piece of furniture, but none the less I followed the unspoken command and sat down. I didn't think I had much of a choice in the matter, so I chose not to fight. Especially with the way Hokama was continuing to look at me. Jason gave me a cursory glance to let me know everything was going to be all right.

Hokama spoke. His voice was powerful and confident. It both terrified me and put me to ease. "I know why you have come here.

Evil has been gaining strength, and now a girl's life is in danger. Yet she is not the cause of her peril. Is she?"

He looked at me and dropped his head, eyes never breaking contact. What does he know? And why is he looking at me like that? Part of me wanted to run, to break through the door and get the hell out of here. Another part wanted to ask him every question I ever had. I had the feeling he would have every answer I would ever need. Jason looked at me. I could still sense the wall in my mind was up strong, and tall. My thoughts weren't getting out. But I think my facial expressions still came out loud and clear because he gave me the slightest shake of his head. As if to say.

*Stay. Don't run. Don't speak.*

Okay, I nodded the tiniest nod I could muster. I would hold my seat and let these elders do the talking. I refused to reveal my secrets that easily. Even though I was pretty sure Hokama already knew everything about me, I just didn't know how.

Hokama continued. "We gather 'round and give thanks to Father Fire. We will be protected and strengthen by the light and warmth of the flames. We cleanse our bodies and minds to prevent evil from penetrating our sacred circle."

As he said this, he scattered bits of something into the flames. It caused a thick smoke to billow up. It filled the room with a heavy scent of sage and maybe lavender. Hokama wafted his hand over the smoke, making tendrils swirl around the room like guppies swimming through the cattails. The smoke fingers weaved around the room in long ribbons. The sweet, fragrant smell of the sage wasn't as overwhelming as it had been a moment ago. It was now a soothing scent, a welcome scent. Hokama spoke again.

"To open our minds and hear the voice within, we ask Mother Earth to guide us, to nurture us. We come to the circle as unformed clay, ready to be molded. We come with humble hearts and quiet souls and thank the Spirit Gods with our reverence. Thank you,

Father Fire." Right after Hokama thanked the Fire Spirit, the flames from our little stone hearth licked up higher. Whipping at the open air until it settled once again into its rock and stone enclosure. After which the crowd responded with.

"Thank you, Father Fire."

Hokama continued to call out to other elements. Again, the crowd would respond with the correct gratitude.

"Thank you, Mother Earth."

The earthen clay under my feet vibrated ever so slightly, causing the soles of my shoes to reverberate with the movement.

"Thank you, Brother Wind."

Instantly, the curtains hanging from the windows jostled as a breeze fluttered into our little hut. The thatched roof swished under the gentle power of the wind.

"Thank you, Sister Water."

As with the other spirits, the water responded. I hadn't noticed the ceramic red pot sitting beside Hokama. It wasn't any larger than the stock pots I've seen group homes use for large stews. A small waterspout twirled and danced inside the basin, kicking up water as the revolutions got stronger and stronger. Just as fast as it developed, it diminished just as quick; the funnel absorbed back into the main body of water. If I hadn't seen it with my own eyes, I would never have believed this could happen. This ceremony enthralled me. My body buzzed as the elemental magic coursed throughout the little cabin. My nerves responded to it. I wanted to be part of it, to embody the elements and be one with them. It took all I had to stay in my seat and not jump up and try to draw the elements into me, to feel them inside me. I knew at that moment I belonged to them. I was them and they were me. I could have moved mountains. I could have called down thunder and lightning.

I needed to control myself. I was spinning out of kilter. This was not the place to reveal who or what I was, but it was so hard.

The elements were calling to me. They wanted me and I needed them. It felt right, but it was not the right time. All this time I've been fighting it; fighting my gifts, my abilities. But coming here, and seeing the elements dance and respond to Hokama, it opened something inside of me, and I never wanted it to be shut again. I tried to control my breathing and steady my heartbeat to continue to listen to Hokama, but at that moment, as I was telling myself to pay attention, he turned abruptly to look me dead in the eye. For the first time that evening, I returned his stare. What I saw I was not prepared for; I was immediately thrown into a vision; Hokama's vision.

It was unlike any other visions I've had before. This was a slide show. Clips of unique life experiences flickered behind my eyes, clear as day. Through this display of static pictures, I knew Hokama wasn't just any man, but a Skin Walker like Jason. He was one of the Original Inhabitants. I saw the beginnings of his people here on the land. The first Alder in the generational line, the Immortal First People. Living their lives, trying to survive, they befriended a group of outsides. Welcomed them into their land and to the use of their resources. There was harmony, there was peace. The leader of the outsiders was a woman, Sonya. I recognized her immediately. They had a fruitful relationship. They shared and learned all about each other, living side by side for many years. It was beautiful. A beautiful depiction of life and harmony, my body wanted to weep from the joy of it all.

Then the pictures changed and morphed into something dark and ugly. I tried to look away. I tried to shake the images out of my mind. It was pointless. I couldn't get away from the gruesome images flashing before me. Death and blood. Broken bodies. Kootenai and Mystics lay broken, and bleeding scattered on the once green meadows where children laughed and played. No one was laughing now. Bodies were so torn there were no distinguishing marks of who was who. What I could see was Lord Nicolai in the center of it all.

Laughing. Laughing at the death and destruction that laid before him.

The images shifted again to reveal the Kootenai's and the Mystic's breaking partnership. The Kootenai retreating deeper into their woods; the Mystics spreading out, dismantled and severed from their once sacred covens. The two becoming strangers, never to be together again.

Finally, the vision was over. New pictures displayed before us, and I knew these pictures were recent, very recent. The images were of a coyote and not just any coyote, a Skin Walker, a young one. A mother, deep in grief over the loss of her son, wept uncontrollably. The young coyote morphed into the body of a young boy, no older than I was, his body was disfigured as if every bone in his body had shattered. Someone left the young boy's body on the road that lead to the tribal lands, which made the whole situation worse. It was deliberate. It was a threat. And I knew this was Nicolai's doing. The picture cleared, and I was back in the circle, back in the cabin, sitting next to Jason. Jason, who looked as if he'd seen a ghost. Jason leaned into me and broke the silence with an unsteady voice.

"Alexandra, are you okay? What happened?" He took my hand, his fingers were so warm against my icy ones. I didn't realize I was shaking till he reached out to steady me. Breathless, I answered him.

"Yeah, I'm fine. I...saw it. I saw everything Jason. Your people, their history, the pain and sufferings that has come from the Dark Coven, from Nicolai. I know now what I need to do. I wasn't ready before, but I'm ready now. This, whatever this is, is far greater than me and my insecurities. I know what I have to do." I sounded a lot more confident than I felt, but I knew it was true.

"Alexandra, what are you saying? Ready for what? You're not making any sense." I wanted to stop and try to explain everything I had yet to tell him, but I could sense that we were running out of time. Instead, I turned toward Hokama, which I now knew meant

Guide, and searched his face. His expression was unreadable; soft yet unrelenting.

"We need to find Chrissy. And we need to rid your lands and all of Mountain Ridge from the evil that has plagued your people and the Mystics for far too long. What can I do?" I lowered my eyes, but this time not out of fear, but out of respect. He lifted a hand and placed it gently on the crown of my head.

"Young Priestess, I sense greatness in you. You are the one the prophesy speaks of. The one who came before and united us so long ago. Welcome Back." I looked up at him with wide eyes and marveled at how he knew something I barely knew myself. He chuckled at the look that was blasting across my face.

"Your spirit is strong young one. There is no hiding it, even if you tried. I was unsure at first, for evil has many disguises and we must use our discernment to keep our people safe. But I can see your true self and you are her. There is no mistaking it." Hokama took his seat, and we finished the ritual.

"In order to locate the girl, we need to offer Father Fire a totem on her behalf. Do you have anything of hers that we can surrender to the fire? Even the smallest of items can be helpful."

I was about to say no when I remembered I had something of hers. Chrissy had taken a page from her journal to write a phone message for me. Clara tried calling me while I was in the shower earlier that morning. She used the main line when I didn't answer my phone. I took a mental note to call her back when I had the chance, but right now, I needed to focus on Chrissy and trying to find her before it was too late. I stuck my hand in my pocket and hopped this half sheet of paper would be enough.

I pulled out the neatly folded notebook paper and looked it over carefully. This was all I had of Chrissy; this one piece of college ruled paper. I knew it was from her journal because I recognized the purple tint to the page and the gold lines that ran across it. Her journal had the same hue and I remember thinking how cool the gold lines looked running through the pages. I wish I knew more about her. These last few weeks we started to become friends. But there was still so much I didn't know about her. Was purple her favorite color, or was this just something she found lying around? Her avoidance of human contact made things a little difficult, but she was working on it, she was trying to build genuine friendships. She was the one who helped me see my true placement as a Mystic. Even if I wasn't ready to hear it at the time and for that, I will forever be thankful. Seeing our friendship reduced to this one piece of purple paper made my heart ache. I vowed I would show her the same kindness she showed me, and when we found her, I would try harder to be a better friend. And now because of me, she was kidnapped, scared, and alone.

I handed the purple paper to Hokama and waited for what he would say next. The following words I heard didn't come from his mouth, but from his mind. Apparently my well constructed wall had no baring here, so I let it go. I let the wall crumble, and I welcomed the vulnerability my open mind created. In my mind, I heard Hokama tell me to place the note in the fire. I did what was asked of me and folded the paper back up into the little square it was before and tossed it into the flame. Instantly, the paper was consumed by the flames. A bluish smoke licked up into the empty space above us. It consumed the entire cabin. It was strange, but honestly, by this point, it was fitting. The blue smoke was whirling around us. It engulfed us in big, luscious waves of carbon and vapors. The smoke was taking on a solid form now, almost as if it was becoming an entity on to itself. It danced it front of us, becoming more and more solid with every swish of movement, like a silk scarf fluttering in the wind. The blue silk scarf of smoke grew to the size of a large pillowcase, a makeshift projector screen. It was completely solid now and on the ethereal, smoky pillowcase projected pictures. I felt like we had front row seats to a spiritual drive-in movie.

The pictures were a little wavy and translucent, but there was no mistaking what was happening before me. Smoke had turned into a movie picture scene. I adjusted my eyes to focus on the fuzzy images to grasp what it was I was looking at. It was a construction site or something — no — it was a railroad depot. Yes, definitely a railroad. I could see the train tracks and old cargo trains standing stagnate in the background. As soon as I could identify the location on the silk screen, the image was gone, and the smoke went with it. No trace of it lingered in the air. Even the fire had gone out. Hokama looked around the room, catching all our gazes. He bent his head and uttered a silent prayer in thanks to all the spirit gods once more. It was Jason who spoke up next.

"I know that place. It's the old Johnston depot down in Troy. Why would they take her there?" I knew the answer before he even finished asking the question.

"It's a trap." I confirmed.

"Alexandra, I won't let anything happen to you. I left you once. I won't do it again." His eyes flicked to Hokama. I wanted to believe the words he was saying, but I also knew the truth. The Kootenai's didn't think too highly of Mystics, and Jason was the next successor to the Kootenai Tribe. He had other obligations that went way beyond whatever feelings we might have for one another. Jason came up next to me and grabbed my hand. He clenched it, looked me in the eye and without moving his lips, I heard him say.

*I'm not going anywhere. There's nowhere for me to go. You are my heart. There is no me without you. I am so sorry, Alex. I was a fool to fight it. You are my destiny just as much as my succession is. If you'll have me, we can figure the rest out later.*

His words blew me away, they were swirling around in my mind. I felt every emotion Jason projected. He was honest, vulnerable, raw. There was no mistaking what he felt for me, with his soul filled confession. I felt the floodgates open inside of me. All the walls I've built to keep people out, to keep myself guarded, to keep me from getting hurt suddenly broke and shattered into a million pieces. I loved Jason; I didn't know how or why, but I knew I loved him, now, then, forever. I had a million things running through my head as to what to say next, but the thing that came out was.

"You called me Alex." Jason smirked and shook his head in a playful display of exasperation.

"I heard it's what you prefer." He gave me his signature smile and raked his fingers through his hair.

"I like Alexandra."

We stared at each other, and it felt like time had stopped just for us. But we knew we couldn't stay here in this bliss bubble forever. As hard as it was, we needed to face the trouble that waited for us outside this cabin. We turned back to Hokama to see what our next steps needed to be. We came up with a plan to get Chrissy the hell out of that freaky railroad, then he gave us his blessings for a quick and safe return. Jason led us out of the tiny cabin, which felt even smaller than it had when we first arrived. The cool late winter air hit us like a waterfall crashing over river rocks. I couldn't wait until the warm air of spring came. I felt the chill down into my bones. The afternoon light pierced through the tree line. Half the day was already over. Was it only yesterday I was last at the manor? Getting our daily chores done, anticipating our evening at the coffeehouse. It felt like weeks has passed. What was waiting for me back there? Where did my housemates think I was? Were they worried about me? Did they notice I wasn't there? Did Ryan? All these questions needed answers, but not now. They could wait. I needed to find Chrissy. She couldn't wait.

It was suggested to head to the train depot by way of Thompson's Falls. It overlooked the old train tracks to the north, giving a bird's-eye view of the depot below. This way we'd have the advantage of higher ground. Or at least that was the hope. Before we mounted the bike, Jason said he needed to make a quick stop. The last thing I heard him not say as the helmet's visor snapped over my eyes was.

*Let's get through today. We'll worry about tomorrow, tomorrow. But today it's you and me.*

# Chapter 45: We're Your Pack

**Jason**

Jason knew he was about to walk Alex into a dangerous situation, but what better way was there to head into a perilous and unknown situation than to drag a few of your closest buddies along with you? And it just so happened that those close friends all held the same magical capabilities, Skin Walking. Which meant that their enhanced predator abilities were great in a fight and as their future Alpha, he knew they would follow them anywhere. So why then did he feel like he would have to convince them?

Jason parked his bike at the head of the trail that leads to the Cub House. The last time he was here, he about nearly knocked the damn thing down out of frustration and rage. Now he was approaching with caution and trepidation. As the next in line to be Alpha, he had a few perks that came with the territory; some were great, and some were not. One good thing was he could *push out* his thoughts to his pack from a much wider distance than the others, which was useful in a battle, being able to call the entire pack at once. Even though he's never needed to use it because of a battle, it was cool when they wanted to start a game of pickup basketball and needed a fourth player. Today he used it so his crew would already be waiting for him at the Cub House. He wanted to do this only once.

He could "hear" the chatter going on inside the Cub House. Word got out that a Charmer was in their midst. The pack knew

Hokama had a sit-in with the Charmer, but they didn't know why, or how she got here, or that she would be showing up in their in Cub House. At least that part Jason would be able to explain it on his own. He knew how the tribe felt about Charmers, and who knows what could have been said or what they would have thought if word got out that he was the one who brought her here? He knew he would have to be the one that told them. It had to come from their Alpha, and therein lies the not so good stuff about being Alpha. If he gave a command in such a way, if he put the correct timber behind his voice, the others would have no choice but to follow. They could not go against him. He hated that part of being Alpha. He wanted people to always keep their free will. To have their autonomy, he hoped there would never come a time where he would have to enforce the Alpha law. But he knew sadly there may come a time when he'd have to.

*Where is she? Why is she here? What could this mean?*

*Nothing good I know that. Where the fuck is Jay? I know he's behind this somehow. How could he do this to us?*

*We don't know anything. There has to be some kind of explanation. He wouldn't do anything that puts our tribe in jeopardy.*

*We don't need to know anything. A damn Charmer has crossed into our land. I knew he'd change once he went to that damn townie school.*

*Ya, what was wrong with our school? What was wrong with the pack? He hasn't been the same since—*

*Cut it out. I think I heard the bike.*

Jason "heard" them as he walked up to the cabin. Which was a good thing, apparently. At least now he knew what he was walking into. It looked like he would have to do some convincing after all. As he approached the door to the Cub House, he blocked his thoughts. This wasn't an entirely out of character thing for him to do. They all knew how he felt about the mind reading business and they were used to his aversion to it by now. But he knew it would draw a bit of suspicions, anyway. Especially since he could feel them trying to get into his thoughts, the closer he got to the door.

Before he opened the door, he turned to Alex and told her. "Let me do the talking. They're — unsure — of you right now and we don't have any time. I'll try to make this quick. Hopefully, I can get them to come with us."

"What if you can't?"

"Then it's just you and me. And I'm okay with that."

Jason squeezed Alex's hand and gave her a look he hoped portrayed how serious he was about following her to the ends of the earth. Alex's eyes glassed over with fresh tears on the brink of falling. Somehow, he knew they weren't tears of sadness. But he wanted to brush them away, anyway. He wanted to take away all her fears and uncertainty. He wanted to love her, and to be loved by her, forever. But to get to forever, he had to get through today. And that started by opening the door and confronting what lay in front of him in the form of his pissed off pack mates. Jason squared his shoulders and hardened his face like he's seen his dad do a thousand times. It was what he does when he addresses the pack at large. Then opened the door.

Immediately, all three members of his pack ambushed him with questions, not even paying attention to the girl at his back who walked in behind him. He knew this had to be quick. He didn't have time to trudge through all the berated questions they were pummeling at him, so he had to do the one thing he rarely did, if ever. Jason spoke in his Alpha tone.

"Enough!"

All at once, they stopped talking and took a step back, bowing their heads in submission to their Alpha. It looked as if some of them tried and failed to fight the urge to submit. But once the Alpha spoke, they must obey. Jason hated to see them like this, but he needed to get their attention quickly and there was no other way to get through to them. He hoped now they would at least listen to him.

Jason looked around the room. All four boys were now in different states of impatience with him. No longer under the Alpha submission, but now at least Jason had their attention. Mato Patrick was pacing back and forth like the bear he was, a trapped bear ready to attack. He was the one who was the most upset about Jason's visitor and would be the hardest one to convince. His family is just as old as Jasons, which was why he was the Beta of Jason's pack. Mikael is Meto's older brother, so they were raised side by side practically like brothers themselves. And like Mikael, he took Tribe Pride to another level. Austin, who stood at the back of the cabin near the only other exit, was Jason's best friend. He wasn't as confident as Jason thought he could be, but maybe it was his coyote. Always just a little nervous. Austin never seemed to believe in himself, he always ended up on the outskirts of the pack. But he was always the first one Jason could confide in. He knew Austin would have his back, no matter what.

Micah was the wildcard. He perched himself on the counter, back against the wall, one leg dangling off the side. He was just as loyal as the others, but more often than not, he looked for a fight. And nine out of ten times; he found one. Micah had a hard life. He was definitely one of the boys and has been friends and pack mates since they were kids, but he never got too close. Like his Spirit Guide, the Hawk, he kept to himself. Jason didn't know what he would do once he told them about Alex.

"Listen, I can't explain everything right now, but eventually I will. Right now, I'm asking you to trust me. Know that I need your help. We need your help. And once we finish doing what must be done. I'll tell you everything you need to know. But right now, you only need to know that I need you, and we need to go. Now."

Jason looked around the room, to the faces that were in front of him. Mato was the first to speak.

"Why should we go anywhere when you're trailing a Charmer behind you? What about Koi? Or have you forgotten his Ina' found his body nearly unrecognizable because of her kind? I don't care what trouble she's got herself in, I won't be a part of it. And neither should you. Jay, I don't even recognize you anymore. Ever since you started hanging out with townies, it's like we don't exist anymore. We're your pack. Not her."

Mato continued his pacing. His circles getting wider and wider like he was trying to get between Jason and Alex. Jason sensed his unease with Alex, and he positioned her so they were practically touching. To act like a barrier between her and Mato. With this slight movement, Mato pushed out his thoughts to Jason.

*She's not one of us. She's a Charmer. She'll bring only death and destruction to our pack. I'm sorry, but I can't be a part of this. And unless you want to make me, there's no reason for me to stay.*

That was the last thing Jason heard before Mato pushed his way past Austin and left the Cub House. An explosion of clothes and fur were left in his wake. The brindle fur of Mato's bear was last seen heading into the forest. Mato's reaction saddened Jason, but he respected his opinion and knew they would need to have a deeper conversation later. But for now, he would let Mato burn off some anger and deal with him later. He turned his attention to Micah.

"And you? What do you say? Are you going to help or not?"

Micah jumped off the counter and slowly began walking towards Jason. Not in a show of aggression, but curiosity. His eyes never left Alex, head tilting from side to side. He never looked more like the bird of prey, then at that moment. He stoppe a few feet away from Jason and spoke.

"I've never once turned down a fight. But only for the ones I knew I'd win. And I don't think the odds are in your favor with this one. You're Alpha, I respect that. But you ain't Alpha yet. And unless you're going to command it, I think I'm going to take my leave while I still can. Sorry Jay. But Mato's right. You've changed."

Micah slowly sauntered out the front door, watching Alex the entire way out.

"And then there was one."

Austin's voice sounded far away, even though he was just across the small house. He moved deeper into the living space, making up his mind that he was going to stay.

"I'll understand if you don't want to get involved. They're right, this isn't your fight, and I shouldn't ask you to put yourself in danger for something you know nothing about."

Jason felt his body relax. The confrontation with his pack mates was a lot more stressful than he realized and now that it was just the three of them, he felt like he could breathe a lot easier.

"You're my Alpha. Where you go, I go. You know that. You don't need to explain anything to me. Do you need my help?"

"Yes"

"Then you got it. My only question is, are we taking your car or mine? The three of us won't fit on the back of your bike."

Jason has never felt more love for his pack mate than now. The undeniable loyalty was beyond measure. There was so much he wanted to tell Austin, but it would all have to wait. Right now, they had to drive to Troy. None of them knew what they would find when they got there. But they all knew they might not all make it back.

# Chapter 46: What's a Skinwalker?

**Alex**

The three of us took off to go find Chrissy. Jason, Austin his pack mate, and me. With nothing more than one full tank of gas and a single braided bracelet of sweet grass wound around my wrist. Hokama gave it to me, saying it would help bring in good spirits and keep out the dark ones. I sent out a quick text to Paige, notifying her we located Chrissy, and we were on our way to bring her back. Winter still held Montana in her grips, which meant our daylight was fading quickly. I hadn't realized how long we'd been in Hokama's hut and the conversation with Jason's pack must have taken longer than I realized. Because night fall was already approaching. My mind was reeling all the way to Troy. It was only a 30-minute drive to Thompson's Falls, but it was the longest one in my life. My mind was making up images and possibilities that would put "Nightline" to shame. We needed to get there, and we weren't going fast enough.

*We'll get there. Nothing's going to happen to her. We'll make it.*

Jason's soothing words in my mind acted like a metaphysical hug around my thoughts. I had to admit that this talking without actually talking has its benefits.

*Hurry Jason.*

Finally, we came across the old railroad. We could see the abandoned depot down below. It was dark and scary looking. From this height, the illumination of the few emergency lampposts cast an eerie glow over the whole place, leaving large pockets of shadows. The perfect scene for anyone or anything to be hiding. Jason pulled over behind a section of collapsed chain-link fence. The fence boarded the entire yard, ending with a mangled gate at the entrance of the depot. The whole place screamed TRAP, but there was nothing we could do but keep moving forward.

All I could see was a dilapidated old platform, the kind of platform that was raised from the ground so passengers can load and unload the trains. I could only image how it once looked in the height of its prime. You could still see some the intricate wooden columns carved to look like Greece pillars complete with fleur-de-lis adorning the capitals of what was left of the structure. I'm sure it looked nothing like it once did. Now it looked like at any moment the wind would collapse the whole damn thing. Leaving only the lamppost stuck in the hard earthen ground below.

Jason and Austin were Spirit Talking while I was taking in our surroundings of the depot. I could tell because even though their mouths didn't move, their heads would nod, or their eyebrows would shift. I don't know what they were talking about, but I could guess it was trying to develop some sort of plan as to what to do next. I didn't know much about Jason and his Skin Walking abilities. I knew he had superhuman healing powers, but I didn't know if his gifts went beyond that. Like could he hear things I couldn't? See things I couldn't? We were farther away from the depot than I would have wanted to be; I wanted to get down there and see if we could find Chrissy. But from up here, everything looked blurry. Could he see down there? Was she there? I promptly realized my thoughts haven't been guarded since before we entered into Homaka's hut because Austin muffled a laugh and commented on my inner turmoil.

"We're here risking our lives and she knows nothing about you? Bro, what do you guys even talk about? Mato would be so pissed.

I can't wait to tell him." Austin laughed again, and this time Jason jokingly punched his arm.

"I don't feel the need to explain my relationship to you. We're — working things out." Jason looked at me and winked. My insides went to mush. Austin interrupted my girly swoon. Did I just hear Jason say we were in a relationship? Before I contemplated any more on that revelation, Austin explained a few things.

"There are a few perks for those of us who can Skin Walk. Apparently, as you know, we can heal superfast. But we also have other enhanced abilities like speed, strength, and our senses are increased. So yeah, we can see from here to the depot a lot better than you probably can. No offense. And the cool thing is, we don't need to be in our Spirit Guide form to access them. I'm probably going to get so much shit for telling you all this, but I figure if we're gonna die, we might as well go all in."

"Do all of you turn into wolves?" I looked at Jason, wondering if it was okay to ask this question. He's been so silent about this side of him. I didn't want it to seem like I was going around him. I was just so curious about all of it. It was Jason who answered me this time.

"We transform into the Spirit who guides us. For some its wolves, for others it's different. With our Spirit Guide, we take on the personality and characteristic of that guide. The eagle is noble, like my grandfather was."

"And he could fly! When he was an eagle, that is. Like Micah, the lucky bastard, I wish I was a hawk."

"What are you?" I asked, super enthralled by this conversation.

"A coyote."

Austin didn't say any more about it, and I could tell I shouldn't press the issue. We moved away from the history lesson and turned our attention back to the railroad. The three of us walked down the hill towards the entrance. We were about to turn and walk around the fence toward the platform when suddenly something moved on the far end of it. I stopped in my tracks and peered into the night sky, forcing my eyes to see beyond the dark and find what had caught my attention. Before I could get a better look, I heard something. A muffled scream from the platform. It was Chrissy. They tied her to some kind of pillar. I was about to run to her, to free her, when Jason caught my arm and spun me around. I was now facing him and in a very harsh whisper, he said.

"It's a trap."

Without even looking, I knew he was right. I didn't see Austin anymore. Jason must have told him to head around back. The two of us retreated to hide behind a prickly shrub.

"Jason, what are we going to do? What if she's hurt? We need to get to her." I was spinning. I needed to get my frantic thoughts under control. I focused instead on ways we could defend ourselves without getting too close. I hated the thought of using a gun, but man, what I would do for a good bow and arrow. It looked really good in the movies. How hard could it be?

"Alexandra. We don't need any weapons. You are a weapon." He was rubbing my shoulders, trying to get my breath to stabilize, to get my heart rate down before I passed out from fear.

"Alex, stay here. I'm going to go around to the other side and see if I can't get to her from there. Austin is surveilling the back field. He'll let me know if he finds anyone. If you see anyone coming, just blast them. Once we get her freed, we'll take off from there." He sounded so sure his plan was going to work. That nothing could go wrong. I wasn't as confident. The gravity of the situation hit me, and it felt like I was drowning.

"Jason, what about you and Austin? What if I blast one of you instead? You can't leave me, you promised me. You promised you wouldn't leave. I can't do this on my own. Last time it was just Neal, and a few little light balls. I can't go up against real Mystics. Against Dark Magic. I can barely control it as it is." He squeezed my shoulders once more, looked me in the eye, and tried to comfort me as best he could.

"Alex, you are a 'Real Mystic'. You can do this; you need to do this. Don't worry about us. Or did you forget we have our own means of protecting ourselves?"

He leaned in and gently kissed my forehead. His lips lingered a little longer than necessary, but it wasn't long enough. He pulled off his sweater and T-shirt, and without another word, he took off toward the platform. The last thing I saw before darkness swallowed him was a tail twitching into the shadows. I repositioned myself so I could jump up if I needed to but lost my balance and hit the fence instead of the bush and made a rather large clanging noise. Which filled the empty space with noise. *Shit.* I held my breath, waiting for my cover to be blown. Nothing happened.

*Alexandra, are you okay?* I heard Jason say in my head.

*Yeah, I'm just clumsy, I'm fine.*

I got my nerves under control and gave myself a little pep talk. Once I stood up, I had all the determination I could muster. I needed to do what I could for Jason and Chrissy. A flash of light caught my attention. A cluster of trees was beyond my vision where I thought it might have come from. I almost chalked it up to being a trick of my imagination, then I saw it again. It wasn't a light; it was a flame. I got ready to conjure up a lightning ball. I was going to do this. I was going to do this for Chrissy and Jason, and Austin. And for me. I was done being scared. I waited. They were going to have to make the first move. I saw them. A cluster of people were moving away from the trees that boarded the depot. I moved away from the bush trying to get the advantage so I could haul my lightning ball at whoever I needed too. I wanted to face them head on, but then I heard something familiar.

"Alex! It's me, Paige."

Paige! Oh my God, was it really her? Paige came at me at a full run and gave me a hug so strong I thought she would break a rib. Right behind her were Ms. Mary and Ms. Terra, along with Ryan and even Nora. I have never been happier to see five people in my life.

"What are you guys doing here?"

"Did you really think we were going to let you play vigilante all by yourself? You may be some High Priestess in training but come on when it comes to having control of your powers, you're just a baby."

Paige's backhanded comment warmed my heart as odd as that sounded. Maybe I really did find friends I could count on after all. Maybe these were my people. It felt weird since I've never had people before. It was definitely something I could get use too. I looked over our small crowd and locked eyes with Ryan. Ryan, who I haven't seen since the café. I didn't know what to say to him. So much has happened in the small amount of time that has passed. I didn't know where to start. I think he felt the same way, because he broke the silence first.

"I was worried about you. I've been beating myself about not insisting I walk you home. Paige filled me in on what happened and I'm glad Jason was there. And I get it. I know it's him. But I need you to know that if it was a competition, I'd put my name in the ring. I like you, Alex, and I'm willing to fight for you. If there's a chance, I'm in. But if you tell me there's no hope, I'll respect that. Just think about it before you decide."

Ryan walked over to stand next to Paige and looked over the scene before us. My head was spinning with his declaration. I didn't know what to think. But I couldn't do anything about it right now. The Matrons were there with Ryan and Paige in what looked to be some sort of war huddle. I was about to go over and participate in the conversation when I felt a light tap on my shoulder. I turned to see Nora standing sheepishly behind me. She didn't look at all like I've seen her before. She was softer, smaller almost. My guard was still up even though she looked like a puppy in the pound. She began to speak.

"Alex, I'm sorry about everything. My brother. Me. Just everything. I don't know how to make it better, but I didn't want this. I'm sorry." I didn't know what to say, so I said what I thought would be best.

"I understand. He's your brother and you love him. But I don't think he's the brother you remember. I'm sorry." We shared an understanding look. We might not be best friends anytime soon, but I think we were on our way to at least being friends.

I told the group everything I knew so far. We devised a rough plan on how to get everyone out safely and then we spread out. Paige and I took off together. We walked around the west side of the tracks so that Chrissy was directly in front of the Matrons. There were going to go directly into the yard to talk some reason into the kidnappers. If they weren't successful, well than the Matrons could perfectly handle themselves. The Matrons were halfway to Chrissy when a voice came out of the darkness.

"Well, well, well, Meriwether and Terracotta, my has it been a long time since our last engagement?" The unnamed goon came out of what was left of the old ticket booth. Looking just as smug as ever.

"Alaric Garrison. It has been a few years, hasn't it? 20, 40 years maybe? Alaric let's stop this nonsense. We were once allies. Why now do you stand against us? We are all one. There is no need for such division." Ms. Terra was as strong and confident as I've ever seen her. Nothing seemed to faze her. Ms. Mary was right next to her, lending her strength. They moved as one solid unit. In a slick, slow, wispy voice, Alaric answered.

"Allies? Allies we are not. We don't align ourselves with Halflings, and Peacekeepers. There is no room in the Ultimate Power for Peacekeepers. You have something we want. The girl will be mine;

I guarantee it." He stopped short, tilted his head like a bird listening for predators. I slowly turned back to look at the Matrons.

"Skin Walkers? You sure do keep strange company these days, Terracotta. Even I have yet to stoop so low as to associate myself with the fellowship of Skin Walkers." Now Ms. Terra was caught off guard. I saw a flicker of confusion cloud her eyes. I hadn't mentioned Jason or Austin to either of them. Too afraid of them having unwarranted bias over people who were here to help. Ms. Mary looked over to the brush where Paige and I had planted ourselves, but only for a moment, careful to not give away our location. Paige looked at me as well, and all I could do was shrug. There was no time to explain myself now. She simply asked.

"What's a Skinwalker? And why do I think you're involved in this somehow?"

# Chapter 47: Marionette Strings

### Alex

That was all Paige had time to say, because right then, an enormous sound captured our attention. We quickly turned back to the platform and out of the shadows came Jason, jaws snapping, and hackles raised. But of course, to everyone else, it was a wolf. A wolf who ran full speed and tackled Alaric head on, head on and ruthlessly. Then all hell broke loose. Everything was happening so fast it was literally spinning right before my eyes. Ms. Mary, seeing the very distracted Alaric, ran to Chrissy to free her from the ropes that bound her. But before she could reach the last knot, something knocked her off the platform, and she landed straight on her back. Falling five feet down, hitting the unforgiving ground. She didn't move.

Ms. Terra let out a scream. A scream buried so deep in her body I felt my heart break. Ms. Terra turned away from her sister's lifeless body back to the platform, looking for the reason for her fall. Out walked a woman, a slim, very angular woman dressed completely in black from her tight leather jacket to her kick ass knee-high boots. Without so much as a hair's breadth of warning, Ms. Terra was on her. She had an affinity for earth, and sure enough, she was no novice to her skill. Earthen rocks had lifted themselves up from their resting place beneath the platform and were flung at the woman. She barely had enough time to duck into the old lobby of the station. Since Ms.

Terra obviously had everything under control, my eyes went back to Chrissy.

She was still trying to undo the ropes, but her hands were shaking from panic, and she couldn't get them untied. I looked over at Paige, and to my surprise, for a girl who comes off as kind of badass, she froze in shock. I shook her shoulders to get her attention, and she finally snapped out of it and looked at me.

"Paige, we have to help. I don't know where Nora and Ryan went, but we have to do something. You need to get to Ms. Mary and see if you can get her to a safe place. I will go to Chrissy and bring her back here. Can you do that?" She looked at me. Her black hair under the moonlight made her skin look even more pale — if that was at all possible.

"Paige! Listen to me, you can do this. Just zap anybody if they come at you. You have an affinity for fire. You can do this." I don't know where this pep talk came from, but suddenly I was filled with so much conviction I knew what needed to be done. And I had all the awareness to know that I could do it. Finally, she spoke.

"But I've never used my powers to fight before. The Matrons always told us not to. I've only used it in little casting circles that Nora and I used to do in the attic. You know, lighting candles without matches and stuff. I can't go against the Dark Coven. I can't Alex."

"Yes, you can, Paige. You don't have a choice."

I saw a tear break free from one of her eyes; I was about to think that maybe I was wrong, that maybe I don't know what I'm doing, and that I was being too hard on this poor girl in front of me. But then she dragged a hand across her face, and I could see the resolve building behind her eyes.

"You're right. I can do this." We left in opposite directions, heading toward our different targets.

Through the melee of rocks and wind and the gnashing of teeth, I saw someone near Chrissy. I tried to run faster while dodging explosions of dirt. I tripped over a pothole created by the rocks Ms. Terra was moving and I hit the ground hard. Luckily, I avoided hitting my chin again. I didn't think my jaw could take another blow. I moved to set my feet underneath me, but I couldn't. I looked to see what was happening. My ankles we being buried in the potholes, and the dirt was constricting my movement. I looked around to see what was happening, and then I saw Neal.

*Crap*

I was going to get this bastard, once and for all. And this time, I wouldn't hesitate. I felt the energy around the dirt particles that were trapping my foot and in one gust; I hurled them all in Neal's face. He groaned, pawing at his face, trying to brush the dirt out of his eyes. I used his momentary distraction and ran toward the platform. Before I heaved myself up onto the stage, I created a light ball full of raw energy and shot it right at Neal. It knocked him to the ground. It gave me a few minutes to get to Chrissy. The figure I saw earlier was Austin. He was already there, getting the last of the rope off from around her legs. I thanked him and gave Chrissy a relieved hug. Not thinking about her aversion to touch. But she returned the embrace. I looked her over quickly, assessing whether or not she was seriously hurt. She looked fine but was probably dealing with a lot of emotional trauma that was going to take years to work through.

"How are you? Are you hurt?"

"I'm fine I think."

"What happened?"

"Right before we were going to leave the café, I remembered I left a book in the library, and I needed it for my midterm. Mrs. Welch gave me a key because I restock the shelves for her, so I tend to go after hours, but on my way there, suddenly I couldn't move anymore. My legs just stopped working. I was frozen stiff. I couldn't run or scream. It felt like someone had turned off the lights and my nerves no longer sent signals for my muscles to move. Then some guys came out of a car and pulled me inside and drove off. That was the last thing I remember before pulling up to you on the street and picking up Neal. They drugged me. I don't remember anything after that. When I woke up, I was being tied to this post. Alex, what's going on? What do they want?"

"Me"

Fear was written all over her face. She was so innocent, so kind, she didn't deserve this. None of us did. I looked over at Austin and gestured for him to help her up. He did without hesitation. Austin managed to get Chrissy off the platform, but the minute he let her go he was caught in a wind tunnel. Separating him from Chrissy. Austin couldn't find his footing and he was fighting to stay upright. The next thing I saw was clothing breaking away from what was Austin, and now in his place was a tawny colored coyote. The coyote dug his claws into the earth to keep himself upright. I looked through the wind and saw a man just a few yards away who I knew caused this mini tornado. Well, he can't get away with that. I decided to give him a taste of his own medicine and pulled the wind tunnel he was creating away from his control and funneled it directly into his path. I was manipulating the wind! Not just energy now, but all the elements were at my control. He wasn't expecting the power my wind tunnel created, and it blew him against one of the relic trains in the station. I heard a sickening thwap and then his body slumped to the ground. He tried to get to his knees, but Austin was on him quicker than the rain. Austin was throwing his body around like a rag doll. He wasn't joking when he said he had heightened strength. I never would have thought a coyote could cause so much damage to a full-grown man.

I checked back with Chrissy, who was using the platform stand to keep herself upright. She didn't look very good, and I didn't know if she could walk on her own. I looked around to see what I could use or who could help me. Ms. Terra was caught in an epic battle between the leather clad lady, and I think Ms. Terra was winning, but it was hard to tell. Ryan, Nora, and Paige were carrying Ms. Mary off to the side and away from the chaos. I saw her chest moving up and down, so hopefully that meant she was breathing. Lastly, I looked for Jason. I wish I hadn't.

I saw Jason caught in between Alaric and now Neal. Neal must have come to the aid of Alaric, who looked a little worse for wear. His clothes were slashed to bits, and he had a huge wound on his upper right arm that was bleeding heavily. Despite all that, Alaric was still throwing fire balls at Jason. But Jason was missing them, mostly. Jason was a predator on the attack. Leaping and clawing, snatching at limbs and leaving disasters in his wake. It was a blur of action. I turned to check on Chrissy. She wasn't looking too well. I focused again on the fight in front of me, deciding I needed to help Jason in any way I could, but I realized the fight was now one on one. Neal was missing.

I knew I needed to help Jason, but I was afraid. Like Paige said, I was a baby priestess. I didn't know if I could control my power enough to hit Alaric and not Jason. I had to try. I couldn't just stand here. Without overthinking it, I focused my attention. I couldn't believe how easy it was now for me to call on my magic. It was like it was always there, just waiting for me to need it. I didn't want to create a lightning ball, too afraid of injuring Jason, so I thought about binding Alaric's movements. If I could control the energy around me and we were made of energy, it made sense to me that, I could manipulate human energy as well. So, I did.

I closed my eyes to steady myself and calmed down my breathing. I reopened my eyes and let them relax and soften as I focused on Alaric. And sure enough, as I did, I saw the soft colors that appeared around him like mirage waves over hot asphalt. It was his spirit taking a physical form; it was his energy. His energy was a muddy green color with yellow edging. He looked sick. It was what I imagined toxic sludge to look like. I didn't know what to do next, so I stopped trying to figure it out and I let my instincts take over. My hands reached out in front of me, as if I could have reached the sparing pair from where I was standing. Once I did, I noticed that the murky colors responded to my movements, like marionette strings. In a sweeping movement I brushed my hand across one arm of Alaric's spirit, and like smoke in the wind, it dissipated. The spirit that surrounded his arm floated away, and once it did, his hand dropped to his side like dead weight. He couldn't regain control of his arm after that. It worked. I did it! I can do this. I am powerful enough to help win this fight. And just like that, I did it again to his other arm, and like before, it dropped dead to his side. Alaric was out of commission. Without the use of his hands, he could no longer control his magic. Jason having realized he was no longer a threat. He whipped his back legs out, and kicked Alaric dead in the chest. He fell to the ground. By this time, Ryan came to Jason's aide and began using the ropes that once bound Chrissy and tied up Alaric. Jason was nowhere to be seen.

I turned my attention quickly back to Chrissy, who was now slumped on the ground, barely able to keep her head in an upright position. Before I could take a step towards her, Austin — who had recovered from being thrown into a train — was by her side, wearing nothing but a pair of sweatpants. He was ever so gingerly gathering her up in his arms, I was so pleased that Austin had come with us. As he tried to stand up with a very small Chrissy cradled against his chest, a railroad tie came careening at his head. He barely dodged it without jostling Chrissy. At that moment, he took off in a run straight for the tree line, Chrissy in still in his arms. I knew Chrissy would be safe with Austin and I felt instant relief that he was there with her, and she was okay. At least I hoped she was okay.

# Chapter 48: Circuit Connection on the Fritz

**Alex**

My head was spinning from all the chaos that surround us in that train depot. There was so much happening I didn't know where to look or who to help. I wanted it all to stop. I was so overwhelmed; it took everything I had to not curl up in a ball and give up. I couldn't give up. I had to help. I had to find Jason. Where did he go? Where was Neal? My gut was telling me Jason needed my help. I couldn't explain it, but somehow, deep inside me, I knew I was running out of time.

I was trying to make sense of the pandemonium around me. I saw Nora, Paige, and Ryan, who looked to be in a battle of their own with people I've never seen before. Fortunately, enough, it looked like they were handling themselves very well and didn't seem to need my help. My anxiety, however, grew over the fact that I couldn't find Jason.

All the horrible scenarios were running through my over reactive brain. Before I allowed myself to get bogged down with worst-case scenarios, a thought came to me. We can communicate with our minds. Jason said he could *hear* others from a greater distance depending on how well he knew them. Maybe that meant I could call him, and he'd hear it and tell me where he was. I also thought about how I can see the energy of everything around me. The Matrons told me that energy can sometimes leave a trace, like footsteps in the sand. What if by focusing on Jason, I can call out to him and use our connection to follow his spirit trail and locate him? It was a long shot, I knew, and I had no idea if this was how the spirit works. But something inside of me told me I was on the right track. That I could do this, and it would work. It would lead me to Jason. I owed it to him to try. With my eyes closed, I called out to him, as if he was standing right next to me.

*Jason, where are you? Are you okay?*

I imagined my words gliding away from me like a gold invisible thread curling out of my mind, out of my spirit. Weaving an ethereal path towards Jason, searching for him. After what felt like an eternity, my confidence waned. Maybe I was asking too much. Maybe this wasn't what spirit could do. I was about to give up, when suddenly I felt a spark, like the shock you get when a thunderstorm brews and you brush your hand over a doorknob, and it bites you back. I felt it again, the spark was growing. It sputtered and flickered like a circuit connection on the fritz. But it was there, a low zing of live energy coming from somewhere far away. I focused harder, holding on to the dull jolt, cupping it in my mind, careful not to disconnect it.

I felt the golden ribbon that was my spirit thread, bobbing and weaving through the dark forest, reaching what I hoped was Jason. Then, as if a 50-volt strike came from deep in the woods, my spirit thread contacted Jason's spirit and our two energy sources fused and twined with each other, making a complete and closed circuit of power. His and my spirit flowing back and forth between us, strong and bright, we could have powered all of Montana. When I knew the connection would hold, I opened my eyes and followed the now visible thread; a golden glowing thin path that sparked and shinned, leading me toward Jason.

My feet having a mind of their own, saw where I needed to go, and went. I followed the path, and strange noises flittered in the air, getting louder and louder with every step. The noises sounded so familiar; I couldn't put my finger on what it could be until a ray of light broke free from deep in the woods. Then my mind was able to marry the two, the flickering glow and the crackling sound. Something was on fire. My feet took off in a run. I had to dodge low-hanging branches and jump over stumps and rocks. A few times, my shins caught the business end of broken twigs and rocks disguised as moss. But I couldn't let it distract me from getting to Jason. I had to get to Jason.

I broke through the forest and came into a clearing that was probably once a beautiful meadow, but now was being consumed by a giant ring of fire. The flames were almost as tall as I was. I tried to look around and through the flames to see if I could make out anything, and sure enough, in the middle of this inferno was Jason, lying frightfully still. He was still in his wolf form, fur matted and caked with blood. His massive wolf's body looked deflated and broken.

*Jason!*

There was no sign of Neal or his goons, or any reason for this giant ring of fire in the middle of the damn forest. But there was no time to decipher the rhyme or reason of this. Because I knew if I took too long to act, the trap that this could be, will catch up to me. And then we'd both be screwed, I needed to act. I needed to get to Jason. This was all my fault. I caused this. I needed to stop the fire. I needed to get to Jason. It doesn't matter who put him here or why. I needed...I don't know what I needed. What the hell am I even doing here? Who the hell was I? Everything came rushing to me like sand in a cave in. Elemental Powers, Reincarnation, Dark Magic, Skin Walkers — I was hyperventilating. My vision was tunneling, this was too much, I was going to break under the pressure. I couldn't take anymore. My knees hit the grass, fingers clawing at the blades like a life saver keeping me afloat. I was searching for air my lungs couldn't find.

*Alexandra. Get up. You can do this, it's who you are — you have to try.*

Jason was in my head. His voice was weak. I had to concentrate just to hear him.

*Jason, I can't! I'm not a High Priestess. I'm just some messed up teen whose under aged mother got freaked out and left her baby on some doorstop. I can't do this! I have to get help. I'll get the Matrons; they'll know what to do.*

I started to get to my feet. I was unbalanced and woozy, but I managed to get upright. With a shaky step a headed away from the meadow and back towards the forest, with the flames at my back. Abruptly in my head was Jason, stronger than he was just a moment before.

*Alexandra, you can do this. You have to try.*

With his simple plea, I felt all the love and confidence he had in me. It was all I needed to get me out of my panic. He was my raft in an ocean of sorrow. I took a deep breath — a few deep breaths — dug my feet into the ground, I was determined to save Jason.

I tried to see into the fire, to see the spirit within the flame. If I could, then I could deconstruct it, similar to what I did to Alaric's arms. Only I couldn't. This fire didn't have an energy source I could access. It wasn't a normal fire and somehow, I knew it was because it was enchanted. It was warded against me.

Okay, new plan. I thought more science than science-fiction. What do you need to stop fire? Water. I knew that I could control all the elements, and I had to put out of my mind that I've never done it before. But like with everything else, I just had to try. The one thing I knew for certain was that I didn't have a lot of time to contemplate whether or not I could Jason's chest, which was moving steadily earlier, was now barely moving at all. My time for thinking was over.

I didn't shut my eyes this time, too afraid to look away from Jason. Thinking if I looked away, he would simply cease to exist. Instead, I thought of water, rushing, gushing, coursing, cold water. I thought about all the surrounding things that were made of water; the blades of grass heavy with moonlight dew, the leaves pulling up water from their roots, the creeks and streams that flow under the forest floor. Everywhere was water. As I began to envision the water, I felt it. Heavy at first, then with the greatest of ease I could draw it in and create huge water bubbles. Massive amounts of bubbles in all varying sizes floated all around me, like magical baubles that glinted in the firelight. With a wave of a hand, the baubles maneuvered themselves over the ring of fire and began to burst. Like water balloons bursting on a hot day during a family BBQ, they smashed into the flames raining down water as they exploded. My water bubbles doused the flames, smothering them instantly. There was nothing left of the fire but a clean, wet smell. I collapsed to the floor, unaware of how much energy it took for me to conjure the water. My breathing was ragged, but I felt my heartbeat stabilizing quickly. I didn't have time to recuperate. I needed to dig deep and find whatever energy was left in my seemingly empty body and get to Jason. I crawled through the dirt and ash onto Jason's wolf's body.

"I'm here Jason, I'm here." I reached out to him, wanting to cradle his wolf form in my lap, but too afraid to move him. I caressed the soft fur under his muzzle instead. He was barely breathing.

*Jason, what can I do?*

I knew his body would naturally heal itself, which is why I was so confused when Jason didn't seem to be getting any better. Maybe it was too much. Maybe his body couldn't heal fast enough to keep up with his injuries. Maybe it was the magic. What if he couldn't heal against magic? I didn't know, but I needed to do something. I didn't know why or when I had closed my eyes, but it helped me slow down my breathing, which kept my anxiety at bay. I needed to be strong for Jason. I needed to get through this. He needed me. I tried to envision his spirit, like I did with Alaric. I needed to see if I could help heal him. When I opened my eyes again, Jason's spirit was visible. He was a beautiful, rich green. It reminded me of his eyes, and the forest he lives in. It was perfect, but it was weak and muted. It was fading. The color was wavering and with every wave, it would grow dimmer and dimmer. I couldn't think about what this meant. I had to keep going. I peered into his spirit, going deeper and deeper into the energy that was Jason, and like watching an MIR screen, I saw into Jason's body. I could see his muscles, bones, and organs.

My eyes went straight to his chest. I couldn't tell right away, but something looked off. His ribs were a shattered mess. Each bone was broken and crushed, shards of bones piercing his lungs, heart, and other organs I couldn't identify. It looked as if his chest took the brunt force of something huge and powerful, like a massive boulder. Neal. Neal and his earth magic must have smashed something into Jason's chest. This looked like life ending injuries. I've seen those medical drama shows. This wasn't something someone walked away from. Aside from the overwhelming number of crush injuries that were plaguing Jason. One of them being the inability to gather air into his lungs because of one having a massive tear from a piece of bone. I finally realized what looked so incredibly odd. Everything in his chest had an orange-brown hue to it. Like there was a noxious gas filling his chest cavity, making everything look like rust. Right then, I knew — magic. This must be Neal's magic trying to prevent Jason from healing.

I had to remove the magic that was poisoning Jason's body. I focused on the gassy cloud. Picturing a strong wind that would blow the mass of energy that was Neals magic out and away from Jason's body, making sure I left behind none of it. Once the murky, rusty cloud was gone, I could finally see the mess of bone and blood that was Jason's destroyed chest cavity. Immediately, I could see the lacerations in Jason's organs knitting themselves closed, and the bleeding was slowing down. But it wasn't happening fast enough. His breathing was rattled, like he was underwater. He was choking on the blood that was filling his lungs. His spirit was just a tint of green now, barely visible. I was losing him. I needed to take matters into my own hands. Maybe I could piece Jason back together, maybe I could help accelerate his healing. I was afraid of what would happen if I didn't try.

Ever so gently, I started with what I thought was the most important issue. His lung. I was in full control of my spirit now, it was like I was spirit, nothing more nothing less. And with such precision I imagined invisible forceps grasping onto the piece of bone that was protruding from Jason's lung and carefully pulled it out. Instantly the lung sealed shut, and I saw it once again filling with air. And that's when I heard Jason let out a gasp. He was breathing! He was breathing. He was going to be okay.

Right then, the color of his spirit deepened. The faint green it was just a moment ago was now darker, more jewel toned, more Jason. He was okay. He was going to be okay. Before I released myself from his spirit, I could see his other injuries piecing themselves back together, bone by bone, muscle by muscle. It was a fascinating thing to witness. I was so grateful to be a Mystic at that moment. That I could heal someone I loved. To save a life.

*Alex*

"Yes Jason, I'm here." Tears fell down my cheek.

*I feel like a herd of elephants smashed into me.*

I couldn't believe it. He was talking again — no; he was joking. I looked down at him through my tears that continued to fall down my checks, leaving hot salty water in their tracks. The color of his fur was brightening, no longer dingy and pale but a beautiful sable brown. His eyes were looking up at me, full of love and comfort.

*You did it Alex; you saved me.*

"I can't believe I could do that. I can't believe anything that has happened in the last 24 hours. Or hell, the last months, years. Just all of it! I can't believe any of it." I was babbling again. My mouth wouldn't stop talking. Until finally, Jason saved me from the endless stream of words that were falling out of my lips. His body was still doing damage control inside of him and he was too weak to change back into his human form. But honestly, it felt like such a natural thing to see him as he was. He was Jason in any form.

*You did it. Maybe now you'll start believing that you are capable of greatness. It's who you are. I never once doubted it.*

Jason, still in his wolf form, stood up on all fours and shook his body like a dog getting out of the bath. His green eyes shining in the moonlight looked right at me. He was so close his breath was hot on my face. The heat radiating from his body was warming my soul. I held my breath, because even though I knew it was Jason and knew he would never hurt me, I was still inches away from an enormous wolf. Then the wolf leaned in closer, if that was even at all possible, and licked my face.

"Ew Jason really! You lick me?" I swear I thought I heard the wolf laugh, actually laugh.

*Got ya! You were scared for a second there, weren't you? Don't try to lie. I can smell fear.*

He laughed again, and I laughed as well. It was kind of funny.

*By the way, would you know where my clothes went off too?*

"They're probably back at the shrubs. Where we first came in."

Which brought me back to Chrissy. We had to get back to make sure everyone else was okay. I had no idea how long we'd been in the woods. Jason, reading my thoughts, was already heading toward the train yard. Somehow, I found the energy to follow in his tracks.

Whether it was because of adrenaline or need, there was no way to know. All I knew was I needed to get back.

# Chapter 49: Super Weird

**Alex**

Within minutes, we were back in the train yard. I didn't know what I was expecting to see, but what I saw was a welcomed surprise. Where before was chaos and mess was now quiet and relief. There was anticipation in the air like the calm before the storm. The feeling around was uncertainty, as if we didn't know if we could let out the breath, we were all holding. But for now, at least we were safe. And we needed to get out of the depot.

Once I got a better look at the surrounding crowd, I could see the fighting had indeed ended. All the Dark Mystics were gone except for one lady, who was currently being bound by ropes and held hostage by my friends. And she looked extremely pissed! It took me an additional second to see Alaric sitting off to the side of the depot, still unable to move his arms and with legs, he was propped up against a lamppost. The person I didn't see was Chrissy. Where was Chrissy! Before my panic could go full tilt, Jason leaned over and gestured to the other side of the train station. I followed his look and sure enough, coming around the corner was a half-naked Austin, and thankfully — albeit a wobbly — Chrissy. Who was leaning onto him heavily but walking on her own two feet. Sort of. I rushed over to Chrissy so fast it felt like I took the entire train yard in less than four strides, but I couldn't stop myself. I ran to her and gave her the biggest bear hug my tired and weak arms could manage. Until she let out a small whimper.

"Oh god. I'm sorry, did I hurt you? Are you okay?"

"I'm fine. Just a little sore and my head feels really dizzy. But I think I'm going to be just fine. Thanks to Austin, he's been so nice to me. He saved my life."

Austin and Chrissy shared a look. I wasn't sure what it meant, but I made a note to ask Chrissy about it later. If I didn't know any better, I think there might have been something brewing between the two of them. Dramatic events have a way of bonding people together. I felt so much relief knowing everyone who I loved was safe, my friends, my boyfriend, the Matrons. The Matrons? I noticed I only saw Ms. Terra. Where was Ms. Mary? And then I remembered she was hurt earlier. I saw her get struck and she fell, hard. My stomach fell to my feet, my whole body went cold. I didn't want to know. I didn't want to look around and see what I knew would be true, and then I saw it. Near the entrance of the gate a brown tarp covering what could only be a Mary sized lump.

All the feeling in my body went numb. The floor dropped from under my feet. I felt myself falling. This was my fault. She was dead because of me. I caused this. My head was spinning, my vision was blurring. I felt an anxiety attack coming. I fell to the ground and started to cry. No, I wept. I wept for Ms. Mary, for Chrissy being kidnapped, for Jason almost dying, I wept for all of us. For the darkness that always seemed to follow me. Even now I couldn't get away. Surrounded by my friends, the darkness was still winning. And that's when I heard Ms. Terra's voice.

"This isn't your fault, child. This is Dark Magic's doing. This was the work of evil. You will not take this on yourself. This is not your battle to fight alone, honey. I loved my cousin deeply, but we both knew the risk we took when we vowed to see the demise of Dark

Magic once and for all. She fought bravely, and with love for all our charges, don't lessen her sacrifice by blaming yourself."

Her voice was steady but somber. Her words were filled with such wisdom, yet I could tell there was so much pain behind them. There were no more tears left for me to cry and I will not allow despair to have any more of my time. I stood up with a new sense of determination. We would have justice for Ms. Mary. We would see the end to Dark Magic. Everything inside me knew this to be true. Once I was upright, I brushed myself off and turned to look at my friends. Ms. Terra took the lead and gave us direction.

"Everyone needs to get back to the manor, including our two new friends here. I've got some questions that could really use some answers. I have called the authorities they are on their, so the less of us here, the better."

"What are the police going to say when they find a dead body?" I had to ask, even though it felt awfully wrong to say it out loud.

"Leave that to me. While I don't condone using spells on our human neighbors, sometimes it is simply unavoidable. Do not worry, everything will be taken care of. Paige, you take the van and everyone else back to the manor. Ryan, will you assist Nora in making sure our extra — companions — get safely into the vehicle? Which brings me to my next point. Miss Alex, since it was your superb spell that bound Alaric's arms, you are the only one who can unbind them. And while I am tempted to keep him as is, he may cooperate a tad better, knowing he has use of his arms once again. But before you do, Nora tie his hands behind his back." Ms. Terra peered over at Alaric, shooting him the deathly-ist of death stares.

"What about his magic? How will you prevent him from fighting back once I unbind his arms?" My concern came out harsher then intended. I didn't want to offend Ms. Terra, but I also didn't want to put anyone in harm's way by having Alaric free to use his magic.

"Do not worry, child, there is a spell for that as well." Right then, Ms. Terra rooted through a small leather satchel that I hadn't noticed until now strung across her chest, and she let out an excited whoop when she came across what she was looking for.

"I'm glad I listened to Mary and threw it in here last minute. She always had a way of knowing what we would need before we ever needed it. This here, my girl, is a tincture of skullcap, valerian, and, well, other magical things we don't need to discuss right now." I wonder what she meant by *other magical things*. Ms. Terra held up a small brown bottle dropper of something milky.

"It's a Mystical suppressant. It locks the magic of the person who has been dosed with it, at least for a time being."

"How are you going to get him to swallow it without spitting it out?" Ryan said, fully convinced there'd be no way we could get Alaric to swallow the spellbinding liquid.

"Well, you see, that's why I was hesitant to bring it at first. Because it is a little hard to administer under certain circumstances. But since he is, for all intents and purposes, paralyzed, we shouldn't have an issue." I was thoroughly confused, and a little baffled as to what she could be talking about.

"This tincture is not meant to be swallowed but dropped into the eye. I've heard it stings for just a moment, but quickly fades. And then the person is rendered magic free for 12 hours. Ryan, if you wouldn't mind, I may need some assistance."

Ms. Terra spoke as if it was completely natural to drop some type of burning magical liquid into the eyes of people. No big deal. There is never a moment where I am not completely surprised by this new world. But nevertheless, Ryan immediately walked over to Ms. Terra's side to accompany her to where Alaric was still sitting in the dirt near the train tracks.

"Get the hell away from me! I will never reveal anything to you, no matter what you do. You might as well just kill me now before

I regain my magic and snap the necks off of all the bleeding heart children you surround yourself with!"

"Now, now, Alaric, there is no need to get so dramatic. I remember when you could barely make a feather float back in the day. Your idol threats mean nothing to me. Eventually, you'll talk. We have a few tricks up our sleeves. Or have you forgotten Venice? That was a fun night, wasn't it? For me at least."

Ms. Terra laughed, a sinister laugh, and I swear I thought I saw Alaric go pale as a ghost. *What happened in Venice?*

"Ryan, if you would be such a dear and get behind him and hold his head in an upright position, and very, very still."

Ryan did as he was told, and Ms. Terra ever so gently hovered over Alaric's face and carefully held his eyelid opened. Then she administered three drops into each of Alaric's eyes. Alaric winced and blinked a few times, water dripping from his closed lids. When he looked up again, I saw his entire eyeball was blue, like someone had poured dye into it. The more times Alaric blinked, the less blue it was. You could see the tincture being absorbed into the eye socket. *Super weird.*

"Alright now that that is done, let's do the same thing to our other friends and get them in the Van. Alex, we'll need you to unbind his arms and please hurry, we haven't much time. And I assume you'll be heading back with Mr. Alder and Mr. Hemlock?"

Ms. Terra was back to business now. Getting the plan and the people moving right along. I didn't know if she disapproved of my company or not, but there would be time to ask those questions later. We needed to get back to the Manor and out of this depot. Disapproving or not, I wasn't letting Jason out of my sight again. I walked over to Alaric and if I didn't know better, would have thought he would reach out and lounge for me, with how much hate was dripping out of his facial expression. It felt counterintuitive to give him back the use of his arms. Nora was there, however, securing his hands with a piece of rope behind his back. Which made me feel a little better about unbinding him, a little.

I took a deep breath and envisioned Alaric's spirit once more. It was still the ugly toxic color, but now it hovered off to the side of him, not above him like it had the first time. I instinctively knew that I had to reset his spirit back to where it belonged. I coaxed his spirit to cover Alaric's body and settle into him once more. Then it was done. Alaric had control of his arms once more.

Our group outside of Ms. Terra all gathered in the van and headed their way back to the Manor. Leaving me, Jason, and Austin in the yard with Ms. Terra. Jason spoke first.

"Alexendra, we'll give you two a second and meet you back in the car."

*Let me know if you need me. I won't be far.*

I nodded my thanks towards Jason and watched him and Austin walk back up the hill to where we had park which felt like days ago. I turned towards Ms. Terra, my eyes heavy with tears now that the adrenaline had completely left my body and the events of the evening sunk in.

"You are an extraordinary young lady. You will be an amazing High Priestess, one it will honor me to follow and fight for. Thank you for tonight." I didn't know what to say. I felt so much love and support from Ms. Terra; it was almost unnerving. I was not used to this feeling. Usually, it was disdain and abandonment I felt. She took me in for a full body embrace, her arms wrapping around me. The feeling of being held together by her strength was cleansing. In my ear, she whispered.

"Sonya's spirit lives in you. You will be powerful one day. Be careful where you lay your trust. Even those who love us can lead us down the wrong path. Use your power wisely, not self-seeking, and use your intuition to know the difference."

We parted. I felt loved, but I also felt warned. What could she mean by that? Before I contemplate anymore on her cryptic message, I heard sirens in the background. Ms. Terra hurried me along before the police arrived in the yard. Jason now back to his true form, we were back in his car, back to where I belonged, back with whom I belong with. We pulled out of the lot and headed towards the manor. Leaving police lights in our rearview mirror. I knew Ms. Terra could handle her own. I only wished I knew what she was warning me against.

# Chapter 50: Not Now
# Not Ever

**Alex**

Jason drove us back to his land to drop Austin off before taking me to the manor. Austin was willing to help, but he was not willing to go back to the manor. I wanted to respect his wishes. I would deal with Ms. Terra if she had a problem. Jason said it was because he wanted to give us some time to talk. And I didn't press the issue, I was not going to force Austin to do anything he wasn't comfortable with. I thanked Austin immensely for everything he did to help us save Chrissy. I would forever be grateful to him. Before he closed the car door, he made sure to ask.

"Will you tell her I hope she's, okay?"

"Of course."

He closed the car door and walked back up the road towards his village. With just the two of us now in the car there was a heaviness in the air that hung between us. I didn't know how to handle it. Several minutes passed in silence. I didn't know what to say, so I kept my words to myself. Jason decided to speak first.

"I meant what I said. You are my heart. There's no fighting it, nor do I want to. I don't care what my father says, he's wrong. There can be peace between our people. There used to be once before. Maybe we are the ones who will bring it back."

Jason was the one who was babbling for a change. I've never seen him nothing but cool and confident, yet this Jason was opened and unguarded. He couldn't hide his emotions. It tugged at my heart. He wanted me; he loved me. I needed to be just as unguarded with him. However, something was plaguing my thoughts, and I had to talk to him about it.

"Jason, I..." He stopped me before I could say anything else.

"It's okay, I know. You don't have to explain anything to me. I don't own you. And I don't blame you."

"Blame me? For what?"

I was trying to not let my temper get the best of me, but sometimes this mind reading thing really had its downsides. If I wanted to have a conversation about something, I wanted to be the one to have it. Not to have the other person already know about it before I could even say it. But then again, maybe it was a good thing. I was dreading having to bring up the fact that not 24 hours ago; I was kissing some other guy. And now here was *this* guy, professing his love. Man, my life was such a mess. I saw Jason flinch as I thought that last part to myself and immediately regretted not making sure my wall was up before, I was so blunt with myself.

"I need to talk about it. Yes. Ryan and I kissed at the café, and I don't know what I think about that. I don't even know how it happened. Or why? But it happened. I was so hurt by you, you left me. You turned your back and walked away, leaving me to believe you couldn't be with me anymore. My world turned upside down, and Ryan was there. He wanted to be there. Jason, I love you. I know that I love you. And I'm sorry. That's all I have to say."

Jason reached for my hand across the seat of the car and held it for a long time before saying anything.

"I know. And I'm sorry. I can't take back the hurt I caused you. But I will forever try to make it up to you. I want to be part of your world in any way you'll have me. We're in this together. You and me. Alpha and Priestess. Ryan — well, let's hope I don't run into him in a dark alley."

"Jason! Stop. Leave poor Ryan alone. It's not his fault he got caught up between two star-crossed lovers."

I laughed and playfully hit his shoulder as he feigned innocence. Together, we got into an easy rhythm of banter and teasing. It felt nice. To be back here again it was easy. It felt right. As much as I loved being in this moment, a part of me couldn't help but to think what happens after we get out of the car. It was easy now to say that nothing matters but us, here in this moment. But that would be wrong. I knew Jason's tribe wouldn't be as welcoming as Jason was. His people have a history of hurt and pain caused by Mystics, and that's what I would be representing. Hurt and pain.

The laughter and smiles we exchanged in the car were mere illusions, concealing the undercurrent of desperation and foreboding that pulsed through our veins. Jason's duty loomed over us like a heavy fog, a suffocating weight that threatened to drown any chance of happiness. His grip on my hand tightened, as if he could anchor me in a moment that was slipping away. For now, it was him and me, and the radio, and the feeling of being indestructible, even if it was for just a moment. Because that was all we needed, just a moment to be untouchable, to be us. Finally, we arrived at the Manor. Jason turned off the ignition but didn't move.

"Alexandra, I don't know what lies ahead for us. With my responsibilities to my people, or the looming threat of Dark Magic. But I am willing to fight for us, even if it means forsaking my duty as Alpha. You are my home. I feel my mother's spirit guiding me to you. I can't walk away, not now, not ever."

Jason turned to me, his touch delicate as he cupped my chin, a tender kiss imprinting a bittersweet promise on my lips. His eyes, once vibrant green, now mirrored the somber depths of the forest he called home. They held the untamed essence of a creature restrained, and they were sad. A single tear escaped, glistening in the moonlight, tracing a path down his cheek. With a gentle touch, I wiped it away, hoping to erase the sadness it carried.

My facade crumbled; I could no longer feign strength. This felt like our last moment, and I surrendered to the recklessness. I grabbed his head, our lips colliding with a hunger I hadn't recognized until that moment. It was feverish, urgent, fueled by the fear of impending separation. I wanted him fiercely, and nothing else mattered. There was an urgency to our kiss, our lips longed for the other, our breath hot and fierce. My hands were full of his hair. His hands traced the skin of my back under my shirt, his fingers felt like flames. Jason's tears dripped down his cheeks. Our kisses tasted like salt and heart and finality. I would fight for us too; I would fight, and we would win. I couldn't let him go, I wouldn't. I pushed my thoughts out to him.

*I want you. I want us. I won't let go. Not now, not ever.*

Our kisses grew deeper. The car confined us, mirroring the constraints of our lives. But in that confined space, I poured my passion into our connection, determined to overcome the hindrances that threatened us. He kissed the skin under my chin and moved down my neck, coming back up the other side. I was hypnotized. The slightest breath left my lips in ecstasy. I heard him groan in approval. Making every hair on my skin stand up. I was so lost in the moment I didn't notice I was reaching out with my Spirit. Not until I felt a tug on the invisible ribbon that tied the two of us together. There was a powerful energy that coursed between us, exemplifying every nerve. It was intoxicating. My heart felt like it would burst out of my chest. Our lips parted, breathless, swollen, and disheveled. We were a testament to the fierce battle we were fighting.

"What was that?" Jason said, his voice coming out husky and low.

"I don't know. I think our spirits connected."

"Well, we gotta do that again."

"You're horrible." I laughed in mock prudishness.

I might have wanted my words to have more decorum, but my thoughts were the exact opposite. I was wondering how hard it would be to convince him to take his shirt off. Jason tried and failed to stifle a laugh at that moment, and my embarrassment went through the roof.

"Hey! You have got to cut that out! That's so unfair." I buried my face in my hands, kicking my feet up on the dash to curl into a ball.

"If you wanted me out of your head, you would block your thoughts. So, I see it as fair game."

"You're such a putz." My muffled voice came out from in between my fingers. But I cocked my head to one side to look at him through slit fingers.

"I honestly try not to listen. I wish I could prevent myself from it. But your thoughts are so loud." I groaned and went back to hiding my face. Feeling the heat of my body rise.

"It will get easier. I promise. And I'll help remind you. This is unfamiliar territory for me as well. I've never needed to be so careful around people before. With the pack, it's almost on instinct now, if they even care at all. You're the first outsider — the first girl — I've been close with, in a really long time. Don't be mad. It's cute. But I don't want to invade your privacy. Promise."

He brushed a hair behind my ear. I turned to look at him. He was so amazingly gorgeous. How could I be mad at him for long? Besides, he sounded genuine. Sincere. I let out a breath and sat up again. Remembering, finally, to block my thoughts. We decided that was a good time to get out of the car. My legs felt weak from all the sitting and all the kissing. He walked me to the bottom of the stairs. There was light beginning to break the horizon. Dawn had come. With the new day, brought new challenges, but we would face them together. So why then did it feel that once we left the car, we left ourselves behind as well? I didn't know what I would find once

I walked into the Manor or what was waiting for Jason back on his land. But a shift happened. I hope that whatever it was, we could get through it together.

Jason gave me one last hug, pressing his lips to the top of my head. I told him not to come inside. That we can face the Matrons together, later. But I should do this one on my own. He promised to call me once he got home, then he turned around and went back to his car and left. There was nothing left for me to do now but head into the house. As I climbed the porch steps, I heard a car pulling in behind me. It was Ms. Terra exiting a yellow cab. She must be coming home from the precinct or wherever she needed to go after we had all left. Ms. Terra looking weary came up behind me with a soft smile on her face.

"Was that Mr. Alder who I saw leaving our driveway just now?"

"Yes, ma'am."

"He's a good kid. Come inside I'll make us some tea." Ms. Terra and I, with the dawn at our back, walked into the house to have a cup of tea.

# Chapter 51: If Wishes Were Fishes

**Alex**

A week went by after that night. The funeral for Ms. Mary came and went. It was a small service; nice, intimate, and filled with every flower imaginable packed into the small rectory. Ms. Mary would have been so pleased. Ms. Terra assured us that Ms. Mary would be back again one day. They believe strongly in reincarnation; the soul is ever eternal and so their journey is never ending. The more powerful the soul, the faster their return to the earth plane would be. If I knew anything, I knew her soul was powerful. I believed we would see her again.

Everything after the funeral seemed so surreal. Even though this immensely tragic event happened in all our lives, the world still spun, school still opened, life still continued. It was odd. We transported the captives we took from the train yard to another residence. Someone who was in the Coven and could further interrogate them, hopefully to get more answers than Ms. Terra could. So far, the only thing we knew was that Lord Nicolai was indeed trying to regain control of Dark Magic, making it more powerful than it's ever been. To finally snuff out the soul of the original High Priestess, aka me. Great! But we didn't know where he was, or how he was planning to do any of this. We knew, however, that Neal drank their punch hook, line, and sinker and was now fully intrenched into their icky ways. I felt bad for Nora, and sort of half expected her to follow in his lead. That's how the days went. Us kids went to school, me constantly checking to see if today would be the day Nora took off. Ms. Terra throwing herself deep into the webs of finding a solution that would appoint us the victors. Intermixed with magic training that now consisted of defensive spell casting. It was almost normal. Almost.

Chrissy was the one who changed the most. Before she was painfully shy, afraid to touch people because of her gift. The gift that caused her to see people's future, and sometimes they're reincarnated past. Now she was strong, outgoing even. She made eye contact and small talk. We baked cookies and went to the movies. I couldn't believe it. And when she wasn't helping with homework or refining her gift — she could now control it to the point where she could physically touch people for short periods of time without being bombarded with visions of their future. She was talking to Austin. Ever since that night, they have been talking quite often. She hasn't seen him since that night, but I think it was just a matter of time before I would see Austin showing up on the front porch.

Everyone else followed their original patterns. Paige, still a sulky anime spitfire, continued with her academic goals and ran for class president. Nora, on the surface, was still her shallow, vain self, but I felt like it was an act. There would be moments where if she thought no one was looking, she would drop the better-than-thou- facial expression. Revealing that of someone who was deeply hurt. She missed her brother. I felt so much sadness for her. Ryan. Ryan was well, Ryan. Still gorgeous and still the nicest guy I've ever met. We tried to not make things weird and awkward, but they were. He found a new Chem partner; I thought it was right I didn't want to lead him on. We would eventually get over it, hopefully, and maybe become good friends. I wouldn't allow myself to be in a room alone with him, but that's a whole different story. But life went on, we all were holding our breath waiting for the other shoe to fall because deep down in all our minds, we knew it would. It was just a matter of when.

Until that shoe decided to drop, we decided to go on with our lives, and that included me and Jason. Jason. He was perfect. I don't know exactly what happened after he got back to his village. I didn't want to know; in case it was something I didn't want to hear. But whatever it was, it didn't prevent him from meeting me every morning at school to walk me to class. Or waiting for me at the end of the day to drive me home. We fell into an easy routine. I rode the bus. I insisted, saying it was easier — but really just wanting a moment to myself. A moment to be a teenage girl and gab with Lissa, about all thing's boys and catty girls. It was nice pretending to be normal for 25 minutes in the morning before school. Jason and I were good, it's like we were a bona fide blue-ribbon couple, complete with stealing kisses in the hallway, passing notes in class, and eating lunch together under the little tree that was now our spot. It was us and, of course, Lissa, who was accompanied by her own beau, a fellow thespian. It was great, it was normal. I felt way out of my comfort level, but it was growing on me. My life had quickly become everything I never knew I always wanted.

It was getting easier now to keep my private thoughts private. Only pushing out the things I wanted Jason to know, and it didn't feel like I was putting up walls. Not anymore. I had no reason now to be guarded or closed off. I finally felt supported, loved, like I belonged. Clara even called me more often now. Knowing that the calls would be just to catch up, and not to convince her to come and get me. I was home. I finally felt like I found somewhere to call home, and I would fight to keep it. I hoped it wouldn't come to that, but like the saying goes, if wishes were fishes. Which is why, I have no words for what happened next. I still can't believe it even happened.

One afternoon, as Jason was dropping me off from school, Ms. Terra met me at the door and asked to see me in her office. Which was strange, for I haven't seen her come out nor anybody go in, in days. I wouldn't classify Ms. Terra as a shut-in, but — she was in her office more after than not these days. She would on occasion come out and have dinner with us or help during study time, but you could always tell she was somewhere else. I knew the mysteries that surrounded Lord Nicolai and whatever evil schemes he was cooking up were always on the forefront of her mind. I also knew she wouldn't give up until she found what they were. She would stop them, once and for all.

"Thank you for coming in so quickly. I will not keep you long for I am sure you have homework that needs doing. Well Alex, I know things around here haven't been, well, they just haven't been now, have they? I am to blame for a part of that, I suppose. The death of my cousin has hit me harder than I ever thought it would, but I need to take solace that I will see her again, either in this life as a newly reincarnated soul, or in the great beyond. I will, however, apologize not only to you but to the others for not maintaining more of a semblance of normalcy. And my first order of business towards that apology will be to bring up the fact that your birthday will be upon us in less than a week's time. You, my dear, will be 18 next week. How about we do something special for you, here at the Manor?"

I was caught off guard, the subject came out of left field. I almost forgot it was my birthday. I have never been one for birthdays in the past. When you shuffle around as much as I have, leaving a trail of fear and destruction in your wake, people aren't lining up to celebrate you. Throw in a little magical battle with good and evil and suddenly blowing out birthday candles doesn't seem very important.

"No, really Ms. Terra, you don't have to do that. It's not a big deal."

"Alex, if you wouldn't mind, I would like to make it a big deal. It would do us all some good, if we had a little something to celebrate. Please, it would mean a lot to mean if I could put a little something together. Besides, Mary was already planning it, so I know it would have meant a lot to her as well." Ms. Terra looked so heartbroken. How could I have refused her?

"Yes, of course. That would be great. I would love to have a small celebration, extra small." I couldn't help but give her a small smile. Who doesn't like the idea of some cake and ice cream? I had to admit; it sounded nice. I reached down, ready to grab my backpack, when she spoke again.

"Now that we have that out of the way, that wasn't the entire reason I called you in here. Alex, when Clara first contacted us about you and your unique situation. All the remarkable incidents that laid claim in your name instantly intrigued Mary and me. Which spurred us to do some digging of our own. Knowing what we know, we thought maybe we'd have better luck discovering who, or what, you are. Even though we may not be a Coven like we once used to be, there are members in our circle who possess certain abilities and remain in practice. Are you following me?"

I could tell Ms. Terra was trying to skirt around the truth, she might not have wanted me to know but needed to give me some of it to carry her story along. I gave her the benefit of the doubt and didn't make this conversation any more awkward than it needed to be.

"You still practice magic under the radar."

"Yes, something like that. Well, one of our members is a powerful seer. Similar to Chrissy and can see both the future and the past of people's lives, as long as they have an item that belonged to the person they're reading."

Ms. Terra paused and opened a drawer in her desk. What she pulled out was the very last thing I would have expected to see in her possession. I almost didn't believe what I was seeing. Laying in front of her was a pale-yellow blanket. I knew if you opened it up, there would be a small hole in the center and one corner of the satin edging frayed and tattered. I knew this because it was my mine. I thought I had safely tucked it away in the bottom of my dresser, but here it was looking out of place in this Victorian styled office. I had no words. I just stared at my blanket, the only thing that has ever been truly mine.

Ms. Terra broke through my stupor. "We've located your mother."

As the shock of her revelation settled in, my mind raced with questions. How? Why now? What does she want? Yet, Ms. Terra's next words cut through the whirlwind of thoughts, leaving me breathless.

"But the truth about your mother, Alex, it's not what you expect. She's not who you think she is. The secrets of your past are far more intricate and dangerous than we anticipated. There's a darkness surrounding her, and it's entangled with your very existence. We need to find her before it consumes everything. Your journey is just beginning, and the shadows of your lineage stretch further than you could ever imagine."

# Epilogue

### Alex

My mother was alive.

This whole time she's been alive, this whole time while I was shuffled and suffered in one awful foster home after another, she was alive. I didn't know if I should be elated or enraged. But she was alive. All Ms. Terra could tell me was, the day my mother left me on the steps of that church, she was running for her life. The seer sensed fear, desperation, and heartache. She was running from something, or someone, and felt she had no other choice but to make the decisions she did. Unfortunately, there was something blocking the seer's vision, making it come in choppy and blurred. She couldn't get a clear enough read, but she knew she was indeed alive. The seer couldn't pinpoint my mother's location, but she thought she might be close, in the same state even. There was hope. There was hope that I could find her.

The seer had a final message for me, one I could tell Ms. Terra was hesitant to give me. She told me what the seer said.

"Be warned, I fear her mother may not be alone. I sense darkness around her. Be careful what your next step may be. Not all those we love are capable of being saved."

I didn't know what to think about that incredibly cryptic message. I was still trying to process the idea that my mother was alive and could be, quite possibly, living somewhere in Montana.

"What does this mean? Where could she be? Do you think she wants to find me?"

There were so many questions running through my head I didn't know how to contain them and prevent them from vomiting all over Ms. Terra's desk. Ms. Terra held up her hand in a silent notion for me to take a breath, then she took over the conversation.

"We need to be very careful about what we do with this information. I believe there is a strong possibility that your mother may be with Lord Nicolai, or someone in his circle. Which means she is either under his influence or being held against her will. Either way, if we jump in and try to find her, we could be walking into a trap if we're not prepared. This is why I have been trying so desperately to identify his weaknesses and find a way to prevail. I am afraid it won't be easy, and there is no guarantee that we will be successful."

A spark of determination ignited within me, and without conscious thought, I implored, "Ms. Terra, how do we defeat Lord Nicolai?" The challenge loomed, a tempest on the horizon, and the journey ahead brimmed with mystery, passion, and the unwavering belief that even in the face of darkness, light could prevail.

### Jason

"You can't be serious, can you? Your dad's gonna flip his lid."

"You don't understand. I almost lost her once. I can't do that again. I won't."

Austin was pacing back and forth, agitated as a trapped animal. While Jason was lying on the sofa tossing a tennis ball into the air as if they were discussing last night's sporting stats. And not the possible dissolution of their pack. Jason and his dad have been at odds ever since the night at the train depot. It was a bold move on Jason's part to walk into a dangerous situation without the full support of his pack mates. Or without telling his father, the Leader aka Alpha of the tribe. But to do it on behalf of a Charmer was downright outrageous, even if he had Hokama's blessing. Joseph wasn't even willing to dive into what that meant for his tribe.

Mato and Micah, in their own ways, had found their paths to reconciliation with Jason. Mato, disapproving of Jason's association with Charmers, had decided to stick around, a silent guardian ensuring Jason wouldn't face the consequences alone, or get his ass kicked. Micah, however, had been quieter since that fateful night, his animosity simmering beneath the surface. Despite being a pack of four for the moment, Jason felt the fragility of their unity, unsure how much longer the pack would remain intact.

The high probability of rejection from his tribe loomed over Jason like a shadow. But he was willing to take the risk. If only they could see Alex as he did, understand the shared pain between their two peoples, then maybe the prejudice would crumble. The healing of his tribe rested on his shoulders, and together, perhaps they could bring down the Dark Coven once and for all. The challenge lay in convincing his tribe, in making them see beyond ingrained beliefs.

But he knew the first step would be to tell his dad. And there was a real possibility he wouldn't survive that fate, or at the very least, he'd be grounded for a millennium. As the weight of his love for a Charmer settled in his chest, Jason knew there was nothing left for him to do but face the storm, admit his feelings, and hope that somewhere in the tempest that was his dad, understanding and acceptance could bloom.

# Don't miss out!

Visit the website below and you can sign up to receive emails whenever Sara Longmate publishes a new book. There's no charge and no obligation.

https://books2read.com/r/B-A-SUHCB-ANRSC

**BOOKS 2 READ**

Connecting independent readers to independent writers.

# About the Author

Welcome to the world of Sara Longmate, a storyteller whose life is a tapestry of motherhood, teaching, and the enchantment found in the quiet moments by the lake. As the proud mother of two beautiful teenage girls and a pair of lively twin boys, Sara's days are filled with the delightful chaos of family life. By profession, she's a dedicated middle school teacher, guiding young minds through the intricacies of learning. Beyond the classroom, you'll find Sara on the baseball field as the devoted team mom, leading her Cub Scouts along scenic trails, or passionately cheering on her kids as they march with the high school band.

Amidst these various roles, Sara discovers solace in her writing, where she intricately weaves tales of love and magic. The serenity of a lake, a cup of coffee in hand, and the gentle glow of the sunrise inspire her creativity. In the midst of life's bustling activities, Sara's stories unfold, inviting readers to immerse themselves in narratives that capture the essence of family, love, and the enchanting moments that make life truly magical.